Date with Responsibility

Character-in-Action Adventure #2

by Elizabeth L. Hamilton

Character-in-Action™

An imprint of *Quiet* Impact® Inc

http://character-in-action.com

Date with Responsibility
Character-in-Action Adventure #2

http://quietimpact.com
http://character-in-action.com

ISBN 0-9713749-0-2

Character-in-Action™ books are an imprint of the publisher, Quiet Impact® Inc.

First Quiet Impact Edition, 2004
Printed in Canada

In memory of
my beloved
father-in-law
and
mother-in-law
whom we remember
with love and appreciation
for their exemplary
lives of character,

and for all those who
aspire to responsibility
and a life of
character-in-action.

The Four McKeans

Alicia

Caleb

Andrew

Cathryn

Valeta Davidson

Acknowledgments

My thanks, first and always, to the Lord God, for giving me creative ideas and the gift to write, as well as health and strength to complete this book.

Second, to my husband, David, for his patience, his loving support, and his encouragement on a daily basis — for editing and proofreading the work with clarity and discernment.

Third, to my beloved father, who first gave me a love for telling a good story, and then showed me how by his great example.

Finally, my thanks to the real girl who, with the man who is now her husband, inspired this story with their unselfish lives, and who continue to live the story beyond the chapters of this book. Thank you for your clear example of true responsibility, and for letting me tell your story.

Table of Contents

Responsibility

(opposite = undependability; unaccountability)

Knowing your obligations and commitments; performing those obligations and commitments in the best possible way and on time, even when it involves personal sacrifice; doing so without reminders or follow up by someone in authority.

Refusing to replace fulfillment of commitments with more interesting pursuits, or to make excuses for duties not performed; accepting consequences of your actions readily.

Responsibility is having <u>knowledge</u> of and taking appropriate and timely <u>action</u> on all commitments and duties.

1

First Kiss

"You always remember your first kiss."

Valeta hurled the magazine at the bedroom door and rolled onto her back with fresh tears.

Her *first* kiss was not the problem! *She* had initiated the first kiss – that day in kindergarten when Jimmy had looked so cute playing on the computer – she had planted a juicy one right on his lips. Jimmy immediately reported this brazen breach of the "personal space rule" to the teacher, of course, and Valeta had been confined to a lonely blue corner for ten minutes. It was a small price to pay for a kiss, in those untroubled days when love consisted of sharing the longest red crayon or a pair of orange-handled scissors.

No, her first kiss was not Valeta's problem. It was her first *adult* kiss – that kiss on the beach last night – that had sprung the lid of Pandora's disaster-filled box.

Date with Responsibility

At sunrise the previous day, Sunday of that last week in February, Valeta awakened with a smile on her perfectly rounded, promising lips. Her sea blue eyes sparkled as a prying sun ray lifted their lids, and she stretched in eager anticipation.

"Edwin's taking me to Senior Luau this evening," she whispered to herself.

The nebulous sheer curtains at the window over her bed swayed, and the trade wind caught her whisper as it brushed her suntanned cheek with a moist kiss. A moist kiss – not a wet kiss. The realization satisfied her. She wanted not the lightest of Hawaiian rains today.

Her mouth's full bow arched upward even farther, and she dared to peer directly into the face of the proud sun. "Ah yes, you look awesome in oranges and yellows," she told it, "but prepare to be jealous, dear sun, when you see my dress for tonight's luau. Everyone will be jealous!"

Valeta sprang her lithe body from the bed trappings, and beckoned to the sun as she flitted across the room to her open closet. "Behold and covet, my fiery friend. Tonight I shall be positively irresistible!"

She draped the long black dress in front of her petite body and gazed into the full mirror. Her hair reflected the creamy yellow of the plumeria that adorned the black skirt, and she piled the golden tresses on top of her head. Dear Edwin. He would give her a yellow plumeria lei this evening, and it would be absolute perfection around the low-necked bodice.

"It's no mystery that I adore yellow plumeria," she told the sun, tilting her head three degrees toward flirtation. "Edwin would buy me nothing else."

Valeta undulated sinuously with the dress, and then hung it back in the closet. She changed to sweats, and padded to her private lanai, punctual as usual for her morning workout.

This exercise thing was Mom's idea in the beginning, back when Valeta had hated exercise. Mom had taken her aside on her twelfth birthday and insisted that Valeta begin to prepare her body for childbirth – for childbirth – at twelve! Silly! "Nevertheless," Mom had told her, "exercise in the teen years will make pregnancy and childbirth easier when the time comes."

The time would never come, if Valeta had anything to say about it. Mom stopped at one child herself, probably because the excruciating pain was more than any woman should bear. So why did Mom think Valeta would want children? Anyway, she had begun to exercise – because Mom demanded it. She continued exercising only because she liked it. It had nothing to do with preparing for child birth. If Edwin wanted a child, which she was sure he never would, he would have to adopt it from Afghanistan or Russia.

Date with Responsibility

Edwin – her mind abandoned the baby for a more palatable subject – tonight's Senior Luau.

The star quarterback had begged to be her date, as had most of the rest of the football squad. How delightful it had been to refuse every last one of them! How absolutely prodigious to spread the word that her escort would be a Marine from the nearby base in Kaneohe!

She giggled, remembering the magnificent round-eyed stares, the wonderful oohs and aahs that her news had garnered. Close friends had known since last June that she was dating the Marine, but her "older man" relationship still impressed them greatly.

As Valeta's lithe young body handled warm-up movements, her mind closed the file of memories and skimmed the day's schedule. She had to attend church first, but she would spend the afternoon shopping for perfect black strap sandals; polishing nails with pearl shimmer; shampooing golden hair; and assuring that Valeta Davidson was totally flawless for this evening's rendezvous.

One more cheerleader toe touch, and then gym ball flexes. The climbing sun mounted the bright orange sphere as Valeta positioned it, but the teen ignored the sun and lay across the ball, five-foot one-inch frame stretched fully, legs bent for balance. The blonde hair swept the weathered wood of the patio as she held the back stretch for

4

30 seconds, rested, and repeated it. Ten repetitions, and she turned to stretch her left side over the ball, then the right side. Finally, she sat astride the big ball and bounced, fully balanced and at ease. Routine completed, she tucked the gym ball into its corner, and turned toward the ocean.

Beach jogging – choice part of the exercises. She opened the arched ornamental gate and slipped through to run lightly across the green naupaka plants to the white sand beach. Running along the ocean's frothy edge would be easier, but dry sand gave a better workout, so she stayed above the high tide line and jogged the length of the beach's gentle arc. Just to the left of that green knoll – jutting into the vast Pacific Ocean – was Kaneohe Bay Marine Corps Base. She paused to conjure a pleasant image of Edwin starting his day.

"I saw you listed in the church program as clarinet soloist, but how do you pronounce your name?" Edwin's first words to her last June. Not very original, since everyone asked, but they sounded positively Promethean coming from the lips of a handsome Marine in Dress Blues.

"It's of Spanish derivation – a ballroom dance. Vuh-lee'-tuh." She stumbled over her own name, but Edwin caught her before she fell.

"An exquisite name – I thought it might be Native American," he said, and invited her to go snorkeling the next day in Hanauma Bay.

Date with Responsibility

"Exquisite name." She confided her secret to the moist ocean air, gave the green knoll one last momentary gaze, then turned and jogged back to the house. Her cardiovascular system yearned for a swim – not an ocean swim – a mellow pool swim.

In her room, she donned a faded green swim suit, so flimsy and comfortable from use it was a wonder it didn't dissolve from her body.

The house overflowed with silence as she tiptoed through the living room and dining area, out into the courtyard.

The morning sun had not stretched high enough to peek over the low roof, so only a nearby thrush saw as Valeta slipped into the pristine blue heated water, swam a few lazy strokes, and drifted onto her back.

Delightfully warm for February, even for Hawaii – forecast to reach the upper seventies by afternoon – which meant it would be perfect this evening – cool enough for a girl to need a cuddling arm around her bare tanned shoulders.

The sea blue eyes retreated as the sun climbed atop the brown shingled roof – retreated, but only from the outside scene.

"Why hasn't he kissed me," she challenged her inner faculties, "instead of always deferring? I understand holding certain things in abeyance, but a kiss? Why wait for my first real kiss from one who is nearly my fiancé? I understand believing in total abstinence until marriage, but where's the wrong in a real kiss instead of dry little pecks on the cheek? He kisses my hand, why not my lips? It is, after all, just a kiss."

It was easy to win the debate with herself, but quite another to win the same debate with Edwin.

Edwin contended that for a man twenty years old – he had just turned twenty – a kiss on her perfect pink lips, tempting as it was, would be much more than "just a kiss" and would change their relationship – make it more serious – move them closer to marriage.

He never said how it would accomplish that. He never explained where a delicate kiss got the extraordinary strength to transport a relationship such as theirs, which was by no means light. Nor did he tell precisely how much of that mysterious power a kiss on the lips had. He simply assured her of its potency, and insisted on unspoken changes that it would make.

Since four years of college separated the present from a potential wedding date, it was far too soon for that kind of kiss, he argued. They would be content with cheek and hand kisses for now – and no, he would not deviate from that.

But she knew otherwise, and she challenged aloud, "You're going to change your mind – tonight."

Date with Responsibility

"I don't know about someone's mind being changed, but your clothes had better be changed soon for breakfast, Valeta."

The blue eyes burst open and darted past a gilded sunbeam. "Grandmother, just how long have you been sitting there spying – and what time is it anyway?"

"Who's spying?" Grandmother bartered question for question, and grinned. "You aren't unique in your adoration of Hawaiian sunrises. If I were still in Colorado, I'd be still in bed, but I'm not – in Colorado or in bed – and these old bare feet love coming outside to greet a February day."

Valeta backstroked to the end of the pool, submerged briefly, and reappeared to repeat her second question. "What time is it, Grandmother?"

"Time for breakfast in fifteen minutes, if we're to get dressed and be at church in time."

Valeta dripped lazily up the stone-set pool steps and grabbed a fluffy beach towel. "I'll be ready before you," she challenged, eyes twinkling, "unless you dare to risk Mom's wrath by arriving at her table in silver nightgown and robe."

Grandmother, rising haughtily from the chaise lounge, took a few quick steps toward her granddaughter as she warned, "I'm not afraid of your mother, but you'd better be afraid of me, or you're going for an unplanned swim."

First Kiss

Valeta giggled and darted away, calling back, "I'll take you on tomorrow, Grandmother." It was hard to believe that such a fun-loving woman as Grandmother had birthed and raised such a crusty old Marine Colonel as Daddy. One more reason for never having children.

* * *

Grandmother had initiated Valeta's church attendance last winter. "I can't have a hibernal home with no hibernal church," she had said, "and I can't walk to church, so someone will have to take me. Who will it be?"

Neither Daddy nor Mom ever went to church, and neither Daddy nor Mom intended to begin going to church, so "Valeta will take you," Daddy ruled – over Valeta's protests that Sunday was the only day, other than Saturday, that she had to shop, and surf, and snorkel, and have fun!

Dear Grandmother took pity on her and sweetened the deal, though, by introducing Valeta to the church orchestra conductor – who needed a clarinetist – thought Valeta was good – invited her to join the orchestra, which she did – and become a church member, which she did – for what that was worth. Of course, its worth increased exponentially when she met Edwin at church.

This morning, Edwin sat with Grandmother during the church service, and Valeta would not see him until after church. Well, she would see him. From her seat in the reed section, she would see everyone until the sermon began, at which time every orchestra member was consigned to a front pew on either side of the aisle.

She tried to keep her thoughts on a short leash while she played – but the eager little daydreams kept racing as far as the leash allowed. Love – she was in love – and tonight was Senior Luau – a luau would be romantic – tonight she would get a true kiss from Edwin – so handsome. He wasn't wearing Dress Blues today. He had gone Hawaiian, donning a black silk aloha shirt, bordered at the bottom with a screen print of blue and mauve palm trees. Additional tiny palms swayed in scattered planting across the muscled black top. Not every man could wear that shirt, but Edwin could, his deep brown hair providing a striking balance for the dark cloth. Of course, it didn't hurt any that he was six-foot three inches tall, had wonderfully broad shoulders, and muscles like bands of steel.

Lance Corporal Edwin Laroque. Someday, four years, three months, and four days from today at the latest, she would be Valeta Laroque.

She moved quietly to a front pew for the sermon, her musings uninterrupted. "It's so exhilarating to think of marriage – exhilarating, yet daunting – or should be daunting."

Friends scoffed at that rationale, as did every character in the books she loved. Juliets perceived only the exhilaration – the sensual elements of marriage – but then – Juliets never experienced real life. In modern, everyday life, from what she heard, marriage involved work. People wrote it in women's magazines; discussed it on TV talk shows: marriage was hard, ongoing work. So the prospect of marriage was supposed to be daunting – but it never was to Valeta.

How could loving Edwin ever be laborious? She never could call it work to wash dishes and do laundry in the new little house Edwin would buy for her. She would be done in a flash, and then they would swim together every morning, snorkel every afternoon, and catch North Shore's big waves every weekend. Marriage would be a long, carefree life of continual bliss, she was certain.

Regardless of that certainty, though, she never could quell the fleeting qualms, and when she thought of divorced people she knew – parents of friends – the qualms strengthened.

Well, but those people chose the wrong mates. She and Edwin had a match that was *ne plus ultra*. Irreconcilable differences were out of the question for them. They never would fight; never would be jealous or unfaithful. They never would have the slightest reason for anything other than eternal marital bliss.

Date with Responsibility

Valeta twisted her wristwatch, and morphed the preacher into a female named Rose – a rose whose thorns had lost their points, she decided, and a rambling rose at that.

She returned to the much more fascinating inner soliloquy. "I'm absolutely certain that I can give Edwin a plausible argument against waiting four years to get married. I won't need a college degree with Edwin a military man. He's going to get the degree – an officer's rank like Daddy has. He won't be harsh like Daddy, though, or content to remain a mere Colonel either. With Edwin's intelligence, he'll achieve five-star General."

A movement on the ceiling caught her eye. "Wow! I wonder if anyone else sees that little green gecko on the rafter above the preacher's head. Oops! Hang on, little fellow. Oh! You almost fell! Stretch, gecko. Stretch upward. Get all four feet back on that beam. Almost.... Uh-ooooooh!"

Valeta's gasp joined a chorus of gasps as the tiny green lizard lost his footing, twisted in midair, spiraled twenty feet downward, and slipped smoothly beneath the loose Hawaiian collar of the man at the pulpit.

The stoical features contorted slightly, a nearly imperceptible spasm tugged one corner of the mouth, and a white hand briefly flicked at the intruder as the preacher's thin lips pressed forward on their predetermined mission.

First Kiss

Little sir gecko, however, had a different mission, and sought shelter on a sun-deprived shoulder as the congregation tittered.

The wooden preacher, strings hopelessly tangled and control gone, gyrated his upper torso, left hand diving beneath the flowered collar, right hand upsetting a water glass. His lips quirked, eyes gaped wildly – and then – all recovered. Only a small tic above the left cheek bone remained as he plunged toward the bottom of his page of notes.

Valeta giggled helplessly into her hands, symptomatic of a disease that spread rapidly. The violinist nudged Valeta in the ribs, extracting a hugely audible burp of laughter. The pew shook with a well-orchestrated echo.

Meanwhile, sir gecko raced downward to the waistband, counterclockwise, clockwise, down, and then – the little lizard pointed his nose toward the one source of fresh air and scampered.

"Oh!" howled the preacher, hastily yanking out his full shirt tail, and hopping awkwardly across the platform.

The solemn service aborted spontaneously. The organist proffered a postlude, but there were no takers. The auditorium percolated laughter.

Valeta jumped to her feet and ran to join Edwin where he stood with Grandmother Davidson, both of them wiping their eyes.

Date with Responsibility

"How funny was that – absolute hysteria!" Valeta exclaimed.

"Not for the preacher," laughed Edwin.

"I didn't realize those gingkos could fall," said Grandmother, dabbing away wet laughter.

"Gecko, not gingko," Valeta corrected as she pantomimed the gecko, "and they do fall at times."

Clumps of churchgoers formed on all sides, everyone embellishing the tale of the gecko's fall, each trying to outdo his neighbor. So entertaining was it all that Valeta nearly forgot they were to meet Daddy and Mom at Officers' Club for Sunday brunch. When she did remember, she ran to put away her clarinet, collected Grandmother from a merry pod of widows, and hurried out to the car.

The taffeta white Accord had been Daddy's gift to her on her sixteenth birthday. She had begged for red, but Daddy required safe white. He won in that as in everything – everything except her decision to date Edwin. Daddy failed there. His orders that she not date a man two years, three months her senior fell on ears deafened by Mom's reminder of Daddy's three-year seniority to Mom.

The white car actually turned out to be Edwin's favorite color, and the front seats adjusted enough for his long legs, which posed a problem in some cars. Of course, back seat passengers had to sit behind Valeta to avoid leg damage.

First Kiss

Today, Edwin helped Grandmother into the back seat, and slid behind the wheel. As he leaned to insert the key in the ignition, he brushed Valeta's cheek with a quick kiss.

"What are you wearing tonight?" he asked, turning his brown eyes to the road.

"Wouldn't you like to know!" she teased.

"I'll bet it's a misty blue muumuu."

"Muumuu? Nobody wears muumuus anymore, Edwin, and you should know that. Haven't you heard what they say about muumuus?"

"My imagination tells me that beautiful young blondes look very feminine in them."

"No – that those who wear them find that they eventually fit, and I really don't think that's the size wife you want, Lance Corporal Laroque."

Edwin gave her an easy laugh. "Excuse me. I'm just completing my first year in Hawaii, ma'am. I'm still a newcomer."

"Newcomers are *malihini*," she told him.

Edwin relinquished the car to a valet and ushered the women into the restaurant.

On the lanai, where Daddy had reserved a table by the golf course, Grandmother confided, "I know the Marines move you often, Donovan, and usually at your request, but I surely would miss this stunning view if you ever leave Hawaii, so you had better be a good boy and stay put this time. Maybe you can have that odd gypsy gene of yours surgically replaced with a homeowner's gene."

Daddy laughed at such an improbability, got to his feet, and led the way to crisp salad and fluffy soft omelettes.

It all looked delicious, and Valeta began to fill her plate, but quickly changed her mind. Senior Luau! She had to get into that long black dress this evening, and a big blueberry muffin buttoned onto each hip would not help. She settled for a small salad beside a spoonful of mushroom omelette, and returned to the table.

When Edwin sat down, hitching his chair closer to hers and cropping the scene to exclude everyone but her, she gave him an impish look. Then, leaning close to deliver the words to his ears only, she whispered, "I can't wait for tonight. I have an awesome surprise for you, and you'll never guess what it is."

He did not stand a chance!

2

Senior Luau

Finding the perfect black sandals presented a challenge, since Hawaii's dark winter fashions had given way to summer styles now that February was closing its doors. Valeta was undaunted by such a challenge, though, knowing how absolutely vital the black sandals were, and determining to ransack every store in Kailua if she must, to find that one perfect pair – or to perish in the effort.

Fortunately, dear Edwin was not there to witness her fastidious attention to detail, for he would have pointed out that she always ended up going barefoot on the beach anyway, so why fret over black sandals – especially sandals with high heels. He seemed to have not a clue when it came to shopping, poor boy. It was his singular failing.

"Which isn't at all bad," she assured herself as she entered the *open sesame* that was Liberty House Department Store.

.

Date with Responsibility

Liberty House abounded with enticing non-essentials, including an irresistible little black bag, but it flunked out on black sandals – as did nine other shops. She finally found the sandals in a tiny boutique, bought them, and glanced at her watch: a mere hour and a half until departure! Racing to the car, she sped home and dashed into the house.

"I'm back," she shouted as she ran through the cool living room to her bedroom.

"Edwin's absolutely frantic about something," Mom called from the kitchen, "and said you were to phone the second you returned."

"He'll see me in an hour, Mom, and I'll never be ready if I take time to call him because...."

"Call him, Valeta."

"Oh, all right." She propelled her bags toward the bed, grabbed her cell phone, and dialed as she ran to start the bath, wondering what was so earth-shaking that it couldn't wait until this evening.

"Hello." His deep baritone resonated in her ear.

"Hi, Edwin, where's the earthquake?"

"Centered between here and Kailua." His voice landed off-key. "I have bad news, Hon."

Valeta caught her breath, knowing instinctively what was coming – the Marines were transitioning him to a remote post, and he would ship out this evening – it could be nothing else.

Senior Luau

"Are you still there, Valeta?"

She slid limply to the tub's porcelain rim and reached for the gilded faucet, wishing the flow of bad news were as easily obstructed as the flow of water. "I'm here," she murmured.

"I don't know how to word this so that you won't misunderstand, but I'll have to miss your Senior Luau this evening to take duty for a sick Marine here at Base."

Hot tears pelted the tepid bath water as she asked, "But why you – can't they get someone else?"

"Me because I have the most understanding girl, Hon, and even if they did try to get someone else, most of the barracks is down with the same thing – food poisoning. It seems eating brunch with you at the Officers' Club was lucky for me."

"I understand," she lied dismally, "and there'll be other luaus, even if I miss this one."

Objections assaulted even as she spoke, demanding answers to how he could put work ahead of her after waiting so long for Senior Luau.

"But," he pleaded, "there's no reason to miss this luau because I made arrangements for you...."

"Whatever they are, it doesn't matter now, thank you," she said, choking determined tears.

"I want you to dress up and go anyway," he continued, "and...."

Date with Responsibility

"Edwin, I don't want to go alone and be a stupid wallflower."

"You won't be a wallflower because I arranged an escort." Edwin's words exploded in her ear.

"How could you," she shrieked, "when we're practically engaged! I can't date another man and even if I could, I don't want to date another man, and furthermore, I don't want you or anyone else arranging my life for me, so just tell Mr. Escort he can go by himself because I'm not budging!"

"Buttercup," Edwin tried again, "you're right. You shouldn't date another guy, and he isn't a date – just a nice guy in bachelor quarters who didn't get food poisoning but doesn't qualify for the night duty shift I'm taking."

"That's the extent of your knowledge – that he's a nice guy who didn't get food poisoning?"

"Valeta, the guy attends church here on base every Sunday, and he never swears or boasts about anything that would qualify him as a degenerate. Come on, Hon, do this for me, please? Your Senior Luau is a once-in-a-lifetime event and I want you to enjoy it. I'll send your lei with him, and you can take a lot of pics to show me later."

Valeta glanced at the silver-rimmed clock, considering how much fun it would be to go out with her friends as planned, and still with a guy who was a Marine, so she'd still have bragging rights – or ignoring rights, if she so chose – and she probably would choose the latter.

"Well, all right, I'll go, but tell him to meet me at the school because if I wait for him here, we'll miss the luau bus, and I'm not riding all the way out there in his car."

"Agreed," Edwin's relief was obvious. "The guy's name is Rick, and he'll be looking for the most beautiful girl in the school, but in case he misses you, watch for his Dress Blues."

"Formal Dress Blues at a Hawaiian luau when I'm wearing a...." She paused, the daydream of the black dress shattered, its purpose – to entice a kiss from Edwin – voided. "I'm wearing a black dress," she continued belatedly, "so Dress Blues will be fine – I have to hurry and get ready – I'll call you tomorrow."

"I'll be counting the minutes," he replied, "and please make it the great evening I know you can make it. Rick's very laid back, so he'll be easy to entertain, probably trying to learn the hula with you – speaking of which, be sure he takes pics of you in that Tahitian dance-off." He paused and finished in a whisper, "I'll be thinking of you all night, and wishing I could be there, but I'm glad you're going. You'll never forget this night."

She thanked him for finding an escort for her, and said a hasty good-bye.

Date with Responsibility

Never forget this night? He was undoubtedly right, since it would be the first night in nine months that she had gone anywhere with anyone other than Edwin Laroque.

She tossed the phone at the bed, turned, and yanked the plug from the bathtub, watching the anticipated bubble bath retreat down the drain in a gurgle of disappointment. Then she turned to the mirror, sighing tragically, "Mirror, mirror, on the wall, who is there that cares at all?"

Edwin had chosen work over their date, so who cared if her nails were pearl shimmer or natural; her hair piled high or hanging loose; her new black sandals and little black bag shiny patent or dirty burlap? She debated throwing on a muu-muu and flip-flops after all, but was too jealous of her reputation to risk it. Homecoming queen, cheerleader squad captain, and girls' track star were not honors to be handled lightly and, with only three more months to receive the adulation of Kailua High School, not to mention the fact that tonight's photos would grace the yearbook, it was hardly the time for a muumuu. The hair could hang loose around her face, though.

She brushed it quickly and reached for the long black dress. Size three petite was a lovely size, a size that guaranteed uniqueness. Nobody else would be wearing a dress like this one tonight. She zipped it from the hips to a spot low on her back, foregoing jewelry. A lei was necklace enough, one more beautiful part of this beautiful island, and long hair precluded the need for more than ear studs. As for rings – she glanced at the unadorned third finger of her left hand – well, maybe tomorrow evening when Edwin was filled with apologies for missing her Senior Luau.

"Valeta, I'll be your chauffeur," Daddy called. He was a dear bit of crustiness, and must have seen her dress – a definite driving hindrance.

"Thanks, Daddy," she called as she slipped into the black sandals and stuffed a few things in the new little black bag. "I have to get my camera, but I'll be there in a second," she assured, knowing that Daddy was at the door, keys in hand, eyes on watch.

"All ready," she announced a moment later, and spun to let Daddy admire her close-fitting dress.

"You're wearing that?" Daddy's bushy brows jerked to attention.

"Mom helped me find it – isn't it gorgeous? I got it for Edwin, but he can't go tonight, so he's sending an escort to take his place, and he's a nice guy who attends church on the base, and doesn't curse or anything – ready?" Her smile, a bit too bright, was parried by Daddy's stern frown.

"Did you feed your kitten?" Mom asked.

Date with Responsibility

"Oh, I forgot Leo! Can you feed him for me, Mom? I know it's my responsibility, and I'll do it from here on, but just this once...?"

"Just this once for the hundredth time since you got him, I'll do it, but he isn't my cat and you simply must take responsibility from now on."

"I will, I will, don't worry," she promised, and then, as Grandmother appeared, "Here goes your Hawaiian granddaughter to her Senior Luau, Grandmother. Wish me luck."

"It isn't luck that you need looking like that," said Grandmother, "but a big brawny bodyguard or two – and a highly trained pit bull."

Daddy put an arm around his daughter and steered her toward the door. "I guess I fit one of those categories," he said with a half laugh, but his eyes brimmed with concern, and he wished he knew more about this escort. Not that he had known much about Edwin either, but Edwin was a man's man, and everything a father could want for his daughter: principled; a brilliant mind – he never would do a thing to hurt Valeta. You could trust your daughter with Edwin any and every day, in any situation, but this escort – well, he probably was okay and it was, after all, a school event with chaperones, so she should be all right....

Nevertheless, as Valeta stepped carefully from the car in the school parking lot, Daddy threw her a word of caution – a poor, brief word that she missed as milling, excited teenagers stomped it into the black asphalt.

Daddy waved, and watched her disappear into a flock of chattering girls. She would be fine. Valeta knew how to take care of herself.

Colonel Davidson went home, and sat down to a delectable dinner of roast lamb.

* * *

"Hey Valeta," said the star quarterback, blocking her way, "that wasn't really you on the news last week, was it – hog-tying that crook?" He slipped an impudent arm around her.

"Sure it was," retorted a bystander, "which you would know if you weren't so mentally declined. Valeta learned hog-tying back in Arizona."

"But you can't be more than 5 foot 1 – 100 pounds at most," he said, intruding further into her personal space and measuring with his shoulder. "The crook was said to be 5 foot 10."

"He was about to steal my car," Valeta said, twisting from the star's eager grasp, "and I wasn't about to let him. I had speed from track training and rope expertise from horse training, so I grabbed my cell phone and rope, chased him about 300 feet, and tackled him. Then I tied his hand and wrapped the rope around his neck. Simple."

"Simple," added her friend. "Undebatably simple to perch atop him in her pajamas, phone the cops, and control him until the cops arrived. She had the coward completely at her mercy."

Jennie interrupted with a squeal. "Hey, there's Valeta's Marine! Wearing Dress Blues. Wow! Sharp!"

"I thought you said he was tall, Val. He's no taller than Maleko," observed Sachi.

"And you didn't tell us he had white hair," giggled Kani.

White hair? Valeta spun to find the object of their gossip. It had to be Rick. He was the only Marine that would be here. None of the other girls dated a Marine. She couldn't see him, though. Where was he? Did he really have white hair? Were they teasing her?

She spun back and laughed, "I thought you really did see my date and I would have to kill him."

"Uh, Valeta. Colonel White Hair's coming this way." Jennie squeezed her best friend's hand.

Valeta stared straight ahead into oblivion. She would rather die than go anywhere with a white-haired man, so she stared a hole into the crowd of teens – and the hole was very small, but so was she. She sprinted for the hole, and would have escaped if the long black dress had not cut her sprint to a tiny step – with an abrupt halt.

"Valeta Davidson?" A strong hand groped for her elbow, and a whining nasal voice drawled, "A lei for someone special." As he draped the lei of yellow plumeria around her neck, he engulfed her with a predatory expression, but she did not see it.

Her blue eyes traveled upward, reached his hungry grin far too soon, and slid back to the heart-sick plumeria flowers as she mumbled her thanks, and wondered why Edwin had not told her that the guy was from the deep south.

"They're loadin' up the wagons," he drawled loudly, "and you and me need to get us a front seat." He tried in vain to catch her hand

She hated the front seat, and had planned on maneuvering to get a back seat so she could have privacy, but not privacy with Rick. "Yes, the front seat's best," she told him and, stealing another quick peek at the dirty old man, found that he did not have white hair at all. He had hair the color of white beach sand, and was young, not old.

"I'm afraid we got off to a bad start with my clumsiness, Rick," she apologized. She lifted the long skirt and mounted the bus steps.

"Don't bother me none," said Rick, "since I'm a big klutz myself, which made boot camp _____, if you'll pardon my French."

Date with Responsibility

How dared he curse! Valeta glared.

"Hey," Rick said glibly, "the guys at Base cuss worse than that, and I just forgot I was with a lady." He sank into the window seat beside her and caught her hand, but only for an instant.

Valeta retrieved the hand as she slid closer to the aisle, craned her neck to find deliverance behind them, and saw Beth. "Oh, Beth, your dress is divine!" Valeta knew Beth only as someone who worked in the nurse's office, but prattled on, "Is your man here yet, or is he driving out to the luau?"

Beth arched a mousy eyebrow and looked from the back of the Marine's sandy head to the frantic face of Kailua's beauty queen. "Oh, my Ryan went early since he's in charge of everything," she chirped. Imagination was a gift most wondrous.

"But of course he did! Wait until he sets eyes on you, though, and that clever hair style – how do you do that?"

Beth stuck out her tongue as she flipped the simple ponytail off her shoulder and purred, "Oh, it's nothing, darling." Valeta and her precious Marine must be quarrelling.

"Then it must be that lipstick – is it the new kind that absolutely never comes off?"

"Of course it is," said Beth, and silently mouthed, "because I was born with it, silly."

Senior Luau

As the bus lurched into motion, Valeta leapt up and began prancing the aisle, laughing wildly at every joke, posing for every pulsing camera. Unobjectionably flirtatious, she giggled as she fell into the quarterback's lap, and blocked his bold kiss. She danced – disarming them – captivating them.

At Paradise Cove, the noisy crowd formed a single file on the long path, reaching for hands fore and aft as they trotted merrily back to Kindergarten days. A quieter Valeta walked in front of Rick with graceful bearing, studiously avoiding his friendly hands and friendlier gestures.

A quaint Hawaiian village at the end of the bumpy trail welcomed them to long tables piled high with juicy pineapples, papayas and mangoes.

Tiki torches burned on the perimeter of the village and Valeta burned with them, thanks to Rick's apology for an offense, coupled with his explanation that it was the result of baked beans he had eaten for lunch. Gross! This "nice guy in bachelor quarters" had better sign a lifetime lease for those quarters because he was going to need it!

Valeta shunned sophomoric Rick, and turned longingly toward the nearby beach where graceful coconut palms bent to catch the spray of white-tossed waves. Flight would not succeed just yet, but she would escape after darkness fell, and stroll the sandy seaside, pretending Edwin was with her, and that she was giving him her surprise.

Date with Responsibility

"Give us a V, give us an A, and an L-E-T-A," chanted a group at a nearby table, interrupting her thoughts. "Sit with us, Valeta."

Valeta led Rick to the wide table and sank onto a white plastic chair, committed to enjoy the luau for Edwin's sake, but....

Actually, this luau was not only her *senior* luau, but her *first* luau. Even though Daddy had been sent to Hawaii two years ago, his work kept him at the Marine Base, and the family didn't get into the local culture very often.

She eyed the curious Hawaiian feast, and joked loudly, "I hope this stuff isn't as digestively challenged as the food in the cafeteria."

"Oh, look!" Katie yelled, gesturing beyond the tables, "they're lifting the pig from the *imu*."

Four men, wearing nothing more than their flowered native skirts, lifted the enormous roasted pig from the underground oven as everyone cheered. Cameras flashed, and laughter bubbled. The *kalua* pig was the main course, baked in the ground with heated rocks and ti leaves and other ingredients. They had studied it in class, but most of the kids knew far more from experience than their Mainland teacher knew from all of his books.

The pig was fabulous – the meat so tender, it literally fell from the bones. Valeta liked the sweet potatoes and Lomi salmon, too.

But then there were *laulau*.

Many students gave the laulau a hot potato treatment, sending them quickly down the table.

"What's in them?"

"*Mephitis mephitis*, judging by the stench!"

The dark green taro and ti leaf bundles, a waiter explained, contained pork and fish steamed together. Valeta declined with a shudder.

But then there was *poi*.

Poi, pronounced like *toy*, was purple.

"Hey, who wants some purple wallpaper paste? Can I sell you a purple mud pack? Here, m'lady. The finest Hawaiian facial!" Every male in the senior class joined the merry torment.

"What *is* that?" Valeta had never seen poi.

"It's made with taro root – like potato," said the waiter, his dark eyes twinkling a bit too much as he answered.

"How do you make it, sir?" drawled Rick, pasting one poi dollop in the too-deep cleft of his chin and another on each rotund cheek.

"You peel the taro, steam it for about thirty minutes, and then pound it with a poi pounder, adding water until it's smooth and sticky." The waiter demonstrated the pounding process, and then showed them how to scoop up the pasty purple poi – not with a spoon – not with a fork – but with their fingers.

"Is this two finger poi or three finger poi?" asked Jenny, three pudgy fingers positioned above the small paper cup she held in the air.

"Oh, I would forget to explain that," said the waiter. "This is two finger poi, the poi's consistency measured by how many fingers you need to get it from the cup to your mouth – one, two, or three." He laughed warmly and moved on between the tables, joking and making sure every young guest was well fed.

Valeta said very little as she ate, watching the sun slide slowly down the evening sky to the restless ocean; watching the passive sky darken; waiting for her opportunity to desert discourteous, macho posturing Rick. She snapped pictures at first, but as couples partnered in Hawaiian games, and giggled at teachers' attempts to do the hula, a crushing loneliness pushed her camera into the new bag. She put the bag under her chair and wrapped her chilly shoulders in deep, watchful silence.

Rick, watching from icy silence beside her, suddenly jumped from his seat and yelled, "Hey, ya'll wanna see me do the hula?" He leaped onto the stage with the performers and began to gyrate, eliciting boisterous guffaws and whistles from the crowd as he mixed clumsy jumping jacks with an elephant waltz.

Senior Luau

How dare he mortify her in front of her class! Enough was enough, and too much was plenty. Valeta slipped off the perfect black sandals, and ran into the darkness with not one backward glance.

She was on the beach in a moment, peace welcoming her warmly, and throwing a light shawl around her. The towering dark palms beckoned her eyes upward, and her body into their shadows. The palms moved with the music of aloha, the music of the islands, and invited her to dance with them.

Her lissome body began to sway, matching its rhythm to the rhythm of the long palm fronds, forgetting Rick. On their own, her graceful arms lifted toward the fronds, trying to weave island history as the hula dancers did. Someday, she would study hula – learn the real hand movements.

The dancing guitars blended gently with the base roll of the waves and the brushing of the fronds. Valeta yielded to it all, imagining she was dancing for Edwin. Her hips moved gently, her long dress swayed, and she welcomed tranquility.

But suddenly, someone grasped the swaying hips – undulated his body against hers – told her that she was wickedly beautiful – far too good for that Marine of hers. "Stop it!" She twisted away.

"You know you like it, sugar. That's why you came out here all alone in the dark. I saw your little come-hither look."

Date with Responsibility

"You saw no such thing. Now go away!"

"I want to give you something." He held her tightly, pulling her deeper into the grove of palms, his smoldering voice insisting, "Y'all would like that Marine of yours to give it to you, but I'm here and he isn't." Fiercely, he forced her slim face close to his own, his breath burning her nostrils as he said, "This is from your goody goody Marine." He pressed his thick lips intensely against her soft ones, suffocating her until she opened her mouth. When he took advantage, she snapped her mouth shut and he yelled. She called on her fleeing strength and fought back, scratching, biting, hitting, and kicking. She stomped her bare feet on his boots, wishing for spike heels.

"You won't hog-tie me, darlin'," he snarled. "I've had five years of judo, and this body's registered with the government as a lethal weapon." Building his passion with heaving breaths of oxygen, the ruthless man wrestled her to the ground, pinned her, knelt over her, and smothered her cries with his left hand. His right hand tore at her long black dress while the wild ocean raged behind him. He cracked a long whip of profanity over her head as he tore, pushing her into the sand, kissing her cruelly and – savagely – biting her nose.

Suddenly – there was an eternity of tearing pain. Valeta managed a single piercing scream, just one, and then he applied a choke hold. She lost all consciousness.

3

Violated

There was very little of Sunday night that she remembered on Monday – so many pieces she could not retrieve. Who found her in the coconut grove, and how did she explain her torn clothing? Did someone call her parents, and did Edwin know?

Valeta cried all day, but did not sleep or eat or speak – did not attend school.

Sometime on Monday, she tried to look at a magazine, her swollen eyes aching to their optic nerves as she pressed one hand against her forehead and turned the pages.

Stay-put lip gloss. Pinstripe denims. Quit smoking secrets. Adorable Australian pets. Spring hair styles. Top musical group.

Petty topics. Prodigal. Page after page of trivial pleasures. Passing fancies. Pure hedonistic frills. Self-tests – everything about the real you.

Date with Responsibility

She closed her eyes, but the hideous dark video of last night was still running in her head, driving her back to the blurry pages.

"You always remember your first kiss."

Valeta hurled the magazine at the bedroom door and rolled onto her back with fresh tears.

Her first kiss – first mature kiss – stolen from her – forcibly stolen from her – stolen, too, from Edwin. After waiting so long – so long. This was all she would have to remember as her first kiss – and she knew she would remember – bitterly – for the rest of her life.

She jumped up, and made her indistinct way from the limp bed to the bath, the softness of the natural-shaped lambskin rug coaxing her bare feet away from the hard white tiles to linger, but only for a moment.

She threw off her pajamas and stepped quickly into the shower, water as hot as she could bear – more soap – more shampoo – more vigorous scrubbing. She lathered the ginger shampoo into her long hair and closed her eyes against the stinging suds, but he was there, still there behind the long lashes, his evil, hard eyes blazing into hers.

Frantically, Valeta threw her head under the water, and opened her eyes, a low prolonged sound of grief and pain filling the shower stall as she sank to the floor. Let the hot water deluge her, mingled hot water and hot tears. Neither could cleanse, but let the hot rain pelt her forever – until they found her corpse, and grieved with her.

"Valeta, there's someone here to see you." Mom's voice drifted vaguely through the veil.

Valeta made no effort to answer.

"Valeta," Mom's voice wore Valium satin, "if you can hear me, turn off the shower, so I know that you are all right."

Slowly, Valeta stood up. She turned off the shower, but did not speak.

"Valeta, Edwin's been waiting for you by the pool. Come out and –" the words confused Mom, "and have lunch with him in the courtyard."

Vacant eyes stared back from the mirror as the petite blonde stepped from the shower stall. She swathed her wet form in a towel, opened the door, and shook her head negatively.

"You really need to see him." Mom's eyes gazed through personal pain. "What have you done to your nose? It's bleeding."

Valeta closed the bathroom door and locked it, felt her way to the chair at the far end of the room and sank down, dropping her wet head onto the white vanity table. The coolness of the wooden table soothed her hot forehead, relieving some of the pain that tortured her swollen sinuses.

Date with Responsibility

"Valeta, I'm going to tell Edwin that you're sleeping, and that he should go home and rest, too." Mom's voice lingered, and Valeta knew that Mom herself lingered outside the bathroom door, but Valeta turned her cheek to the soothing cool wood and said not a word.

How long she sat there, wrapped only in the thick blue towel, Valeta could not guess. Nor could she guess why she finally stood. She simply found herself dressing slowly in fresh pajamas, putting a large, clear Band-Aid on her tiny nose, and shuffling back to the bedroom, her hair in gnarled, ignored tangles. She pulled her white silk robe from the closet and wrapped it over her pink pajamas.

When her cell phone rang for the umpteenth time, she launched it into the living room, slammed the door, and then viciously kicked a mostly-empty pizza box under the bed.

Beyond the window, fog swirled across the ocean waves, up the beach and into her mind. So different from yesterday. So different. Yesterday was perfection – but today....

Her hands knotted and re-knotted the ties of the pure silk robe, crushing the work of the tiny silk worms. She caught the hands at it, and angrily making them stop and undo every pinched knot, she stroked the demure orchids that embroidered the collar, remembering when Edwin gave her this robe last Christmas, just two brief months ago when life was exciting and full of promise. He loved to see her in white, he said, and in green, blue, pink, and.... He had named every color in Crayola's Top 50 Box, and she had giggled at his attempt to remember *laser lemon* and *electric lime*.

The memory of it refreshed her sobs. She would never see Edwin again. He was here today only to accuse and berate her – to break off their relationship and retrieve his friendship bracelet. She was certain of it – as certain as she would have been had his own lips told her. Hot, salty tears stained the chaste orchids and she gazed at them in dismay. Their beauty was defiled, besmirched. Their innocent purity was gone forever.

Her fretful mind returned to the cluster of palms on the luau beach. What had she done? Was it the dress? Was it too tight? It had to be the dress. She had given him no reason to think she liked him. She had not worn the *Wicked Wahine* perfume that she had planned to wear. Maybe it was the lilt of the hula music. The hula was seductive. She knew that. She was not naive. She thought she was alone when she danced, but she should have been more careful. She should have been sure nobody was watching before she swayed her hips that way. He had to do what he did. She made him do it.

As she sank into the wicker chair by the window, throwing her head back, she became aware of the sun's blood-red glow on the white curtains.

Date with Responsibility

Red glow. What was it about that red glow? There had been a red glow last night. Where? Memory faltered. A tiki torch at the luau? No, it was brighter. Hotter. After the luau.

Suddenly, Memory shouted in her brain, *"Fire! There was a huge fire last night!"*

She started in the chair, remembering. Of course. It erupted in the wee, dark hours of this morning – Monday. How did she block it from her thoughts? She stared at the red-soaked curtains. Daddy and Mom had been in bed when she got home from the luau last night. At least, as far as she knew, they had been in bed. Closing her eyes, Valeta trailed Memory back in time – back to last night's luau – back to the sandy beach.

In the moonless night, a huge man hovered over her like a big Hawaiian *kahuna*, a dark flowered *lavalava* barely meeting around his paunch. Would he use witchery to heal her or, more likely, would he sacrifice her to a descended spirit?

"We go already," he said. That was all. He bent his huge bulk, scooped her from the damp sand and, despite his size, ran easily along the tide line, her weight seemingly nothing to him. Reaching a narrow, steep trail between rocks, he left the beach and carried her upward to a dark, deserted field where, without a word, he opened a car door with one hand, set her inside, and closed the door. Then he heaved himself into the driver's seat.

Violated

"Yo' stay living in Honolulu?" the man asked in deep Pidgin.

Valeta shrank against the passenger door, aghast at the thought of what he might do to her. She could not run from him in the tight dress and even if she could, she knew neither where she was nor where she could go. "Kailua," she whimpered.

Without a reply, the big man urged the car's engine to action. It hacked lustily, but adjusted to a somewhat steady rhythm as he flicked on the lights. A dim ceiling bulb revealed a repulsive, dingy gray blanket and pillow wallowing together between the seats, trying unsuccessfully to conceal empty takeout boxes and squashed cups – how many days' worth, she did not care to know.

The driver struggled to pull his lavalava over hairy, knobby knees, and rumbled, "Yo' come tankful dat somebody going find yo'. Dark night to swim. Where yo' stay living in Kailua?"

He seemed to think she had gone for a late night swim, so perhaps he really did mean to take her home. Brokenly, she stammered out her home address, and then shrank from him again, turning her face to the food-smeared window. She refused to utter another word during the long drive – even when he had to stop for gas, and asked if she would like a cold soda – even when at last he stopped in front of her house and asked in his rough Pidgin, "This yo' hale (hah-lay)?"

Date with Responsibility

Valeta nodded to agree that it was her home, but offered no "thank you" as she leapt from the car, ignoring the battered door that remained open, and racing away as fast as the desecrated dress would allow. She heard the man close the door, but realized that he made no move to go. She wanted to shriek at him – tell him to get out of here NOW!

She staggered barefoot across the lawn – felt him watching as she fumbled with the front door, found it unlocked, and stepped inside. She secured the lock behind her, and lurched drunkenly through the living room to her bedroom, hungry for its security. She longed to turn on the lamp, but chose darkness rather than let him know where she was in the house. The clock's pale green LED, nearly at 3 AM, would have to suffice. She sank onto the bed and listened to the heavy silence that concealed the Hawaiian man's thoughts as well as his actions. Surely, he would go now, unless he was spying on her. She barely breathed as she waited.

When the eventual cough of an engine marked the filthy car's departure, she sighed in relief and then, suddenly racked with sobs, fumbled out of the mangled dress, took a long, hot shower and put on her blue satin pajamas, only to stand in the middle of the room and stare. She dared not go to bed, or try to sleep. She stuffed the ruined dress in the darkest corner of her closet, and realized for the first time that the black sandals and little black purse were gone. Had Jennie or another friend picked them up for her – or were they in the big kahuna's possession? She shivered.

Still crying, she moved to the living room, closer to Daddy, and curled herself deep into a blue and white chair. The chair faced the French doors leading to the courtyard, but heavy blue drapes offered protection from the forbidding darkness.

Leo jumped onto her chair, issuing a string of commands and questions as he licked at her nose, his little tongue strangely painful.

Valeta hugged the kitten close, her fingers obediently stroking his fur, her thoughts still accompanied by sobbing. If only she had refused to go to the luau, stayed home to take care of Leo, and called Edwin to talk during his break. If only.... She would have her perfect black sandals, her black bag, and the size three petite dress – all new and perfect – for her next date with Edwin. But now, dates with Edwin were out of the question.

She looked down, fingering a red spot on the little Himalayan's white fur, and then raised her head. The drapes, too, were reddish-orange.

Valeta jumped to her feet, dumped Leo to the chair, and yanked open the heavy drapes. Unmistakable flames, accompanied by screams, erupted from the opposite side of the courtyard. Fire! The master bedroom was on fire! Mom and Daddy were running toward the garage.

Date with Responsibility

Valeta whirled as a chilly hand touched her shoulder from behind.

"What's happening, Valeta?" Grandmother Davidson blinked sleepily. "Why did you scream?"

Scream? She did not remember screaming. Mutely, she pointed at the flames.

"Call 911!" Grandmother ordered.

But Valeta did not move.

"Valeta!" Grandmother shook her, but Valeta only stared. "Oh, I'll call," said the older woman. "Grab a robe and get out of the house. Hurry! Go out on your patio!"

Valeta stared at the flames, paralyzed. They seemed to be tiki torches. Dozens of tiki torches. Closer. Burning brighter. Orange sabers slashing the sky. A figure dancing in the light of the flames. A man. A strong, athletic man. Running.

Grandmother made the call and returned, but Valeta still stood where she had left her. "Valeta! The firefighters are on the way. We must get out of the house." Grandmother threw a lap robe over the girl's shoulders and pulled her away from the French doors. "Hurry! Here's your kitten." She plucked Leo from the chair and thrust him at Valeta. "Go out through your bedroom. Out on the patio." She coughed as acrid smoke filtered into the room. "Hurry, child!"

Violated

Valeta felt her body being propelled toward the bedroom. Her feet moved to keep up.

The light of the orange sabers stabbed the night darkness – stabbed at the tiny ball of fur in her arms. An indignant meow quivered on his pink lips. She drew the kitten closer, hurrying ahead of Grandmother. They reached the patio as sirens pierced the smoky night air, and Valeta craned to see over the wall. She could not see the master suite from here – could see only flames and the pulsing red strobes of the fire engines. Were Mom and Daddy safe?

Grandmother Davidson led her to a patio chair and answered the unspoken question. "Your father and mother got the cars out of the garage. I saw them parking them down the street. We all are safe, and the firemen will have the fire contained soon. I wonder how it started."

Valeta gazed unseeingly. Her eyes, aching from the prolonged crying, were swollen and red. Her mind rebelled at the thought that began to form within it. No! Surely not. She could not know how the fire started. She did not see anyone – or did she? The thought tormented her as they waited until finally, with the fire chief's permission, they joined Daddy and Mom in the courtyard. The crew had nearly finished their work and the pool, so clean and sparkling a few hours ago, was sodden with ashes and debris.

Date with Responsibility

The fire chief gave a few final words of direction to his crew, and hurried to the Davidsons, skirting the dirty pool to bring a report.

"The good news is that the fire is now fully contained," he told them. "The bad news is that there is clear evidence of arson. The fire crew found what appears to be an incendiary device tied to a pipe inside the sauna. A police arson investigation will be opened soon, of course, but if you know who might have wanted to make trouble, we can look for the individual right away."

The fire chief peered straight into Valeta's eyes. Did he suspect that she knew who it was? How could she know?

Rick! The truth exploded in her brain. It was so obvious! He knew where she lived. Edwin had given him the address, so he knew the house, but not the room. Had he known the room, she would not be standing here draped in blue pajamas and a white robe – she would be lying over by the fire engine, zipped into a black body bag.

Icy fear moved her closer to Daddy. They did not know what happened at the luau. Daddy might question why she stayed out so late, but he would never suspect that Rick had ....

Her mind repelled the frightful word, and suggested a second possibility – the big local man that brought her home from the beach!

The fire chief pursued his questioning. "Are you sure that nobody has a personal vendetta against one of you?" His eyes returned to Valeta. "Is there anyone who would want to hurt you?"

Daddy snorted. "No. Not unless the Honolulu police freed that robber Valeta captured."

Valeta nodded at the ground, and silently twisted a few strands of blonde hair.

"We haven't made enemies here." Mom's voice shook. "We hardly know anyone outside of the military, and none of them would do this. Why would someone try to murder us?" Tears gathered in her throat.

"Ma'am, we don't know that the motive was murder. It could be mere youth vandalism – done out of boredom or thrill-seeking. It could be revenge against the military taking Hawaiian land, or it might stem from mental illness. There may be no criminal motivation at all, but we won't know until after the investigation."

The fire chief's questioning was interrupted by the arrival of a Honolulu police officer. The officer thanked the fire chief, and suggested that the family go inside. "Our personnel will need to do a thorough search of the property," he said, "as well as take photographs and collect samples, so they will need access to the entire area. I will let you know what we find."

Date with Responsibility

Mom resisted – the officer insisted – and they all were ushered into the house.

Daddy and Grandmother exchanged views on the arson quietly, but Mom became irrational, demanding, "How will we sleep at night? I'm sure they meant to kill me. They'll come back. We have to go to a hotel. We have to leave Hawaii."

"Don't panic, Marjorie." Daddy tried to quiet her. "They didn't try to kill you."

"Of course they did!" Mom's fear increased in volume. "The fire started in the sauna, didn't it, and who uses the sauna? I do. They tried to kill me, Donovan."

Daddy turned her from the door, pulled her against himself, and raised martial eyebrows. "They used the sauna because it was wood and there was a suitable place to attach their bomb."

"Bomb?" Mom actually screeched. "Bomb? Oh, Donovan, we're going to die!"

It was easy for Valeta to be silent with Mom blabbering in a delirium of terror.

Daddy's every attempt at comfort failed, and he finally gave up. "I need to get over to the base."

"You can't leave me alone!" Mom shrilled, clutching him. A second thought struck her and she pushed him away. "You can't get dressed for work! Your uniforms were destroyed! My clothing destroyed. Everything is gone!" The enormity of the fire registered in Mom's green eyes. "*Everything*! Our clothing – our photos – our wedding photo – my beautiful wedding gown. Oh, Valeta! The wedding gown was going to be yours – for your wedding to Edwin! It's gone! Everything's gone!"

Mom's eyes glazed over and she stared ineloquently toward the ashes of her proud life for a moment before turning. She felt her way grayly to the couch, and fainted across it, only to revive and begin screaming hysterically.

Daddy watched for five seconds, then kicked into Colonel mode. Tightening his jaw, he strode to the kitchen phone. Brusquely, he asked for Dr. Soo, summarized their situation, and requesting a sedative for his wife, hung up. He told his mother he would get whatever he needed at the Base, and hurried out, clad only in pajamas and robe.

Within twenty minutes, the Valium was delivered, and Grandmother led Mom to the guest room, where she administered it directly. As the hysteria gradually subsided, Mom fell asleep, and Grandmother went to the kitchen.

Valeta was left alone. She had not spoken a word the whole time, but nobody seemed to notice. Her persistent sobbing also had gone unnoticed. Mom's performance had driven from their minds any questions about Valeta. So now she stood, still holding Leo, and wandered into her bedroom.

Date with Responsibility

The fire was her fault. Rick undoubtedly believed that she would report him to the Marine Corps and that he would receive a court martial. She could hear Daddy's voice, speaking from last summer, telling them about a Marine who received a court martial for rape.

"He's despicable!" exclaimed Daddy, "and under the *Uniform Code of Military Justice*, the military's maximum punishment for rape is death."

"That's extreme," Mom had replied.

"Extreme?" Daddy had bellowed. "Death should be the *minimum* punishment for such a heinous act, not the *maximum*! If any man ever dared do that to my daughter, I would be certain he got death, even if I had to storm the Pentagon to achieve it!"

Valeta shuddered, and put Leo on the bed. Rick was not taking chances with a court martial. That was why he lit the fire. He decided to cover his first crime with a second – arson and intent to murder.

Well, two could play at that game. She was not sure how, but she was up to the challenge.

She went to the closet and pulled out her running shoes. Tying them on quickly, she reached for a jacket. The pre-dawn air would be damp and cold down on the beach.

4

Inquisition

Kailua High School buzzed with speculation Monday morning: Valeta Davidson absent for the first time this year – and on the most auspicious day of the year – when she was to be announced Homecoming Queen!

The absence of any other student might go unremarked, but not that of the Homecoming Queen. Moreover, even the absence of the queen would engender less intrigue was there no more gossip involved, but there was more – much more.

- √   Valeta left the luau early.
- √   Valeta's Marine left the luau early.
- √   The Marine never returned to Base.
- √   A fire erupted at Valeta's home.
- √   Someone found a corpse on the beach.
- √   The corpse was the Marine.
- √   Valeta must be involved.

Date with Responsibility

As locker doors banged between class hours, scandal littered the air:

"She didn't stop with hog-tying this time!"

"That guy was a loser with a capital L!"

"But Valeta didn't have to kill him!"

"Hey, she's innocent until proven guilty."

"If she didn't kill ol' Rick, who did?"

"Maybe the arsonist killed him."

"Yeah? So, who's the arsonist?

"Maybe Valeta's the arsonist."

"Burn her own home?"

"Nobody's hurt, and insurance will pay for it."

Valeta had no knowledge of the gossip, of course. Oh, she was not so naive that she did not know there would be gossip – that was one of the reasons she stayed home today, although not the only reason. The events of Sunday night, the lack of sleep, and the tears that refused to stop had left her exhausted, not to mention the disaster scene that was her face.

She had gone to the beach hoping the cold predawn ocean air would make her stop crying, tighten her pores, clear her mind – but it had been in vain and everything remained obscure.

She never stopped to think, in the chilly darkness preceding sunrise, that she might meet someone on the beach – especially him.

Inquisition

She shuddered and whispered softly to the listening walls, "Too late now. Can't turn back the clock – and nobody will believe me – nobody will believe any of what happened."

She got up to soak a thick blue face cloth in cold water and then, pressing it against her eyes, returned to the chair. A sudden knock on the door made her catch her breath.

"Valeta, open the door." Daddy. He was not supposed to be home until dinner time.

"Valeta, may I come in?"

Valeta remained silent, counting on Daddy's personal code of behavior that prevented him from opening her door without permission.

"Valeta." Daddy's voice was strained. "A police officer wants to talk to you."

A police officer! Valeta said nothing.

"Valeta, I must make an exception and open your door." The knob turned, Daddy crossed the room in three strides, handed his daughter a small, laminated gray card and whispered, "Give no information. Just read what is on this card."

Valeta stared at the card, her eyes aching so that she could barely focus on the small print, and read "Legal Aid." She tossed the face cloth at the sink, and submitted to Daddy's command.

Date with Responsibility

The Colonel led her to the living room, and gestured for them all to sit.

"Valeta," said Officer Lee, "I will begin by reading your *Miranda Rights*. Please listen." He read from his own small card, and Valeta nodded after each of the first five questions:

1. You have the right to remain silent and refuse to answer questions. Do you understand?
2. Anything you do say may be used against you in a court of law. Do you understand?
3. You have the right to consult an attorney before speaking to the police and to have an attorney present during questioning now or in the future. Do you understand?
4. If you cannot afford an attorney, one will be appointed for you before any questioning if you wish. Do you understand?
5. If you decide to answer questions now without an attorney present you will still have the right to stop answering at any time until you talk to an attorney. Do you understand?
6. Knowing and understanding your rights as I have explained them to you, are you willing to answer my questions without an attorney present?

Officer Lee raised his head at the end of the final question, and waited.

Valeta stared, dumbfounded for a moment, and then looking down at Daddy's legal card, she read in a shaky voice:

"If it is your intention to question, detain or arrest me, please allow me to call an attorney immediately."

Inquisition

Officer Lee sighed. "I'll wait," he said.

Valeta looked up, surprised. She had not expected him to wait. She turned to Daddy.

"I'll call," Daddy said. "Wait in your room."

"I'm afraid I'll have to ask her to wait here," interrupted the officer, "since Valeta is being questioned on suspicion of murder."

Murder! The word struck with the force of a fully loaded freight train, and Valeta fell back into her chair. Murder!

"Say nothing!" Daddy barked the words as he reached for his cell phone. He selected a speed dial number and, in moments, had convinced his attorney to come immediately.

The Colonel closed the phone and turned to confront the officer. "Who was murdered and why is Valeta a suspect?" he demanded tightly.

"A young Marine," said Lee, "who escorted your daughter to the high school's Senior Luau, where they both disappeared. His body was found on the beach early this morning and, although the tide had washed away all footprints, we found a pair of women's sandals and a purse nearby. We have reason to believe they may belong to Valeta."

The officer opened a large bag and produced the black sandals and purse, each sealed carefully in a labeled plastic bag.

Date with Responsibility

A gasp escaped Valeta's lips. They were hers! But she left them under her chair at the luau table. Where did the police get them?

"Do you know anything about the murder?" He risked charges of police misconduct in asking.

Murder. Valeta stared straight ahead. Her escort had been murdered. Rick was dead.

"I was on the beach..." The words began tumbling forth of their own volition.

Daddy jumped up to silence her, but it was not necessary. The words stopped as abruptly as they had begun.

Valeta made not another sound until the attorney arrived, and the hour after he did arrive had the intense irrationality of a dream.

Harsh and relentless questions flew. She answered a few. She left many unanswered.

"What is your name?"

"Valeta Davidson."

"What is your address?"

She told him.

"Where were you on Sunday night?"

"At Senior Luau."

"Who was your date?"

Inquisition

Valeta looked at the floor and her attorney stated sharply, "My client wishes to maintain her right to silence."

"Your date was Rick, wasn't it? What is Rick's last name? You don't know, do you? All you know is that he took the place of the Marine you wanted to be with. Isn't that right?"

"As I said, my client wishes to maintain her right to silence," reminded the attorney.

The police officer ignored him. "You left the luau with the deceased, went to the beach, had a fight with him – which explains the wound on your nose – and then you killed him, didn't you?"

Perspiration beaded on her forehead, but she said nothing as the attorney reiterated in mounting anger, "She wishes to remain silent!"

The officer's tanned face contorted with displeasure. "Miss Davidson, you might as well come clean, because your classmates implicated you already," he lied. "I have spoken, also, to luau workers who saw you leave with the deceased. You do understand, don't you, that cooperation will make things much easier for you?"

Valeta wanted to cooperate, but Daddy's attorney intervened, telling the officer, "We will not cooperate in your attempt to get a confession or a statement of any kind. Furthermore, we will sort out this matter in court, not here."

Date with Responsibility

The officer apologized, and changed tactics, smiling warmly at Valeta as he said, "You are a wise young woman with a wise solicitor, and you have begun to convince me that you are not guilty. The only problem is that when you maintain your right to silence, it makes you *appear* guilty."

He moved to a different chair – made it impossible for Valeta to see him and the attorney at the same time as he tapped his note pad with his pen. "If I have to write in my report that you hid behind your Miranda Rights, it won't look good, Valeta, so let's begin again – and let's not turn an easy case into a difficult one."

This time, the officer used statements instead of questions, and each statement was cloaked in the softest of words. It must have been awful to accept a substitute date for her Senior Luau. And what a shame that the substitute date was such a buffoon. That could spoil the evening for any girl, let alone the Homecoming Queen. Why, just to know that everyone was watching her – thinking that jerk was her boyfriend....

He paused, studying Valeta closely, and then continued. On and on he talked, weaving a story of a young girl given no choice but to shoot her escort with his own gun.

Finally, Officer Lee fell silent, waiting for Valeta to volunteer a statement; counting on the tension and discomfort to produce a confession.

Inquisition

Valeta avoided the officer's trap, but only by remembering a magazine story about police interrogation. The suspect had picked a spot on the wall behind the interrogator, imagined the words "no comment" painted there in fluorescent yellow, and stared at it for the entire interview.

She raised her head. Behind Officer Lee hung an oil painting Mom had bought – a fiery representation of the Big Island's main volcano. Intently, she imagined "NO COMMENT" burned into the black lava in flaming letters, and then began to stare fixedly at the words.

The peace officer returned to his harsher style of questioning, but Valeta simply stared at the imaginary words and ignored him.

"Don't toy with me, young lady," said the officer. "I can make things tough for you."

"Are you threatening my client, sir?" The attorney leaned toward the officer with a crooked grin. "I remind you that you have no warrant for her arrest, and to get such a warrant, you must show probable cause. I suggest you go home and memorize the *Fourth Amendment*. Then we can talk rationally about the matter."

Officer Lee stood up and jammed his small notebook into a pocket. "I will be back – *with* a warrant of arrest," he shouted. "I'll be back!" He was out the door before the last word faded.

Date with Responsibility

The attorney got to his feet. "You have raised a strong young woman, Colonel," he said, admiration clear in his voice. "She has nothing to fear with a backbone like that. I will be back early tomorrow morning to hear her story in detail and negotiate our plan of action."

"We will cooperate fully," said Daddy, "but I must make one request. Don't let her mother or grandmother hear anything about this. My wife is distraught enough with the fire. I don't think she could handle the possibility of her daughter being arrested. And my mother – well, she doesn't need to know that her granddaughter ever has been a suspect in such a thing."

"I'm sure we can do that. In fact, I'm fairly certain we can keep it out of the papers, and off of the news entirely, if Valeta truly is innocent."

The attorney turned to encourage Valeta, but she was gone.

5

Circumstantial Evidence

Killed with his own gun.

The words rang a death knell in her mind. She did not think he would die – could not have hoped for such good luck, but really, it was his own fault – carrying a loaded hand weapon to a high school luau – and carrying it in the ready-to-fire mode. Obviously a rotten decision.

She noticed the M9 pistol when he got up to dance the hula, if those gyrations could be dignified by the word *dance*. It protruded only for a moment from under his Dress Blues, but she saw it – and recognized it as the same kind Edwin let her shoot once. Edwin gave her lessons in basic pistol training for self defense last autumn, then let her try his M9 just for the experience.

It was nothing like the one she used in class at the weapons academy. It had such an enormous circumference, she could barely get her tiny hand around it, let alone shoot it with confidence. She laughed about it with Edwin, and vowed she would never use such a pistol again – self defense or not. She meant it, too.

Nevertheless, when a man is shoving a girl into the damp beach on a moonless night, she will use anything she can get.

Valeta washed her face, and painfully combed each snarl from her long blonde hair, studying the desolate reflection in the mirror above the sink. What must Officer Lee have thought? Her wound oozed from under the Band-Aid, and her eyes! Had she not possessed such naturally enormous ones, they would have disappeared between the blotchy red of her eyelids. Her inflated lips were no prize, either. She touched them with a finger – more cracks than a Saharan riverbed. No chance of anyone kissing those. Edwin certainly would not want to kiss her today. She brushed at fresh tears. Edwin would never want to kiss her again – never. She dropped the brush, letting it lie where it landed as she wandered back to the window, and watched afternoon shadows lengthen on the beach. It would be dark out there in a few hours.

Rick was dead. Killed with his own gun.

The leaden words burrowed into her mind. She must have been the one who killed him – her new sandals and handbag were near the scene, but she did not remember killing him. Could you shoot a man to death and not remember?

A knock at the door derailed her train of thought, and she opened the door mutely.

"Valeta, the attorney wants to talk to you again." Daddy led her to the dining table.

Another surreal hour with the attorney unraveled more of the riddle, but did not solve it. He had discussed the evidence with the police – and all of it was circumstantial.

"Rick's body, his service gun and dog tags missing, was found on the beach near the site of the luau, all footprints in the vicinity washed away by the tide, but clear footprints fifty yards down the beach – bare footprints. Your sandals and purse were found at the luau site, but there were no witnesses, despite what the officer told us, and nobody saw you leave the luau. Nor did anybody see Rick leave the luau. The first anyone noticed that you both were missing was when the bus was ready to depart for Kailua, and they assumed you and Rick had gone home, so they left without much of a search." The attorney paused and took his legal pad from his briefcase.

"All of that is circumstantial evidence?" Valeta asked. "And what is the legal definition of circumstantial evidence?"

Date with Responsibility

"The easiest way to explain circumstantial evidence is to say what it is not – it is not direct evidence from a witness who saw or heard, but it is fact – fact that can be used to infer another fact."

"So the facts that Rick is dead, his own gun is missing, and my sandals are nearby, can be used to infer that I killed Rick?"

The lawyer helped himself to a chocolate covered macadamia nut from Mom's crystal bowl. "Right. Another fact is evidence of a severe struggle under the palms – boot prints and two sets of bare foot prints, one small and one large."

Valeta pulled her tiny feet up under her on the hard wooden chair as the attorney continued.

"One thing in our favor," he said, "is that Rick was still wearing his military boots, so the large bare footprints are not his. There were no prints on the beach – not even leading from the luau site to the location of the corpse."

"So that proves I'm not guilty!" She keenly wanted him to agree.

"Not really," he replied. "It's still possible to infer that you voluntarily went to the beach with a larger man; Rick came to find you and fought with the man; during the struggle, he lost his pistol, which you grabbed. In anger, you chased Rick down the beach, killed him with a single shot to the head, and left with the other man."

Circumstantial Evidence

"But I would never do that," she whispered.

"You completed weapons training with top grades, didn't you? And you hog-tied a robber not long ago. The court will take both of those into consideration. They will try, too, to determine if the other man was Edwin."

"No! No! Edwin was on duty!"

Daddy spoke up. "What about the fire here? Is that part of the circumstantial evidence?"

"I think it will be. The arson investigation is not complete, but along with the simple bomb in the sauna, they found shoe prints leading from your gate down to the beach. Again, there were two sets of prints – one large and one small. They overlapped at times, as though the smaller were following the larger. It could be inferred that Valeta had a rendezvous with the arsonist."

The attorney spoke at length about other bits of evidence, then stopped and directed his gaze at the teen. "If I am to defend you and, hopefully, keep this thing out of the courts, Valeta, I must hear everything you can tell me about what happened – every detail from the moment you met Rick until you talked to the police officer."

Valeta squirmed uncomfortably.

"It's all right, Valeta," Daddy said. He sat down beside her. "We know you aren't guilty."

Valeta's entire crushed being rebelled. She could not do it. "Perhaps," she said in a strained voice, "it won't go to court anyway."

"The only way it won't go to court is if you can provide proof to me that you are innocent," said the attorney. "Now, let's begin when you met Rick." He reached for a small tape recorder, set it to record, and then grabbed more nuts.

"I really don't remember everything," said Valeta. She glanced at Daddy. If only he would leave. She could not tell Daddy what Rick had done.

"Just tell what you do remember," urged Daddy, leaning forward, his face pensive.

"All right." Valeta sank back into her chair, picked a brick in the fireplace behind the lawyer, and told the brick the whole story. Occasionally, the attorney asked her to speak up, or interrupted for clarification, but otherwise, only Valeta spoke.

She told of Rick being an embarrassment to her from the beginning, and gave examples. She related how she had waited for darkness, to get away from everyone and be alone – how she saw the pistol when Rick got up to dance – went to the beach while he danced on stage – how he found her, forced her to the sand, and....

The word assaulted her vocal cords and tightened around them. She glanced at Daddy, and beads of perspiration formed on her forehead.

Daddy's clenched hands gleamed white at the knuckles, deep red along each finger. A spot on his left jaw twitched and his eyes flashed. His lips curled in disgust, but he said nothing.

"Please continue," said the lawyer.

Valeta found the brick again, and confided in a whisper that Rick had raped her.

"I'm sorry, but you'll have to repeat that more loudly." The lawyer gestured to his recorder.

Valeta's ashen face flushed as she said, "He wrestled me to the ground, tore my new dress, kissed me and bit my nose. Then – then – then." She took a shaky breath. "He raped me."

Daddy leapt to his feet, his eyes blazing murderously. "He's lucky someone already killed him!" Daddy shouted as he pounded a big fist on the table. "It was far too merciful to kill him with one shot, though." He stormed across the room and back. "He deserved a slow, torturous death!"

"Please let her continue," said the attorney.

Valeta looked at Daddy, and seeing his broad frame shoulder her burden, told the brick that she must have lost consciousness when Rick choked her, because she had no memory of him leaving. She did remember that she felt strangely disembodied for a long time, and then awakened to a huge Hawaiian man bending over her.

The attorney sat up and leaned forward excitedly. "A large man found you?" he asked,

Valeta nodded and Daddy paced again.

"How much later would that have been?"

"I don't know. It must have been a long time. He carried me up the beach and across a field to his car – and brought me back to Kailua."

The attorney leaped beyond excitement now. "Valeta, what did you do with the torn dress?"

"It's in my closet."

"Go and get it!" He punched the recorder's buttons as she got to her feet. When she returned, he examined the dress carefully. "This is perfect. We'll have DNA tests run, and establish that Rick raped you."

"Will that prove that I didn't shoot him?"

"No, but I think we may have found the killer. The police have casts of the footprints on the beach, and we'll match them to the man that brought you home, check for powder burns on his hands, and investigate whether or not he has Rick's missing watch and military ID. All we have to do is find the big Hawaiian man." The lawyer beamed. "Give me a description of the big man – a complete description," he said. He reached for the small recorder again, and stuffed his cheeks with another handful of chocolate macadamia nuts.

"I'm afraid I can't do that," said Valeta. "All I can tell you is that he was huge – a big belly and very tall – barefoot – and he wore a lavalava with no shirt. Oh, and he spoke really strong Pidgin. I think he was pure Hawaiian."

"Can you describe his lavalava?"

"It was dark, with a dark flower pattern."

"Describe his voice for me."

"He had a very deep voice, but he didn't say much. He just picked me up and said *'we go already'* as he started up the beach. He didn't ask if I wanted to go or not. In the car, he asked if I lived in Honolulu, and I told him Kailua. He said something about it being a dark night to swim, and that I should be thankful somebody found me. I guess he didn't know what happened. He seemed to think I'd gone for a midnight swim. The only other time he spoke was when he got here, and he asked if this was my home."

"What can you tell me about his car?"

Valeta's wounded nose wrinkled, and she shuddered, wrapping protective arms around her body. "His car looked like a junk yard reject. He had trouble starting it, and the inside might be home to his pigs, for all I know – a dirty blanket, a greasy pillow, and a lot of old wrappers and cups and things from takeout food. It positively reeked."

"That helps," said the lawyer. "True, many locals on the Waianae Coast live in cars, but not so many that we can't check out all of them. I'll get on this right away."

"What about the fire?" Daddy hurled his big body back to the table to ask.

Valeta shrank. "Rick didn't set the fire. He couldn't have." She looked from Daddy, who was gritting his perfect teeth – to the attorney, who was licking chocolate from a ragged fingernail. "Could he have set it? When was he shot?"

"We don't know yet," said the attorney. "The coroner's report will determine the time of death, but I don't think he started the fire, since he'd have no reason to return to the beach after coming all this way to plant a bomb."

"Unless!" Daddy's mouth tightened into a stubborn line. "Unless he was unsure Valeta would come home, and went back to the Waianae Coast area to check on her. If his main objective was to silence Valeta, he would want to be sure he got her – either here or out there."

"You mean Rick tried to kill me?" She recoiled in horror.

"Yes. He probably realized soon after his assault that there would be heavy consequences for what he had done, so he decided to cover the crime by destroying the only witness – you."

Daddy grabbed the attorney's yellow legal pad and scribbled a quick map of Oahu, under which he began to write.

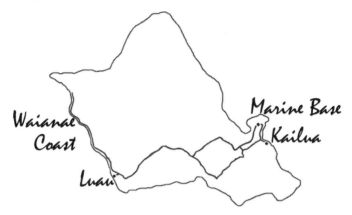

"Rick assaults Valeta sometime near the end of the luau," he said. "Germaine's hosts the Senior Luau, and they end special programs around 10 PM, so the attack occurs sometime just before 10 PM. He chokes Valeta so that she loses consciousness, and then he heads out toward the highway to catch a bus. It takes maybe a half hour or so to get the next eastbound bus, and he has to make several transfers to reach Kailua, so it probably takes him an hour and a half to get back to Kailua, making it close to midnight." Daddy connected the two sites with his pen, then paused. "He drove his own car to the high school before the luau, didn't he, Valeta?"

"He left his car in the high school parking lot," Valeta remembered.

71

The pen scratched across the paper again. "He gets off the bus at the high school, retrieves his car and goes somewhere to get materials for his bomb, or to get a bomb that he already has constructed for some other purpose. Let's give him a half hour to an hour. He comes to our home...."

He paused again. "Did Rick know where we live, Valeta?"

Valeta swallowed dryly and nodded. "Yes. Edwin gave him directions so he could pick me up, but I told him to meet me at school instead."

Knew the address, noted the Colonel. "He comes here and finds the family asleep, since it's now at least 1 AM – possibly later. He plants the bomb, setting the timer for 4 AM, which gives him time to get back to the beach, and then home to bachelor quarters on the Marine Base."

Daddy's pen dashed across the map. "Rick drives back to the Leeward side and goes to the beach. He finds a man – an enormous guardian angel – standing over Valeta. The man realizes that Rick is the rapist and chases him. They fight in the sand – the man kills Rick. Then the man returns to wait for Valeta to regain consciousness."

"Wait a minute," interrupted the attorney. "Would Valeta still be unconscious? It's more than an hour to the luau site from here, so it's been at least four hours since the assault."

"She probably is not truly unconscious," the Colonel replied. "More likely, she is voluntarily unconscious – her brain not wanting to deal with the reality of the rape. She could be difficult to rouse, or completely unresponsive, but still not technically comatose."

"Wouldn't a gun shot have awakened me?" pursued Valeta. "I must have heard it."

"Not if you don't want to be awake. You've been through a traumatic attack. Also, there's the possibility that Rick has slipped a rape drug into your tropical punch at the luau."

Daddy went back to his story. "When Valeta opens her eyes, the big man carries her to his car and drives her home. She comes in and the big man drives away. The bomb in the sauna ignites, but it takes a while for the fire to grow and reach the master suite. By the time my mother places a 911 call, it is near 4:30 AM. It seems clear to me that Rick set the fire and the big man killed Rick in defense of Valeta – and maybe in self-defense." A vein in Daddy's neck pulsed dangerously.

Valeta sat forward. "There's something else I didn't tell you, though," she said. "When I came home, I noticed the clock. It was just before 3 AM. That means the big man took me from the beach before Rick could have gotten back there. And after the fire, I went down to the beach back of our house here, to get away from everything. It was still pretty dark, but beginning to get light – after you went to the Base, Daddy. I had barely gotten down there when I saw someone coming toward me. I recognized the lavalava, and knew it was the big Hawaiian who had brought me home."

Daddy stiffened. "He was on our beach?"

"Yes, Daddy. He was wearing shoes by then, and he lumbered along the beach, looking toward our house. When he saw me, he ran right at me and took a swing at me for some reason, so I sprang directly at him and clapped my hands over both of his ears at once, the way we were taught in self defense class – I may have damaged his hearing permanently. I'm afraid I broke your code of honor."

"If your life or body is in serious danger," said Daddy, "there's no code of honor that you must live by. Your assailant broke the code the moment he attacked you."

The attorney stood up, pushed his legal pad and recorder into the stuffed briefcase, and reached for the father's hand. "Your hypothesis has possibilities, Colonel," he said, "but we still don't know who killed Rick. What we do know is that even if Valeta were guilty, she would have a plea of self defense, not murder. I'll work on what we have and get back to you in the morning."

6

Influenza

The end of February and first two weeks of March formed a blur – a blur of avoiding Edwin, though she wanted desperately to see him – a blur of multiple meetings with the police and the lawyer – a blur of ongoing influenza.

The lawyer worked feverishly to keep Valeta's name out of newspapers, and Valeta out of jail, ordering tests on the dress, and proving that the DNA was Rick's. He got the forensic pathologist's report, in which the time of death was estimated to be sometime near 3 AM, and found a bus driver who remembered a disheveled Marine riding his eastbound bus to Kailua after 11 PM. A police report showed Rick cited for speeding westbound at 2:48 AM near the luau exit. Amazingly, the lawyer even managed to find a witness who knew the huge man who came to Valeta's aid, and identified him as a worker who cleaned up after the luaus, usually going to the beach for a swim after work. The man himself verified Valeta's story, including the meeting on the Kailua beach, the clincher being that he had great difficulty hearing the attorney's questions, and attributed it to Valeta's self defense move.

The big Hawaiian had meant to protect Valeta, not hurt her. He had seen a man lurking near her house, and was trying to find him. He did not want to alert him by shouting, so decided to swing at Valeta, hoping she would duck and run back to the house where she would be safe. He never expected her to fight back.

The evidence piled up in her favor, somehow the lawyer avoided a warrant for her arrest, and they all avoided telling Mom or Grandmother.

When the police tried to produce Valeta's sandals and purse as *probable cause*, the calm attorney pointed out that many people leave things behind at luaus, and that the murder took place much farther down the beach from where Valeta's things were found. That argument, along with other findings, convinced the judge not to issue a warrant for her arrest. The lavalava man supplied a detail that Valeta had forgotten – the stop in Pearl City for gas. The station attendant was witness to the time, the fact that Valeta was in the car, and that they were eastbound when they left his station. Neither Valeta nor her big guardian angel were suspects any longer.

Influenza

For a few days, question remained as to whether they both might be guilty of arson, but shoe prints found near the sauna and outside the gate matched neither Valeta's shoes nor those of the lavalava man. The tire tread evidence matched neither of their cars either, so they were exonerated.

The attorney brought the news on March fifteenth, announcing with barely-contained joy, "Time to celebrate, Valeta! I just got wonderful news! You are officially back to normal life."

Valeta did not smile. "Beware the Ides of March," she intoned, her face haggard with worry.

The attorney laughed. "As Julius Caesar said, 'The Ides of March are come'."

"And as Spurrina answered Julius Caesar, 'Yes, they are come, but they are not past'."

She didn't know why she said it. Maybe it was that nagging feeling that she would never experience a return to normal life, or maybe it was because she was sick of seeing the attorney and had ceased to be civil to him.

"Good news?" she asked herself. "Good that I won't have to stand trial, but other than that? Sure, Mr. Attorney can return to normal life, but I can't. Mom still is spaced out on sedatives, and Leo spends most waking moments running to his cities of refuge – furniture. Daddy rants about the local police force and asserts that the Marines would have long since solved the twin cases, while Edwin comes every day and sits by the pool waiting in vain for me to appear. Grandmother tries to be a rock for us all, still without knowledge of the rape, carrying messages among us because we all are at each other like cats and dogs. Furthermore, Mr. Big-shot Attorney," she continued silently, "I skip church every Sunday, which means Grandmother stays home, too. I skip school, thanks to my note with Mom's forged signature – ill – no study – no guests – no phone. Rick's picture is all over local TV news and the daily papers. You must have bought off the media with Daddy's money, because my name is never connected to the story, but everyone at the luau knows I was with Rick that night, so they naturally suspect the worst. What's normal about a life like that?" She spoke the last question aloud, glowering darkly at the waiting professional, and brazenly daring him to open his thick lips with anything other than the deepest commiseration.

And then suddenly, as quickly as she had capsized into it, she popped up out of her mood and told the poor lawyer, "You're right, I must get back to normal." She affected a bright smile and added, "Normal, Illinois, that is – just north of Bloomington. I'll pack and leave immediately."

The attorney did a confused double take, and then gave her an enthusiastic grin.

Influenza

"What's so funny?" Valeta snapped at him, her face flushing with indignation. "At least if I went to Normal, people wouldn't stare at me as though I were NOT normal!" She stomped into her bedroom and slammed the door behind her.

That was the last she saw of the attorney.

* * *

Valeta skipped church again that Sunday, arriving at breakfast in a shabby purple sweat suit.

"One more Sunday, Grandmother," she begged, nibbling on dry toast. "My embouchure is so rusty that I couldn't play a note on my clarinet. Besides, I'm not ready to see people. I'm tired."

"*You're* tired?" Mom was sitting across the table wrapped in her newest gray Valium mist. "*You're* tired? What do you think about me? I'm exhausted. Arson investigators, cleaning crews, police – and now decorators. I haven't had a minute to myself. And I haven't slept a mite since the fire." Mom yawned and rubbed a hand across features that looked quite refreshed.

Grandmother sent a knowing wink past Mom's veiled eyes, and said "Valeta, being ready to see people again is not a right, or a gift that's going to drop into your lap. It just doesn't happen that way. It will be your responsibility to *make* yourself ready to meet people, and one way to do that is to dress up for Sunday brunch today."

Date with Responsibility

"There's no reason to dress for brunch," said Valeta, backing into her shell. "We aren't having guests, are we? Daddy will be out on the golf course, Mom probably thinks my purple sweat suit is a lace blouse with velvet pants, and I just don't have the energy to dress up, Grandmother. I think I'll spend the morning in my room."

"Not in your room, Valeta," Mom said slowly, "You look pale. You need exercise. Don't let something like a fire ruin your life."

"You're one to talk, Mom," Valeta barked. Her face flushed and she jumped up from the table, tossing the dry toast at her plate.

"Today is special...." Grandmother began.

Valeta's face drained of the quick color. A trapdoor opened in her stomach, and the few bites of toast rose rapidly on a tide of bitterness. She flew to her room, into the bathroom, and bent over the toilet, pulling back long hair with a quick hand. As suddenly as it had risen, however, the nausea subsided, never reaching her lips. She rinsed her mouth with a glass of cool water and draped herself across the bed.

"Great! The last thing I need now is the flu." She rolled carefully onto her side as she whispered it. "Make it through the entire winter without so much as a tiny head cold and then, just when life might turn toward normal, I have to get the flu."

Influenza

She closed her eyes, but the trap door opened again, so hand over her mouth, in extreme slow motion, she rose carefully to her feet and walked gingerly into the bathroom, but by the time she got there, the awful sensation had passed once more.

Odd, how tired she felt lately. Normally, she had a warning – an overture – before the flu hit her this way. "But nothing is normal these days," she told the kitten under the chair. She looked at the clock. 8:35 AM. If she went back to bed, maybe she would feel better by noon.

She crawled slowly beneath the comforter, felt the purple sweat pants twist around her legs, and doubled over to tweak them, but immediately thought better of it. "Top ten reasons you should never get the flu," she muttered into her pillow. "The sweat pants can just stay twisted. Now. Count to ten without thinking about a stomach."

"Meow." Leo came out from under the chair and jumped on top of his companion. "Meow."

"Oh, Leo, you haven't had breakfast yet. Can you wait just a few minutes? Come here, little prince, and please, please don't shake the bed." Opening her eyes slightly, she pulled the kitten from her back, and snuggled his soft white face against one cheek. A tiny pink tongue ventured out to lick her nose, but retracted quickly when a big sneeze exploded. The kitten spat.

"Don't worry," she reassured him. "You're all right." She pulled him against her face again and closed her eyes. "Just let me sleep."

Leo curled into a regal ball and began a leisurely bath. He was hungry, but he would wait, as long as his servant did not forget entirely.

For an hour, they lay that way – Valeta on her stomach, the little Himalayan curled against her side, in a house that was quiet for the time being, as was her stomach. Her mind caught a thermal, and glided effortlessly higher and higher, into a peaceful place far above the troubles of the last three weeks.

Suddenly, she screamed. He was there again – Rick – bending over her – cursing her!

She threw back the comforter, tossing the kitten with it, and jumped to the floor, her eyes darting wildly toward the far window, a chill creeping stealthily up her arms under the purple sweat shirt. Someone was out there. She could feel it. Someone was on the beach, only a stone's throw from her window.

The chill inched toward her throat, bugling ominous warnings, demanding that she check the patio door – be sure it was locked – be sure the security alarm was set.

A light knock startled her, and the glossy white door to the living room opened slowly.

Influenza

"Mind if I visit?" Grandmother asked.

Valeta shivered and sat down on the bed. "Come in." She pulled the comforter around her arms and stretched to look out the window above the bed.

"He won't return." Grandmother sat down.

"Who?" Did Grandmother know?

"Whoever set the fire. We've had so many police officers around here, nobody would dare return, no matter what their motive."

"Oh." Small consolation. Grandmother did not know. She could not know. She led a genteel life. She never danced under the palms at night on a wild beach; never fought off a stranger beneath coconut palms; never felt the pain.

"Are you all right, Valeta?" Grandmother's eyes gazed intently.

Valeta looked up, her own blue eyes wide. "Oh, I was just thinking – is Jean Luc preparing brunch today or are we just going to snack when we're hungry? I'm not sure I can eat much."

"Jean Luc is preparing an Irish brunch in honor of St. Patrick's Day." Grandmother smiled.

"This isn't St. Patrick's Day, is it?" Valeta turned toward the wall calendar. "St. Patrick's Day is tomorrow. Look."

Date with Responsibility

Grandmother stood. "It is tomorrow, but Jean Luc has the day off tomorrow, and your Daddy's coming home at noon today, so we're doing the Irish brunch today. That's what I was trying to tell you earlier when you dashed away from the table. That's why you should dress nicely for brunch – maybe in something green?"

The older woman stepped toward the door, one hand in her pocket. "Oh, dear." She stopped. "I've been carrying this around for weeks now, and I keep forgetting to give it to you."

She tugged a small packet from the pocket. "Your cousin Andrew sent you a gift from New Zealand, but you mustn't open it until tomorrow. See. He wrote on the back: *Do not open until St. Patrick's Day.*"

Valeta shrugged. "It's probably a lucky leprechaun," she said sarcastically.

Grandmother smiled. "Could be." She handed Valeta the package, and went to the kitchen to oversee brunch.

Valeta turned the box over. From Andrew McKean? Mom had told her that Andrew went to New Zealand as an exchange student – had some kind of trouble – had to go home to Delaware. Why would he send her a gift? They hadn't seen each other in two years – not since Daddy transitioned to Hawaii. Wait a minute. Andrew was sixteen by now, wasn't he? That explained it. This was some stupid gag from a high school junior.

She set the little package in front of the computer monitor and promised curiosity that she would open it after midnight. She would be awake, no doubt about that since she was awake at midnight and long after every night. In fact, she would not allow herself to go to sleep until daybreak.

Speaking of sleep.... She looked at the clock. Two hours until brunch. A huge yawn forced the decision. She stretched across the bed again, and was soon asleep.

The next look at the clock showed 11:30 AM. Valeta jumped up, influenza forgotten. Irish brunch! In the big bathroom mirror, a real smile appeared for the first time in three weeks. She showered quickly, actually humming four ragged bars of *Danny Boy*, breathing in the perfume of the green soap saved for this one time of the year.

She luxuriated in a brief giggle when Leo haughtily shook off the droplets falling from her wet hair, his black-tipped tail quivering. "You just watch Daddy at brunch, Leo. It'll be your first time to see how he reacts to the word *Irish*. I wonder why he never noticed that he was falling in love with an Irish girl. Do you suppose he thought that Marjorie O'Hearn was a Scottish name?"

She turned sideways and eyed her bare body in the mirror. "Still firm, but I really must get back to exercising. I haven't gone jogging even once since...." Her smile and her voice faded.

Leo used the silence to remind in clear Himalayan that his meal must be served – now. But Valeta only half listened as she combed her hair and dried it into soft, loose curls.

The absence of that semi-smiling mask from the mirrored reflection accentuated wan reality. Where was the burnished tan she had purchased with those hours of hot sun and bottles of fragrant coconut oil? Had that glorious bronze really turned to this sallow beige?

She picked up her toothbrush and squeezed blue mint gel onto it. "You've got to go out once in a while," she admonished the reflection. "You don't have to go to the beach. You can get a tan on your patio, but you must have a tan if you're going to look good in white as Homecoming Queen."

The toothbrush paused, then dropped into the sink. "I'm not going to be Homecoming Queen. I don't want a tan. I don't want to wear white. I can't wear white. I won't even be able to wear white when I get married – if I ever get married."

Bitter huge tears cascaded over her pale face – unrestrained – convulsive – turbulent.

"Edwin will never marry me now. Nobody will marry me. Nobody wants damaged goods." She dropped to the bare tile floor and wept.

Influenza

Eight full minutes she wept, everything other than the rape forgotten, but then the storm ceased as suddenly as it had begun.

Valeta Davidson got to her feet, went to her closet, and began to dress. She put pale green silk underneath; petite Kelly green cotton shorts over her toned thighs; a slightly lighter Kelly green V-necked tee top above those; and a delicate gold chain around her neck – only after removing the chain's tiny gold heart. Her feet remained bare, but she picked up green flip-flops to wear from the outside door to the courtyard table.

Not once did she return to the mirror. It held nothing now but sad memories of the past.

Leo, pupils still hugely dilated, sat and watched as she dressed. Mistress would live, he decided at last, and would feed him soon. He set his tail at full mast and trotted to the bathroom to shred a roll of pale blue tissue. Tiring of this, he climbed the hand towel to the sink and licked the fallen toothbrush. His tail trembled and he shook his head at the sting of mint flavoring. He left the toothbrush and stalked a fly across the counter top, chattering loudly at it. Finally, he ran back to the bedroom to find his beloved servant, but she had gone to brunch without him.

"Happy Saint Patrick's Day," Valeta told Mom. Mom didn't know one day from another, but who cared? "Did Jean Luc make fruit salad bread?"

Date with Responsibility

"Of course!" Grandmother answered with a smile. Unlike her son, she was happy to celebrate an Irish holiday. "Happy Saint Patrick's Day, Val."

She presented a handmade, wistful greeting card to her granddaughter. Tiny fairies of silver and gold danced lightly in its field of verdant shamrocks, each delicate pastel gown matched perfectly to its wearer's gossamer wings, faces radiating sunbeams.

Valeta's face brightened involuntarily as she opened the parchment card. She read aloud:

> *Always remember to forget,*
> *The things that made you sad.*
> *But never forget to remember*
> *The things that made you glad.*
> *Always remember to forget*
> *The friends that proved untrue.*
> *But never forget to remember*
> *Those that have stuck by you.*
> *Always remember to forget*
> *The troubles that passed away.*
> *But never forget to remember*
> *The blessings that come each day.*

The brightness disappeared behind a bank of clouds, but Grandmother led her through them to a chair near the pool.

As she sat down, Jean Luc arrived bearing Mom's Irish china – each shamrock-rimmed plate loaded with tantalizing food.

Influenza

Warm fruit salad bread overflowed with dark raisins – perfect tiny potato cubes dotted the fluffy yellow omelette – broiled Irish sausages lay in a bed of tomato slices – sweetness beckoned from each teacup, curling fingers of steam that wafted upward and disappeared into thin air.

"What's so special about Patrick?" Daddy arrived bearing St. Patrick's day gloom. "If he had been at all skilled, he'd have rid the entire world of snakes, and not stopped with Ireland. If snakes were bad for one country, they were bad for every country, weren't they?"

Daddy sat down firmly and reached for his cup. "What's this stuff? Tea? No self-respecting Marine drinks tea! Where's my coffee?"

"That is your coffee, Donovan, and you know it." Grandmother was not beyond taking her son to task, Colonel or not. "It's Irish coffee, too, so don't get carried away."

"How can you get carried away with this?" Daddy stabbed a large finger at the cup. "If it's coffee, it belongs in a mug, not a thimble with green stuff growing around the edges."

Valeta could not help yielding to a small smile as she teased, "Daddy, I've always wondered about something – why does Mom have red hair?"

"She dyes it," said Daddy, "pure and simple. Why she dyes it, I don't know. She thinks she's

Irish, but anyone who knows anything about the Irish knows that an Irish woman would never want red hair. The Irish have superstitions about red hair. If an Irishman is going on a trip and sees a woman with red hair, he goes home and starts again. If I had any smarts, that's what I'd have done, too!"

Mom gave Daddy a detached, benign smile, and invited him to propose a toast.

"Certainly, my dear. A toast to your coffin! May it be made of 100 year old oak. And may we plant the tree together, tomorrow." Seeing Mom's frown, he continued, "May misfortune follow you the rest of your life, but never catch up."

Grandmother prayed then, and they settled into small talk, Daddy noting for their education that St. Patrick was actually a Scotsman, captured by the Irish when he was young. He escaped, but returned to Ireland later as a Catholic missionary.

Valeta cautiously sipped tea as she listened, hoping the influenza virus would not rebel at something so bland. When it did not, she decided to risk the fruit salad bread, which she dearly loved, and took a small bite. The warm sweet bread was just caressing the taste buds at the tip of her tongue when, appallingly, nausea overwhelmed her, and Edwin stepped into the courtyard.

7

Butterfly Pendant

"Hi, Valeta." Edwin crossed the space to her chair in two strides and kissed a single curl on her pale forehead.

"Edwin, I...." Her eyes found his and lost them in the same instant as she put her snowy white Irish linen napkin on the immaculate Irish linen tablecloth and pushed back her chair.

His strong hands helped her up, and his right hand reached for her quivering chin, gently trying to tilt her face toward his. "I've missed our Sunday brunches at the Base, so I couldn't refuse when your grandmother invited me to an Irish brunch. May I stay?"

"Excuse me," she managed, and fled to her bathroom. The toilet seat flipped upward quickly at her touch, and she sank to the floor beside it, poised for a volume of disgorged matter, but unable to throw up, despite remaining queasiness.

Date with Responsibility

"So much for breakfast," she thought grimly, "and so much for Edwin, for he's sure to think I was running from him." Slowly, she got to her feet and closed the toilet lid but, on second thought, opened it again – just in case.

She brushed her teeth, never noticing that she had to retrieve her toothbrush from the sink, so happy was she that the blue gel banished the bitter taste of bile – at least temporarily.

Leo had shadowed her from the table, and studied her visage with two blue question marks.

"Well, I don't have to worry about making conversation with Edwin, now do I?" she asked him. "It feels as though I just met him for the first time, only worse, and it's weird how he's like a stranger, but not a stranger. I can't look at him because Daddy's sure to have told him, even if he did keep it from Mom and Grandmother."

The Himalayan kitten decided to climb her bare leg. "Ouch! Leo, that hurts! Get down!" New nausea seeped into her mouth. "This flu should buy me another week away from school, Leo. Mom won't notice, and Daddy can't send me to school with Asian flu." She scooped up little Leo and sank onto the bed, closing her eyes so that she could concentrate on erasing her mental chalkboard, but the effort proved futile. The unseen hand of life wrote on its own, covering the board with dark words and darker graphics.

Suddenly, uneasiness crept across the bed, eyes studying her – from outside the window or here in her room? She had not taken time to close the bedroom door.

Slowly, Valeta turned toward the open door, unbalancing the nausea scales in the process. Edwin stood just beyond the threshold.

"I think I've got the flu," she murmured weakly. "Every time I move, I feel nauseous."

"I'm sorry, Hon," he said. "Can I get you something? Some dry toast? Some tea?"

"No. Eating makes it worse – usually. It isn't like last year's flu. It comes and goes throughout the day, and I never quite throw up, but I keep feeling as though I will." She sat up slowly.

"I thought we could talk today, but if you don't feel well...."

Valeta stretched out a hand and hesitantly gestured him over the threshold into a place he had never before ventured. "I'm sorry, Edwin," she said softly, her lips trembling. "I wanted to talk to you, but I didn't think you wanted to talk to me."

"Didn't anyone tell you that I've spent hours here every single day, hoping you would come out?"

"Grandmother told me, but I didn't believe her, and when Mom told me, I figured she was too spaced out to know what she was saying."

Date with Responsibility

A moment of fragile silence stretched between them as he stepped cautiously into her room, stood by the bed and took her small hands into his large hands. "It's all right," he said huskily.

Valeta closed her eyes, feeling warmth flow from his hands into hers and straightway to her heart, calming its fears, encouraging her to speak, to ask him about that night. "Do you know what happened at the luau?" she asked, eyes still closed.

"Everyone knows about Rick's death, Hon."

"I mean before that. Has Daddy told you that Rick...." The horrid word still choked her.

"He hasn't told me anything, Hon. Did Rick do something? Is that why someone killed him? Did he do something at the luau?"

Edwin's look of confusion convinced her that he did not know, but she had to tell him now that she had planted the question – had to give him the answer.

Her finger traced a russet seashell on the comforter, and her eyes lowered to watch the finger. Seashell pattern – beach – palms – dance – her mind followed the thread back through three weeks and she began to tremble.

"What is it, Valeta?" Edwin put an arm around her shoulders, but avoided sitting on her bed, pulling her to her feet instead. "Tell me."

"I – I can't," she stammered. Her eyes, haunted by inner pain, avoided his searching gaze.

"Honey, did Rick do something to you?" Edwin turned her so that he could see her face more fully. His voice tightened. "Did he hurt you?"

She pulled her flushed face away from him and hid it with her hands. "I can't tell you. You'll have to ask Daddy. He and the lawyer are the only ones that know."

Edwin's eyes narrowed. "I'll be back," he said. He turned and marched out toward the courtyard with a firm military gait.

Valeta looked after him, wrestling between being present or being absent when Edwin learned the truth. She finally decided on presence, and walked slowly to the courtyard, but Edwin had gone – and so had Daddy.

* * *

On Monday, it being Jean Luc's day off, and Mom being in no condition to cook, Daddy decreed that they would go to the Officers' Club for the evening meal. The chef served a continental cuisine buffet on Mondays, and it would give them all an opportunity to get out of the house.

Valeta protested to Daddy, in private, that she did not feel well, neither the murderer nor the arsonist had been caught, and she was afraid.

Date with Responsibility

She had not seen Edwin since he learned about Rick, and a public restaurant was neither the best location nor the best time. Daddy could see that, or could he?

Daddy could not or would not. He went to work, and Valeta spent the day in bed – worrying surpassingly – sleeping infrequently.

As the sun dropped low in the sky, she got up and got dressed, putting on yesterday's green outfit, since this was officially St. Patrick's Day.

Edwin was waiting in the Officers' Club when they got there, at their usual table, and stood as they approached, his eyes meeting hers for the first time since he heard. He smiled, and there was a new tenderness in his smile, but there was something else – something she could not define. She tried to turn from it, but it drew her back.

"Happy St. Patrick's Day," he said. His left hand disappeared into a deep pocket, somewhere in the leg of his khaki cargo pants, and withdrew a beautiful glass pendant on a black satin cord.

"Oh!" Valeta reached out both hands to take the bubble, and stared into its clear rounded front. "How exquisite! There's a real butterfly in it. How do they get it in there? How do they shrink it? It can't be more than a quarter of an inch long. It looks as though it's fluttering through a blue and silver universe." She held the pendant toward the window and a ray of sunlight formed a miniature rainbow above the butterfly. "Oh, look, Edwin! Just like Hawaii – an impromptu rainbow."

Edwin spoke huskily to the top of her blond curls. "Do you like it?"

"I love it!" She hesitated and sobered. "You shouldn't, though. I mean, you shouldn't give a gift to me." She held the pendant toward him.

"Valeta Davidson, don't be that way," Mom said brusquely. "I declare, you've been acting weird ever since the fire. Now stop insulting Edwin and take the jewelry." She patted Edwin's arm. "If she won't take it, I will," she offered.

Valeta looked from Edwin to Mom, and then turned to Daddy for help, but Daddy was talking to a friend at a nearby table.

She pulled her arm back and gazed into the beautiful glass again. "Where did you get it?"

"I bought it at an amazing little craft stand near the beach – it's handmade – butterfly and uinverse of glass, flecked with real silver. The artisan melts the glass with a high temperature torch and forms it into various shapes. I went to his web site and ordered two others for you."

She gave him a shy smile. "Are they both universe butterflies like this?" She felt the smooth glass of the little treasure, and looked again at the tiny Monarch hovering over silver planets.

"No, one is a caramel mushroom in clear glass, and the other is a glass turtle of dark greens and blues."

Edwin held her chair for her, and then took the beautiful pendant. "May I?" Without waiting for an answer, he draped the satin cord around her neck, tying it in back, and letting the cool glass pendant fall toward the V of her tee top.

Valeta looked up at him, confused again. "Thank you so much, Edwin." She hoped it did not sound as stilted to his ears as it did to hers.

Colonel Daddy finished his conversation, sat down next to Valeta, and approved the new glass pendant as though he were its creator. He insisted that Valeta go around the table so that each one could look closely at the gift, which sparked comments that began with the utter impossibility of someone crafting such a beautiful piece, and moved on to cocoons and their Monarch butterflies. At least they all were safe topics....

Until Grandmother went too far and said, "Remember the wedding I went to at the church last spring? At the reception, the bride and groom opened a release box, and 100 beautiful Monarch butterflies flew into the air. It was absolutely breathtaking, and since everyone was draped with leis, they fluttered around for the whole reception. I'll never forget it, and I don't suppose the bride and groom will either."

Valeta flushed. Marriage was *not* a safe subject – definitely not a safe subject! Marriage was out of the question now, and Grandmother should not talk about it in Edwin's presence. She stretched a foot in the older woman's direction, but remembered that Grandmother had no way of knowing that marriage was out, had not heard what happened with Rick, so a well-placed kick would only spawn questions.

Valeta retrieved the foot and introduced a more banal topic. "I wonder if they have Seared Ahi Salad this evening." The effort miscarried.

"I want to hear more about the butterflies," Mom protested. "Butterflies are so pretty. What kind did you say they were? Monarchs?"

Daddy made the rescue. "Let's pray so we can eat."

As usual, Grandmother was asked to pray. Valeta listened for the "amen" and raised her head to find Edwin looking at her. He smiled – but that new element registered again in his smile.

"Well, let's see if the buffet has roast prime rib today." Daddy stood to lead the way.

"I'm not really hungry," Valeta looked up at Daddy. "Maybe I should take the bus home."

"What do you mean? You're a growing girl. Of course you're hungry," said Daddy.

Date with Responsibility

Actually, she was hungry – very hungry, with her stomach growling the message every thirty seconds, but the message might become garbled if she tried to eat.

Edwin stood and bowed beside her chair. "May I accompany you to the salad bar, Madame Butterfly?" The teasing eyes matched the new note in his voice.

Valeta was tempted by the possibility of Seared Island Ahi rubbed with cajun spices and served on a bed of crisp greens, but she protested. "I really do have the flu, Edwin. I'm afraid to eat."

His hand touched her forehead, then pulled her to her feet. "Must have been twenty-four hour flu," he said softly, "because you aren't hot. Try a bite for me and if you get sick, I'll take you home."

Without waiting for an answer, Edwin guided her to the buffet, selected a small Ahi Salad for her and blackened *sashimi pupus* for himself, and popped a small pupu into her mouth as he said, "If this appetizer stays down, the rest of the meal will, too."

It stayed down – it tasted wonderful – even though it was raw fish. The whole meal stayed down, and with each bite, she felt much better.

As she ate the final bite of beef, she turned to Edwin and said, "Did you notice if they have pineapple Crème Brulée on the dessert table?"

Butterfly Pendant

They did, and she topped off a rather large dinner by sharing with Edwin a big Crème Brulée, softly folded with caramelized pineapple, and served in a half pineapple shell.

After dinner, they left the family and walked on the beach under a full moon, Valeta fingering the treasured glass pendant in silence.

Edwin, too, was silent, and uneasy with the silence. Every thirty seconds, he glanced toward the girl at his side as though he would speak, but then he looked again at the moon's path on the troubled waves. If she had taken her fingers from the pendant, or looked at him, his lips might have found the strength to break their bonds, but she did neither. So they walked on in pregnant silence.

At last, Edwin said, "I've been studying this peninsula's history for an article in the Marine Corps news. Marine Corps Base Hawaii sits on what once was sacred ground to native Hawaiians. The royalty ruled here, warriors trained here, and their ancestors were laid to rest here."

Valeta shivered. "Let's not talk about dead people, especially in connection with beaches."

He put a protective arm around her waist. "Valeta, I hardly know where to begin to tell you the emotions I felt when your Dad told me what happened – the emotions that still churn inside me. I'm a mass of agony, rage, frustration...."

She laid a finger on his lips, and then pulled away from his grasp as she said, "Please, Edwin. Don't say anything. Let's just walk."

"But Valeta, we need to...."

She sprinted away, some part of her crying to listen to him, but a stronger part afraid to hear.

Edwin caught up to her in a few strides, and taking her hand, walked again in strained silence, seeking but not finding a way to make her hear how he felt.

At last, he returned to the safer topic and said, "There will be a festival here in October to celebrate the beginning of Hawaiian New Year, and they've invited the Marines to join them."

"Will you go?" Her subdued question reflected the staggering realization that she no longer had a right to go – at least not with Edwin.

"Probably – especially if the paper prints my article. They said it's an ancient festival dedicated to Lono, the deified guardian of agriculture, rain, health and peace." He sounded as though he had memorized it from a reference book. "It's Makahiki season, which coincides with their New Year."

"I remember reading a little about Lono in Hawaii History class," she offered quietly. "About how he has influenced Hawaiian thinking for 2,000 years – but I forget what Makahiki is."

Edwin stopped and pointed toward the sky. "See that cluster of stars – the Pleiades? It's that bunch that looks like a swarm of fireflies."

"You mean the Seven Sisters?" Valeta asked.

He nodded. "Hawaiians believe that was where their ancestors lived before they came to earth. They consider winter officially begun when it rises at sunset, sets at dawn, and is visible most of the night. They set aside four months after that for peace, and to thank Lono for his gifts from the land and sea. They say that Makahiki belongs to Lono, so they temporarily put aside some of their more rigid *kapu* – their taboos – and celebrate."

Valeta stopped, gazing abstractedly at a moon beam caught in her pendant as she asked, "What do they do at the celebration?"

"The way I understand it, they start just before sunset, out near Pyramid Rock Beach, with a formal ceremony to recognize Makahiki and the New Year. Someone blows a big conch shell, and then a group does an ancient Hawaiian chant. Next, they tell stories about their ancestors – and they do this on each of the seven islands."

The moonbeam remained. "All seven?"

"All seven. In fact, when Captain Cook first arrived on the Big Island in 1778, it was Makahiki season, and the Hawaiians mistook him for Lono."

Date with Responsibility

"They knew how Lono looked?"

"They thought so. They used to carve his image on top of a long wooden staff, attach a cross pole below the carving and hang long sheets of white *tapa* on it – to represent clouds. Tradition said that fair-skinned Lono would return to the islands, so when they saw the sails and masts on Cook's ships, and it was during Makahiki, they thought it was Lono returning."

The two had reached the end of the sandy crescent now, and retracing their steps, each deep in thought, they returned to the Officers' Club where Edwin glanced at his watch and said, "I guess your ride left, but it's almost time for the bus. I'll go back with you, so you aren't out alone."

Valeta nodded, and they walked to the bus stop where they soon boarded the nearly empty bus, taking a back seat for the short ride.

"I leave in the morning for jungle training," he told her as the bus started, "but I'll be back for Easter brunch on April 21. It will give us both time to think about where we go from here."

She nodded, and stood as the bus stopped in front of her home.

Asking the driver to give him one minute, Edwin hurried her to the door, kissed her on the cheek, and was gone.

8

Edwin's Absurdity

That night, holding sleep in abeyance until the safety of dawn, Valeta tiptoed into the living room, looking for something to read. On the table beside Daddy's leather recliner, she found a newspaper, but not the local paper. This was the *Ryukyu Shimpo* – however one pronounced that.

She took it to her room and flopped across the bed, judging from the content that it was a newspaper from Japan, but in English, and from August of 2000 – almost three years ago. Why would Daddy be reading this?

Her eyes scanned the thin paper, finding little of interest at first, but suddenly screeching to a halt and opening wide as she read:

Marine gets 4 years for rape

She leapt up and circled the bedroom, cautiously checking doors and windows, and then resetting the security alarm for the eighth time. Pulling the shades tightly shut, she returned to the bed and began to read.

> *A US Marine Corps private first class, aged 19, was sentenced by a military court on August 2, on a charge of rape.... He has been sentenced to a four-year prison term without parole ... deprived of salary and other allowances, demoted to the lowest rank ... and will receive a dishonorable discharge from the service.*

She stared at the paper. It went on to tell how the victim at first had declined to press charges, not wanting to face the assailant in court but, being urged to do so, finally agreed. Now he was in a prison....

Valeta stopped reading. If Rick had not been killed, Daddy would have made her press charges. She shuddered and opened the paper, looking for a different subject. A manual fell from the folds of the newspaper and she picked it up. "What's this, Leo?" She read the title:

<u>U.S.A. Uniform Code of Military Justice</u>

A bookmark led her curiosity inside, where she skimmed the page:

Any person... guilty of rape... punished by death.

She dropped the manual. Daddy was not kidding! Rick really could have been put to death. No wonder he acted quickly to destroy her – the sole witness! He knew the penalty. He would have studied the manual in boot camp – reviewed it and discussed it with other people. Stress creased her smooth brow. The death penalty, which she had always opposed in school debates, arguing that civilized societies should respect life, suddenly took on a different meaning. Without a death penalty, where was the respect for *her* life? Had Rick lived, he would have made sure that *she* did not live. Should he then not have paid for *her* life, for his lack of respect for her life?

The question was moot. Rick had paid – not at the hands of government, but at the hands of .... She stopped. At whose hands? Who killed Rick? The police still did not know.

Her bare feet paced the room as she tried to focus on the unanswered question, to remember someone, anyone, who might have been at the scene. She chewed the right corner of her lower lip. There was a shadowy figure present when she opened her eyes before the Hawaiian came – not long before – someone was nearby and there were angry voices: Rick's and.... The phantom image faded as quickly as it had come, and she could remember no more. Perhaps it was not her memory, but rather her vivid imagination.

She sat down and picked up the manual. How could a man do that – when he knew the penalty was death? Even if the penalty was only incarceration – was that not enough to deter the crime? The idea that a person could be stripped of everything he had, denied freedom, and locked in a cell ought to provide some measure of deterrent.

Leo opened big blue eyes to stare at her from a king-size bed by her pillow, and then stood, stretched, curled his backbone the opposite way and re-settled himself pompously.

Valeta moved to a spot beside the kitten and petted his soft white coat as she continued thinking. Rick had been so juvenile at the luau. Maybe that was the best explanation. Maybe he gave no thought to the penalty, like a juvenile driving a car too fast and thinking that accidents happen to older people but not to youth, because youth is invincible. Maybe Rick thought prison or death happened only to other people – or that rape usually went unpunished and he had nothing to fear – realized only after he assaulted her that he was not invincible and did have reason to fear.

"Or maybe," Valeta whispered in the kitten's soft ear, "Rick simply did not care, and now he is dead. Injustice meets justice."

She looked at the clock – 3:45 AM – another three hours until sunrise. Maybe she could find something of interest on TV. She moved the white wicker chair closer to the set and reached for the remote control, but it was slim pickings at this time of the morning: *Hawaii Five-O – Rugrats*.

She flicked the channel button. *Can't Cook, Won't Cook* – infomercial for cookware – Hawaiian word of the day.... She paused.

"This morning's word of the day," chirped the sanguine TV host, "is *hapai hao*, which means *to lift*, as in weights.

"Good idea." Valeta turned off the television and started toward the patio, only to swerve back to the wicker chair and curl her body back into its protective arms. "Not a good idea." She picked up the clock and gazed at it absent-mindedly. 4 AM.

She turned on the TV again, and surfed the channels, settling on the Hawaiian music channel and closing her eyes. With her bedroom in this wing, separated from the rest of the bedrooms, nobody else could hear as long as she kept the volume low. She hummed sadly and softly to a familiar tune that she had not heard in weeks.

Suddenly, she began to shake. "Stop it," she cried out. "Go away!" Her lips felt his lips hard against them, suffocating her, and she opened her mouth, snapped it shut, and opened it again. "Go away! Go away!" She screamed now, and thrust her slim arms in front of her, clawing the air, biting, thrashing, crying, her eyes still closed.

"Valeta!" Daddy hurried across the room. "Valeta, what is it? Why are you screaming?"

Her eyes flew open, but she did not see.

Daddy put his arms around her. "Were you dreaming? Did you have a nightmare?"

Valeta peered about wild-eyed. "Where is he? Stop him! Stop him! He raped me!"

Daddy shook her gently. "Rick isn't here, Valeta. He is dead. You're safe. I'm here to take care of you." He pulled her from the chair and led her to the bed, where he cradled her against his broad shoulder.

Slowly, Valeta's eyes focused again on her surroundings, and a look of bewilderment replaced the wild-eyed stare. "What happened, Daddy?"

"I think you had a flashback. That often happens when someone is beginning to heal after a trauma. Something reminded you." He looked around the room. "Maybe it was triggered by the music from the TV. Was *Sweet Leilani* the song you were dancing to under the palms?"

Valeta looked at the TV set. "I don't know. I don't remember what song was playing when it started. I was just sitting here with my eyes closed, and then I was fighting him again."

"I think you need to put some time between you and it before you go back to sleep," he said. "Let's see what we can find in the refrigerator."

Sleep? Little did Daddy know. She allowed him to take her to the kitchen in his protection.

Edwin's Absurdity

Daddy dished out mango ice cream and sat down at the counter with her, studiously avoiding the subject of Rick; talking about work on Base; musing on the possibility of another relocation.

"What would you think of moving to Japan, specifically a base on Okinawa? I have a few months left in Hawaii, but I could put in for an early assignment if you would like it."

Valeta shook her head and let the spoonful of sweet mango cream sit on her tongue for a long, sweet moment. "Mom would hate it," she said, "as would Grandmother, who is infatuated with Hawaii. Where would she winter?"

"She could visit my brother for a change." Daddy grinned smugly. "She would be almost as warm in Phoenix as she is here."

Valeta curled her lips. "Phoenix? Oh, she will just love brown everywhere she looks; dirt everywhere she walks; and the companionship of spiders, scorpions, and rattlesnakes, won't she? I don't think so, Daddy."

"It isn't that bad."

"It's like where we lived in Yuma, isn't it?"

Daddy scraped up the last of his ice cream and put the dish in the sink for Jean Luc. "Well, think about Okinawa," he said. "By the way, the attorney called. They think they may have a lead on both the murder and the arson. They've been interviewing every one of your senior class, it seems, and someone finally gave them a clue."

Valeta blanched. "Someone in the senior class? There was an eye witness, Daddy?" She shrank away. Had someone seen her shoot Rick?

"The lawyer said there was no eye witness, but a cheerleader overheard the football squad talking on their way into the locker room, and one of the guys said something that may implicate a team member." Daddy stood up. "Don't worry. They'll find him. The Marines would have had him long ago, but eventually Hawaii Five-O will get their man. Are you all right now?"

Valeta assured Daddy she was fine, and shuffled back to her bedroom, viewing a mental lineup. The man that she heard fighting with Rick on the beach – the man that she saw running from the fire – a football player? She did not know.

She spent the remaining hours of darkness watching reruns of sitcoms, unaware that her face was twisted in anguish rather than amusement.

At 6:30 AM, she opened the white mini blind beside the bed and looked out across the ocean. A rosy-orange hue heralded the coming of the monarch of the sky. Valeta sighed and stretched her weary body beside the feline monarch on her bed. At last, she could sleep.

Edwin's Absurdity

* * *

The weeks until Easter dragged. Daddy was not on jungle training, but might as well be since he seemed to be at Base 24/7. Mom continued to walk through tranquilized mists as she directed remodeling of the garage and master wing, and Grandmother departed on a long-awaited South Seas cruise with friends from the church.

None of them noticed that Valeta remained truant from school – the forged note kept school authorities at bay, and her actions kept Mom and Daddy at bay. She departed each morning at the usual time, dressed appropriately and backpack on her shoulder, only to return through her private patio door and go to bed, Leo at her side. There she stayed until late afternoon, and still she felt tired. The lifelike flashbacks continued to shatter her calm on a frequent basis, but she muffled them into her pillows and told no one.

Easter Sunday arrived at last, but it was a strange Easter Sunday with Grandmother gone and nobody attending church, so Valeta spent the day alone in her room.

Easter Monday, April 21, Edwin came for brunch – as promised – and Jean Luc tried to spoil him – as usual. He started with apple-mustard glazed ham, one of Edwin's favorites, to which he added French toast made of Italian bread that he dipped in a mixture of egg and orange juice, and then sprinkled with powdered sugar. As though this were insufficient, he served an egg and broccoli casserole, and a bowl of Hawaiian fruit salad.

"I'm not sure he prepared enough for you to have any, Valeta," teased Edwin.

She stomped his boot in pretended anger.

"Hey! Take it easy on the spit shine." Edwin wrestled her into a chair. "It took me an hour to accomplish that. Don't you know that a Marine's quality is often measured by his spit shine?"

"Ah! We sleep safe! Our Marines have great spit shines." As Edwin's eyes glinted with pleasure, she felt sudden guilt. She should not lead him on. She forced a smile and studied her plate.

Opportunely, the rest of the family arrived before Edwin could question her behavior, Daddy asked Edwin to pray, and then Daddy led the conversation as they began to eat. Valeta spread a flowered napkin on her lap, and taking hearty portions of everything, felt a tide of well-being wash over her. It was good to have Edwin back, and she did not feel ill today. She applied herself to the glazed ham, laying aside a bright red, spiced apple ring for later. The glaze teased her taste buds, promising sweet, then tangy, and delivering both. She swallowed the morsel of ham and cut a bite of French toast, but with the fork halfway to her mouth, she had a sudden change of mind.

"Excuse me," she said. She bolted to the bathroom – and had another change of mind. She could not throw up, despite the strong urge.

"Are you sick again, Hon?" Edwin stood in the doorway. "Because, if you are, I think you should see a doctor. This can't still be the flu."

"What could it be if it isn't the flu?"

"Pregnancy."

Valeta's face glazed with shock and her blue eyes widened with alarm as the words tolled in her ears. Pregnancy. Pregnancy. She shook her head. "That is an absolute absurdity," she said.

Edwin crossed the room and led her to a chair. "I want you to go to Base Clinic today," he said, easing her gently into the seat. "I don't have duty until this afternoon, so I can take you. That's the only way we'll know if it's absurd or not."

Valeta gaped at him in silence.

"Listen, Hon, the influenza virus doesn't last for a month, and it doesn't act like this. You don't get sick in the morning, then get well and have an enormous appetite in the evening."

Valeta's skin grew clammy and a cold fist entrapped her pounding heart.

"I know you'd rather not think about such a possibility, but ignoring it won't help. You should have gone to a doctor immediately – the night that it happened. I understand why you didn't – the Hawaiian man, the fire, and all – but I want you to go now – for me. We can leave right away. We don't have to tell your family. We can pretend we're going out for some air to make you feel better, and if you're afraid someone will know you at Base Clinic, I'll make an appointment for tomorrow with a doctor on the other side of the island instead."

Her voice returned, much weaker than when it left. "I don't need a doctor to know it's the flu. I just have to rest a while and I'll be better. I'm not pregnant." A sickening wave of terror welled up from her belly as she spoke the word.

"Do you have any reason to know for sure that you aren't pregnant?"

Valeta knew what he meant, and shook her head. "That's no proof, though, at my age."

"You need to see a doctor. Is it OK if I make an appointment?"

"I'm sure any doctor will say it's the flu, but...." She dropped her head and nodded slowly.

9

Misty Blue Muumuu

Edwin, true to his word, found a doctor on the other side of the island. Hawaii Kai was some twenty-five minutes down the coast and around the southern end of the island. Her appointment was for the following morning.

Valeta showered early, wrapped herself in a big peach towel, and going to her closet, scanned the colorful apparel. Purposefully, she slid aside hanger after hanger – blouses, shorts, skirts, dresses, and jeans – until she reached the closet's innermost corner. The misty blue muumuu. It was very acceptable for today – in a few weeks, it might be much more than acceptable, if Edwin's so absurd suspicion proved to be right. She stood in the deep closet and began to dress – a short process, since the full muumuu required nearly nothing underneath. As usual, she had slept only after dawn. Wearily, she carried the muumuu from the closet, sat down on the edge of the wicker chair, and pulled the long, bell-shaped garment over her head. Waves of airy, pale blue cotton floated over her, piling in drifts around her hips. She stood and let the flowered fabric fall to her ankles. Two slim hands grasped the side seams and pulled the muumuu to its full width.

She chewed the corner of her upper lip. "Valeta Davidson, I hope for your sake that there's always ample hip room in this thing." She found the butterfly pendant where she had left it on the bedside stand, and fingered it gently, its incredible beauty striking her anew, and calling forth the response of a small, tentative smile. She had decided to wear it everyday – as long as Edwin remained in her life – which might be no longer than today. The smile faded. She would put it on last. She tucked the deep cobalt blue, glass bubble into the muumuu's single pocket.

Last of all, she brushed her golden hair and pulled it into a long ponytail at the back of her head. She applied a light pink lipstick without glancing in the mirror, and turned to look at the time: twenty minutes until Edwin would come. She pulled the butterfly from its pocket and tied the cord at the back of her neck. The beautiful ornament touched her just above the muumuu, fluttering softly against her skin. Valeta looked around. Blue sandals waited by the bed, along with her blue cotton tote bag. She was ready for her doctor's appointment – at least outwardly.

"Meow."

"Oh, Leo. Why do I keep forgetting to feed you? It isn't that I don't love you, little one. I just have other things on my mind. You understand, don't you?" She padded on bare feet to the closet and got out a small can of kitten food. She lifted the lid, and dumping moist food into a red plastic pet bowl, carried it to the bathroom, put it on the floor, and refilled a red water dish. Then she turned to call the kitten.

But Leo needed no call. He dashed past her, not pausing for his usual perfunctory ankle rub, tucked his triangular little face into the dish, and began guzzling the food.

"You're welcome, ungrateful little feline," she said. "Not that you bothered to thank me."

She watched the kitten absently. "You would think that I, growing up in a Marine colonel's home, would have procrastination drilled out of me, but still I put off things – even the important things like feeding you. If I ever do have a baby, it will starve to death."

She walked to the computer desk and reached to turn on the monitor. There sat the small package from her cousin Andrew. "Oh great," she said. "St. Patrick's Day gift becomes an Easter gift. He probably wonders why I haven't thanked him." Well, better late than never. Carrying it to the chair by the window, she unsealed it carefully. Inside was a plain white box about three inches square. She lifted the lid, felt through piles of shredded green tissue paper, and discovered a small soft object about two inches long.

"A lamb – attached to a key ring." She took it from its tissue grass and read the attached note.

> *Hi, Cous! Saw this, thought of what*
> *a lamb you are, and decided to send*
> *it to you. It's real lamb's wool, and*
> *the definitive NZ mascot.*

Valeta grinned. "Not bad. And I expected something stupid." She dangled the little white lamb from its silver ring. Two blue bead eyes peered at her from above a pink felt nose. A tiny tail flopped in back. "Well, little white lamb, you shall guard my keys then," she said, "though you don't look a bit ferocious." She took her keys from the bag on the bed and transferred each one to the new ring. When she looked at the lamb again, she had to cry – inexplicably. A moment later, she chortled at the little lamb, still chuckling when Edwin arrived, and they got in the car.

"You look happy today," he said as he started the engine. "How do you feel?"

"Marvelous at the moment. Four minutes ago – lousy. Four minutes from now – who knows?" She stared out the window at the lush mountains. "What doctor are we going to?"

"One who is professional, expensive, and discreet." He placed in her lap the mushroom and turtle pendants, which had arrived during his absence. "I called Tripler Hospital, pretended the appointment was for my wife, and asked them for a referral to a good doctor."

Valeta startled herself with a spontaneous giggle, and a flip of her ponytail. "Edwin Laroque! Shame on you," she scolded. "You never told me you were a married man." She picked up the glass pendants and held them to the car window. "They're beautiful. The butterfly is my favorite, but these are great, too. Thank you so much!"

Edwin grinned, but soon afterward frowned. "I don't want to lie to the doctor, Valeta. Whatever she says, I want to be honest about this."

"You plan to tell her I was raped?" Valeta flinched. "She doesn't need to know that. Isn't that the whole reason for choosing a doctor a half hour from home – to avoid the rape gossip? I don't want to tell anyone about it, Edwin. I want to forget it. I just want to get on with my life and never think about it again. Please don't tell."

Edwin gazed across the beach where they used to body surf, his dark eyes straining to see through the gathering salt deposited by the breeze.

Valeta noticed, and reached to flick the windshield washer. Her hand bumped the lamb, dangling helplessly from its tether, and she wondered why Edwin had not commented about her new key chain. The washer fluid moved the salt spray to the outer limits of the windshield, and the blue ocean extended its mystery into the car as they continued along the rugged coastline, deepening the silence she had spawned with her refusal of Edwin's request for honesty. They passed *Sea Life Park* and rounded the island's southeastern tip without speaking. They passed a complex of marina front condominiums, each boasting its own boat dock and lush gardens. Still they did not speak. They drove down Hawaii Kai's main route – left side adorned by a sparkling blue-green bay filled with crisp sailboats and sleek outrigger canoes – the right side dressed in specialty shops and eateries. A few minutes later, Edwin turned the car toward an elegant low-rise professional building.

Then they spoke, but not about the doctor. A few murmurs passed between them as they walked to the building, icy hand in warm hand.

In a large room of polished island wood and gleaming bronze, they registered and sat down to complete the lengthy medical history form: name, address, date of birth, etc.

He tried to lighten the mood by teasing about her being married at age seventeen, but she was in no mood for lightness.

She finished the form – got a magazine from the table – held it – listened to Edwin – looked at the clock – re-checked the form for error – chided the clock – turned magazine pages – studied the clock – then suggested they leave.

"This is waste time," she said in Pidgin.

"It won't be long now," he told her.

On which cue, a nurse appeared and called out Valeta's name. She led Valeta to a sterile white examination room, gave her a small paper cup, and indicated the restroom. Meekly, Valeta obeyed, although the sample was meaningless if this was the flu, and she still could not believe it was anything else. She returned to the aseptic room, and followed instructions to disrobe and don the paper dressing gown. The nurse drew blood, then left her to shiver through the passage of time until the physician's arrival.

"Valeta Davidson? I'm glad to meet you, and sorry to keep you waiting." A slim, olive-skinned woman extended her hand in brief greeting, and scanned her clipboard. "Age seventeen. How are you feeling this morning, Valeta?"

"I think I have the flu." That shriveled voice. Whose voice was that?

The doctor produced the inevitable tongue depressor and asked, "What makes you think you have the flu?"

Date with Responsibility

Valeta waited until the depressor left her mouth to reply, "I've been nauseous off and on, pretty much every time I try to eat. I don't vomit, but I come close." Her shrunken voice grew even smaller. "It's been going on for about five weeks."

"Why did you come to a gynecologist for the flu? Don't you and Edwin have a family doctor?"

This was a gynecologist? Valeta's face flushed. "Actually, Edwin made the appointment for me. I guess he didn't realize," she said, but she knew that Edwin was not that naive.

The physician continued her examination, increasing the humiliation as she went. Finally, she helped Valeta sit up. "You can get dressed now, and I'll have your husband join you." The polished professional gave no sign of seeing anything but her unblushing clipboard.

As the door closed, the teen hustled into her clothing, straightening the muumuu over her hips just as Edwin was ushered into the room.

He rushed forward, taking both of her hands and asking, "What did she say?"

"Nothing. She just prodded and probed. I want to go home, Edwin. I don't want to wait." Valeta's forlorn eyes glistened with blue-tinted tears, and she tugged on his firm, strong hands. "She isn't the best doctor, Edwin. I'm not sure she even knows what it is. Let's go."

Edwin pulled her into his embrace and leaned against the examination table, hushing her. "It won't be long, Buttercup."

The gynecologist knocked briefly and opened the door, silently gesturing them into the twin chairs as she smiled warmly.

"Congratulations, Mr. and Mrs. Davidson," she said. "You're going to have a baby – about the end of November." Edwin's brown eyes dilated into black holes. His right hand tightened on Valeta's shoulder. He sucked in an enormous breath, and immediately needed another.

The doctor rattled off details: difficult to tell exact date with first child – anytime between Thanksgiving and Christmas – blood test sent to lab – will confirm tomorrow AM – fairly certain of results – regular prenatal visits – vitamins to be prescribed – no smoking – no alcohol...."

Perspiration covered Edwin's brow. Maybe his little Buttercup was right – maybe this doctor did not know what she was doing. He had little knowledge of her qualifications, and money to rent a prestigious office did not a good physician make. He glanced down at a too quiet Valeta. Her skin had managed a shade somewhere between pale dull spring and pale weak yellow. Her eyes emitted little more than a dull cyan. What had he done? Why did he bring her here? He should have insisted on the Base doctor, and would insist now, but that he knew she would never go. His hand left her small, trembling shoulder, dropping to his side.

Valeta felt the hand leave and tensed. Edwin would tell now. He would tell the doctor that it was not his baby – that they were not really married – that it was fathered by a felon who was now dead and buried. Her breathing seemed destined to perish, but the strength needed to revive it was concentrated entirely on the talking lips above the white starched jacket before her.

The doctor completed her pithy recital of instructions, handing them the small comfort of a booklet and pamphlets they could study at home. She paused for questions and, when neither of them spoke, concluded by repeating, "The birth date is impossible to predict, so just plan on late November and you'll be all right." She smiled briefly. "Again, congratulations! I know you have a lot to discuss, this being the first child. Your baby will be beautiful, though – tall with Daddy's brown eyes and dark hair – or short with Mommy's blue eyes and blond hair. You're a lovely couple, and we'll do all we can to make your pregnancy a happy one. I'll want to see you again on May 21, so be sure to schedule your appointment at the desk." She left abruptly, closing the door on both herself and all communication.

Edwin's unanswered questions bombarded the closed door, but Valeta – Valeta's mind would not craft a single question. "Having a baby changes everything," she murmured,

Edwin nodded, but let silence stretch a net of unspoken thoughts between them. Her high school education was incomplete, college education unbegun – friendships and popularity relinquished. Edwin's officer training was interrupted. No more spontaneous surfing days. Strained finances. Loss of freedom....

Valeta almost said, "Our marriage is ended before it began, Edwin," but instead, she retreated further into the jumble of thoughts. Her new little baby – exciting cherub – product of crime – sweet, happy innocent – reminder of trauma – token of stolen virginity – bitter fruit of a felonious seed.

Edwin stabbed at the jumble. "We should go." He opened the door.

"Should I make another appointment here or go to our family doctor in Kailua?"

"I guess that's up to you." Edwin stared blankly into the empty hall.

"Up to me?" Her eyes swelled with tears.

"It isn't my baby." The words sliced through the air and pierced her to the heart.

For a moment, her face lifted – gave him a chance to retrieve the sword – but the moment was gone before he realized what he had done.

Date with Responsibility

Valeta stumbled past him to the reception area. She stuttered her request alone – received the appointment card alone. She walked with him to the white taffeta Accord – but did not hold his hand. He opened the car door for her – but closed it on the misty blue muumuu.

Baby. The Accord was too small to contain the thought – far too small to examine it.

"I'm so sorry, Valeta." The words faltered from his lips with stiff self-consciousness.

"It isn't your fault," she whispered numbly.

"It wouldn't have happened if I had gone to the luau with you." He backed the car from the space and turned toward Diamond Head.

"You're going the wrong way." Valeta's keen sense of direction automated the words.

"I thought I'd take your favorite route and go back over Pali Highway."

"Oh." She stared at the silent scenery.

"Waikiki's getting busier." Edwin nodded toward the famous white sands as they passed, but she only stared straight ahead.

Then Edwin, too, fell silent as he drove the three miles through Honolulu's crowded streets and turned onto the Pali Highway – first road built to cross the steep mountains – connect Honolulu and the Windward side of the island.

It was famous for its breathtaking scenery, and Valeta usually loved the drive – loved to stop at the Pali overlook, clinging to Edwin in the strong wind, and gazing out over the northeast coast to the Pacific. She always tried to relive in imagination what it must have been like for the Hawaiian warriors who Kamehameha the Great chased up here, then pushed off the high cliff to their deaths – or, in the version of the story that she preferred, warriors who leaped to their death rather than be captured.

Today, they had gone only four minutes up the highway, were still in the residential area, and were in the left lane passing a long line of slower traffic, when she suddenly said, "Oh, stop!"

"Stop?"

"I'm really going to be sick this time. I have to get out. Now!"

Edwin accelerated, found a small hole in the traffic to his right, and darted into it. Horns blew, but he ignored them and, in another swift move, pulled off of the highway and stopped. Valeta flung open the door and leaned out.

Nausea, for the first time, carried out its sickening threat, and in view of Queen Emma's Summer Palace, Valeta threw up violently and repeatedly. When she could throw up no more, she gagged, and ended with hiccupping.

"Are you all right?" Edwin's voice tendered concern.

She nodded, and reached into the back seat, feeling blindly for the tub of moist towelettes they kept on the floor.

Edwin found them for her and she wiped her mouth and hands, stuffing the used towelette into the litterbin. When she finally closed the car door, she was crying uncontrollably.

"I don't want a baby, Edwin," she sobbed. "A baby will change everything. It will ruin our lives, but I don't know what to do, and I don't know who to ask what to do. I can't even *tell* Mom, let alone ask her for help, because she understands nothing about me. I can't tell Daddy either, unless I want a full-scale war. Grandmother is out of the question, too, because I don't want to worry her with my problems. I have nobody – nobody."

"You have me," he said.

"No, I don't," Valeta blubbered. "This isn't your baby."

10

Kitty Litter

Edwin's preoccupied mind, on auto-pilot, managed to get them safely home and into the newly rebuilt garage. He handed Valeta the little lamb key chain, and got out of the car, but Valeta did not move. Hunched and still, eyes still drenched in tears, she sat in dark despair.

He opened the door and took her hand. "Come on, Valeta. You need to go in. You don't have to tell them right away. You can wait until you've had a rest. You need something to eat, too. Things will look different after you've eaten."

Valeta did not move.

"Your grandmother will be back today. Tell her first. I know you don't want to worry her with it, but she can help tell your parents. She's a wise woman, and she will know how to break the news." Edwin unsnapped the teen's seat belt as he spoke, and extended a hand to help her from the car.

Date with Responsibility

Valeta would not look at him, but asked, "Will you tell Grandmother for me?"

"I can't. I have to get back to Base, but you can do it." He lifted her from the car, set her on her feet, and closed the door.

Valeta clung to his arm. "Take me to the base with you. I'll wait until you're off duty. I'll sit in the library and read. You can pick me up there when you're ready, and we can come back and tell them together."

Edwin's eyes clouded with confusion. What could he say to her – his sweet little teen – the girl he had planned to marry? "I need time to think," he blurted abruptly. "I'll call you later." He kissed her on the forehead and hurried away.

She watched until he was almost to the bus stop, then fled to her bedroom and locked the door. She would never see him again. She knew. She noted their final meeting on her calendar:

April 22, 2003 – 12:23 PM

* * *

At 6:30 PM, Grandmother knocked – and knocked – and knocked until Valeta relented. "Going to dinner with me?" Grandmother reached in and took her hand. "I missed you. There was lots of company on the cruise, but none like yours." She led Valeta from the room. "You are very good company, and I'm going to need good company at dinner – someone who isn't fixated on interior decorating. Your mom's a mess. I almost wish we could put her back on Valium. I simply cannot imagine how you and your daddy are living through this decorating frenzy. That master suite will be gold-plated by the time she's done. And with her timetable and Donovan's luck, she's likely to finish one day before he gets a new assignment and you all have to move to Timbuktu."

Valeta shrugged. "It keeps her occupied." She followed Grandmother to the dining room where Jean Luc had spread a festive Mexican tablecloth. The bright bold stripes read like a Mexican menu: hot sauce, guacamole, olives, cheeses, dried fish and dried peppers.

Daddy sat down at one end of the table and Valeta sat down at the other, just in case she had to leave suddenly. Grandmother prayed, and Jean Luc began to serve enchiladas.

"Mrs. Davidson's late," Jean Luc worried.

"Marjorie! Come!" Daddy's barked order got an immediate result.

"I'm here." Mom held a decorator's catalog between Daddy and his enchilada. "Do you like this tile mural for the master bath? I know orchids in a pond are inaccurate, but don't you think it's delightful with those tiny tree frogs swinging on the leaves – purple orchids and green frogs?"

"It would be more delightful if thrown into the pool," Valeta growled under her breath.

"Marjorie, I want to eat," Daddy said.

"Well! If you aren't interested, just tell me!"

"OK. We aren't interested." Valeta took undue satisfaction in Mom's irritation.

Mom glared. Just once, her daughter should be like her. Just once!

Despite Valeta's morning episode by Queen Emma's Palace, she could not resist the spicy hot enchiladas. She had two: one beef and one chicken, interspersing crisp salad to cool her palate. She relaxed as her stomach accepted it all, right down to the final sip of iced raspberry tea.

After the meal, she followed Jean Luc to the kitchen. "I'll load the dishwasher," she offered. "I need responsibility now that I'm not in school."

"You aren't in school?" Mom had followed her. "What do you mean, young lady? Where do you go every morning if not to school?" Her voice rapidly interrupted the flow of air in the kitchen, spiraling upward with each question. "And why aren't you going to school? Hasn't it been eight weeks since the fire? Wasn't I the intended victim of the fire? If I can get over it, can't you? How many times have I told you that your education is important? How do you expect to graduate?"

Kitty Litter

Valeta rinsed tomato sauce from oval plates and arranged the plates noisily in the dishwasher as she sang in a tight voice:

Who knows all about you?
Whose fine product are you?
Who knows everything will be
The way she told you – your mother.

"Valeta, you listen to me!"

Valeta dumped a handful of strident knives and forks into the dishwasher basket:

Who has always loved you?
Always worried 'bout you?
Who will smother the life
Out of you – your mother.

"You might try to ignore me, but you won't be able to ignore the University of Hawaii when they reject you. You don't get into college by being a high school dropout, missy, and I intend to see that you aren't one."

Valeta stopped singing abruptly and said in measured tones, "School is my business." She slammed the dishwasher door shut. "Mine. Do you understand? I'll take care of the little things in my life like school work, and you worry about the big things in my life like wall tile murals."

Mom frowned. "I just don't think...."

"That's your trouble. You just don't think!"

Date with Responsibility

Mom glowered. "What I mean is that I just don't think you should be skipping school because you need an education, and you'll get nowhere without an education. You have a good mind and you need to develop it. Why, you could be so many things. You have advantages that I never had. I had to stop with high school because my parents couldn't afford to send me to college, but if you graduate from high school *and* college, you get a better job, with more pay. It might be possible to leave school and blaze a successful trail on your own, but that doesn't happen often, and it isn't easy. You can't keep your perspective. I know that you plan to marry Edwin and you don't think you need a career, but even if you do marry Edwin and settle down to raise a family, you will be a better mother if...."

Valeta twisted the dishwasher knob to "start" and ran to her room, singing loudly. Mom's voice pursued like a storm tide, unleashing its fury and force at her, but Valeta locked the door, and scooped the kitten into her arms as she crossed the room.

"Mom calls that the gift of eloquence, Prince Leo, acquired when she kissed an image of the Blarney Stone on the Internet. She never kissed the real Blarney Stone in Ireland, and you wouldn't think an Internet graphic would have any effect, but Mom swears by it. The rest of us simply swear *about* it."

Kitty Litter

Valeta locked the patio door, and then took a hot shower, following which she sat down to read the information given to her by the doctor. One pamphlet broke the news that morning sickness could occur at any time of the day, and might last through the entire nine months. She read some of the suggestions that might alleviate it:

- Avoid spicy foods – ha! Like enchiladas?
- Move slowly when you get up.
- Eat dry pretzels before getting out of bed.

Pretzels. Daddy insisted that there always be pretzels in the house. She would get some from the kitchen after the family went to bed.

She looked at the next pamphlet: *Baby Name Finder*. What could you name such a child, and how could you name such a child? The last name would be Davidson, she supposed – would have to be Davidson because it could not be Rick's last name. True, it was Rick's child, but Rick was gone – and besides, nobody needed to know about that – if indeed she was pregnant – and she still was very certain that she was not pregnant.

The remaining pamphlets warned that girls younger than 19 are physically less ready to have a baby, resulting in a greater possibility of death for the baby as well as the mother. They told about health concerns; the importance of not smoking; the expense of raising a child without its father; the danger of changing your cat's litter box.

Date with Responsibility

What? Danger in changing the cat's litter box? That sounded ridiculous. She read the title again: *Is it safe to change my cat's litter box during pregnancy?*

She laid aside the rest of the stack and opened the thin pamphlet.

> *The warning given to pregnant women about contact with cat litter is due to a concern about a disease called toxoplasmosis. More than 60 million people in the United States have been infected with this disease and do not know it.*

Valeta read more rapidly, skimming the page for the chief ideas.

> *If you contract toxoplasmosis ... it can reach your baby, and possibly cause miscarriage, brain damage, serious illness. One source of this infection is cat litter boxes. Litter boxes must be kept very clean ... clean at least once a day and wear gloves when you clean them.*

Valeta looked at her growing kitten. "Leo. You're the villain." Her eyes flew across the page.

> *If you are infected..., you may have flu-like symptoms, ... that last for a few days to a month or more.*

Valeta sat bolt upright. Flu-like symptoms? Last for a month or more? Why – then – she was right! She was not pregnant! She was not! Her flu-like symptoms were toxoplasmosis. She just had an infection from kitty litter! She grabbed up the little white prince and whirled into a circle of dancing. Edwin would be so relieved – *she* was so relieved! What a fright! All this time wondering why her flu lasted longer than anyone else's flu lasted – why she was nauseous off and on – Edwin worrying that she had become pregnant – and it all was just an infection from Leo's litter box.

She plopped Leo on the bed and grabbed her cell phone. She had to tell Edwin, had to share this stupendous news. She dialed Edwin's number at the barracks, and paced the floor as she waited, but the answering voice said that Edwin would not be off duty for another half hour. Another half hour? Another half hour? How could she wait another half hour? She left a message for Edwin to call her, and went to the bathroom. She lifted her pajama top and scrutinized herself again in the mirror, but there was not the tiniest sign of pregnancy – not the slightest bulge. Once she got treatment for this cat disease, she would get over being tired and nauseous, and once the police found the man who killed Rick and set the fire, she could get back to total normalcy.

Dancing into the bedroom, she turned on the TV set, after asking the kitten, "May I have permission, your highness? I'll fly into a zillion pieces if I don't do something." She sat on the bed, surfing the channels. A commercial. Flick. Another commercial. Flick. Real estate. Flick. Sports. Flick. Wait a minute. That was last year's cheerleading competition. National championships. She leaned forward as a huge guy hurled a tiny flyer into the air. Very impressive! She would like to be a flyer in college – and she could go now. First, she would finish high school on the Internet. She had found an online high school already. She would get her diploma there, apply to college – and nobody would ever know what had happened. She gasped as the guy sent the flyer soaring like a graduation cap.

In the middle of the soar, Edwin called and she bubbled out her news. "I'm not pregnant, and you'll never believe why I've been nauseous and tired. Listen to this." She read the pamphlet to him – every word of every sentence, and concluded with a happy, "So I'm not pregnant – I'm not pregnant — simply an infection from being too careless when I cleaned Leo's litter." She giggled.

"But there's still the doctor's diagnosis," he said. His voice traveled with guards fore and aft.

"That doctor said she was *fairly* certain," she reminded him impatiently, "not certain."

"Only because she wanted to wait until the blood test came back from the lab," he replied.

"Sure. She said it would confirm pregnancy, but I think it will confirm a naughty little parasite, compliments of Leo. Oh Edwin, I'm so happy!"

Silence bombarded her ear.

"Say something, Edwin." She bit her lip.

"What do you want me to say?" His low voice tightened. "I'm not a doctor. I don't know what the blood test will show. That pamphlet says that the infection gives flu-like symptoms, but you're leaving out part of the warning. It also says those symptoms are *if* – and it's a big if – *if* you are infected for the first time during pregnancy. I'll call tomorrow to get the test results." He hung up.

Valeta closed the phone and put it on the bedside stand. "Well, he will see tomorrow, Leo. I won't come right out and say, 'I told you so' but he will find out that I am right."

* * *

Tomorrow remained in chains for hours and, when it was released, approached in slow, measured steps. Valeta waited for it in the white wicker chair, her knees draped across the chair arm, her eyes re-reading every word of the pamphlet on toxoplasmosis. She had read so fast before – could Edwin be right? She read more slowly.

> *If you are infected for the first time <u>during pregnancy</u>, you may have flu-like symptoms... and pains that last for a few days to several weeks. However, most people who become infected ... don't know it.*

Date with Responsibility

You probably did *not* have symptoms if you were *not* pregnant, and you might or might not have symptoms if you were pregnant.

Valeta laid aside the pamphlet and gazed at the humming TV. Feverishly, she snatched up the remote and flicked from one weeping channel to the next, her thoughts dancing, whirling and screaming in agitation. Pregnant. Expecting. Containing unborn young within the body. Me. Valeta. The girl who has absolutely everything except a baby – and does not want a baby. The girl who vowed never to have a baby – to talk her husband into adoption if he insisted on children. The girl who exercised her body for child-bearing, but with no intent of bearing – only to quiet a harping mother. How could this be?

The TV screen swam into focus, displaying a young woman with distended stomach covered in stretch marks – a fate worse than death, to hear the advertiser tell it – a fate that awaited her.

Information bites from sex-education class swarmed like bees: teenage mothers are a burden to society; teenage mothers never complete high school; teenage mothers never attend college. They were truisms – too obvious to mention – but the teacher did – *ad nauseam*.

Valeta rubbed her hands across her belly. Good-bye favorite jeans and old green swim suit that felt like her skin. No more wars with Daddy over chic, midriff baring tops and hip riding pants. Her misty eyes closed as she thought through her wardrobe. Just as well that the slinky black dress with the yellow plumeria was gone.

The thought struck her to the ground, with Rick standing over her. "No," she groaned, "I didn't wear the dress for you, nor did I dance for you. No! Go away! Leave me alone!" She fell from the chair, face covered with her hands, rolling back and forth. "No, Rick! Get away from me! Go away!" She trembled violently as she screamed out, "Stop it!" His lips bit into hers – bit her nose. His hands closed around her neck. "Go away!" She screamed, her hands slashing the air.

A loud knock on her door went unheard, but Grandmother hurried in. "Valeta! What is it? What's the matter?"

Valeta continued to writhe, her eyes tightly closed. "Go away! Go away! Go away!"

"It's Grandmother Davidson, dear." Grandmother knelt beside her, reaching for a slashing hand and holding it in both of hers. "Valeta, open your eyes and listen to me. You're all right. Open your eyes. Look at me." Grandmother massaged the hand. "Open your eyes, dear."

Valeta opened her eyes, but could not see through the tears. "Make him leave me alone! Make him go away! Please make him go away, whoever you are." She rubbed her free hand across her eyes, but succeeded only in soaking the hand.

Pulling a clean handkerchief from her pocket, Grandmother pushed it into Valeta's hand and urged her to sit up. "Tell me what you were dreaming," she said.

Slowly, Valeta sat up, holding the snowy handkerchief to her streaming eyes, but she neither spoke nor looked toward Grandmother.

"I heard you scream Rick's name," said Grandmother. "Did Rick hurt you?"

Valeta lowered the handkerchief and stared dumbly until her eyes gradually focused and then, when Grandmother restated the question, she nodded her head. "He raped me. And now I – I may be pregnant."

11

Bitter Fruit

Grandmother Davidson helped Valeta from the floor to the bed, then sank into the wicker chair by the window, remaining silent for a while, and gazing sadly at the crying girl. At last, she said quietly, "Would you like to tell me?"

Valeta did not move at first. Sobbing had given birth to hiccups, and the conversation of those two between themselves precluded any conversation with Grandmother.

"I'm sure it would help to talk about such an awful experience, Valeta."

"But aren't you ashamed of me? (Hiccup) I thought you might despise me when you learned about it, because you never would have made a man rape you, and I should have listened to you (Hiccup) when you said what you did about the black dress and a body guard, because you knew what you were talking about, and you were right."

Date with Responsibility

Grandmother's loving heart frowned past her high moral standards, and she replied, "I don't know that I would have done anything differently when I was a teen, so let's talk about it."

"It happened the night of Senior Luau."

Grandmother glanced toward the window, and then back at her granddaughter to ask, "Wasn't that the night of the fire?"

"Yes, and the investigators think there may be a connection," said Valeta, blowing into a paper tissue and taking a trembling breath.

"You got the arson report while I was on the cruise? Oh, but we can talk about that later – go on – I'm listening," said Grandmother, and she pulled an aqua lap robe over her knees.

"Well, you know that Edwin couldn't go to Senior Luau." With such a brief sentence, Valeta began – and talked until 2:30 AM, Grandmother spending the hours in the wicker chair, and Valeta restlessly changing from one position to another.

"Edwin got me a blind date – Rick."

She reached into her mind and took out the details of Senior Luau. One by one, she unwrapped them and set them before Grandmother. One by one, they examined each detail and discussed it. They began with the black dress – stylish and slinky – any man would believe himself seduced.

They laid it aside and unwrapped Rick's vulgar actions, dreadful language, luau drink – alcoholic and refilled more than once. Next came Valeta's drink – virgin fruit punch – perhaps with a date rape drug. There was no way to know. Had she gone to a doctor immediately – but she had not. They laid it aside and moved on. Grandmother nodded gently when Valeta took out her longing for Edwin, the soft Hawaiian night, the swaying palms and the hula music – winced in pain when her granddaughter unwrapped the actual rape. They examined the Hawaiian man's kindness, the fire, the Hawaiian man on the beach, the police questioning, and Valeta's confession to Daddy and the attorney. Last came the pregnancy test, the results of which would be known in a few hours.

But, before she took out that, she told Grandmother what she had told no one else: that she had a vague memory of someone fighting with Rick before the Hawaiian man came. She was trying to remember – she heard voices yelling. Sometimes she thought she was about to make out his face in her imagination, but she could not.

"Valeta, do you remember whether they were both male voices?"

"Yes – Rick's voice and another one – a more familiar voice. It said..... I forget."

"Well," Grandmother comforted her, "You will remember later, after you have healed." But to herself she said, "A voice that was familiar – as familiar as Edwin's?" She mused in silence. Surely, by now, they had established Edwin's whereabouts and vindicated him.

Grandmother listened as Valeta completed the recital, and shook her head as she said, "It's no wonder that you didn't want to leave the house, but I wish you had told me sooner." She paused, listening to a bird that cried in its sleep beyond the window, and then continued, "I can't believe that your mother has not even mentioned this. Does she know about the rape?"

"No, she doesn't know," said Valeta, eyes widening with alarm, "and you must never tell!"

"This is your mother we're talking about."

"This is my business we're talking about."

"She has to know sooner or later."

"Later is sooner than soon enough," she said, and then swung her legs over the side of the bed, sitting up quickly and leaning toward the older woman. The movement, too fast, caused the latch on her stomach to fly open.

Grandmother followed her to the bathroom, held back the long hair, and stayed with her until the vomiting subsided – a reminder of childhood days, although she had never been sick like this in childhood days. Childhood sickness followed rules, but there were no rules for morning sickness, if this was, indeed, morning sickness. Morning sickness was allowed to strike long before morning dawned; to strike simply because you sat up quickly; and to strike even when you had not eaten for hours. She began to cry at the total unfairness of it all.

After a few minutes, she stopped crying, and wondered why she had begun. The nausea had passed, and Grandmother was sitting on the edge of the bathtub, her face etched with fresh sorrow. Valeta stood slowly, washed her face, and smiled encouragement at Grandmother.

"Please don't look so sad," she said. "I'll get into fresh pajamas, we'll go have a snack, and then you need to get some sleep."

Grandmother raised an eyebrow, but got up and went into the other room while Valeta changed. Then she accompanied Valeta to the sleeping kitchen, and sat quietly while the teen raided the refrigerator. When they had eaten, they returned arm in arm, and Grandmother fell asleep on one side of the big double bed.

Valeta spent the remainder of the night in the chair, the TV silenced and the light dimmed for Grandmother's sake. Leo condescended to keep her company for a while, demanding his share of the lap throw, but he ended up in his normal spot on the bed, accepting Grandmother's company in lieu of Valeta's. When she was certain that her grandmother was asleep, Valeta covered her with the warm seashell comforter, and then returned to the chair where she snuggled under the lap robe.

The ringing cell phone awakened them both at 7 AM, but Valeta, getting up slowly and cautiously, a stopper in her yawn, only wondered what had awakened her. When she realized, she reached quietly for the phone, looked at the caller ID, and then looked at Grandmother.

"It's the doctor's office," she said, the words hanging frozen in the morning air.

"You are going to answer, aren't you?"

Valeta nodded and made the connection.

"Mrs. Davidson?"

"Yes." Valeta carefully ignored the error.

"Mrs. Davidson, I hope I'm not calling too early, but the doctor has asked me to tell you that your blood test is back from the lab, and it has confirmed your pregnancy."

Valeta gave a startled gasp, dropped the phone, and backed hastily away.

"Mrs. Davidson?" The connection remained open, but the caller got no response.

Valeta gaped, stunned, still wanting it to be no more than a simple cat infection, but knowing that it was not, and knowing that the test was accurately confirmed, that she was pregnant with Rick's child – the bitter fruit of his rape.

She slumped down onto the thick, marine blue carpet, the swirls of its texture doubling and tripling in mist, spiraling her down into a foreign land – the land of pregnancy. The tiny monarch growing within handed down a sentence, decreeing that Valeta remain imprisoned for the next seven months, eating that which was best for the monarch's health; wearing that which would provide the monarch comfort; sleeping sufficient hours for the monarch's well-being; exercising only with the frequency and in the manner that were best for the monarch; and giving priority to the monarch in every aspect of her life. Valeta buried her head deeper in the blue pile carpet.

"It will all work out, dear, but we need to tell your parents right away – and Edwin."

"I can't tell Daddy and Mom," came the muffled response, "and I can't tell Edwin, either, because it isn't his baby, and he won't want to talk about it." Her sobbing voice regressed to a childish moan.

Grandmother settled beside her, supplying tissues and comfort until the tears finally ended.

At 9 AM, the phone rang again and, as Edwin's phone number displayed on the caller ID, Valeta pushed the phone toward Grandmother.

Date with Responsibility

"Who is it?" Grandmother asked.

"It's Edwin."

"He doesn't want to talk to *me*."

"It's you or nobody." Valeta pressed the ringing instrument into Grandmother's hand.

"Hello?" Grandmother's voice was edged with tension, despite her attempt to smile at the phone. "Hello, Edwin. Valeta can't talk to you now, but she'll call later."

Valeta shook her head violently, but the older woman ignored her and invited, "Why don't you stop for lunch or dinner?"

Valeta's mouth formed a big "No!"

"Yes," Grandmother told the phone, "they called at 7 AM, but I'll have to let Valeta answer your question." A pause ensued, after which Grandmother said that, although Valeta was sick earlier, she should feel up to talking by the time that Edwin arrived, and she would see him then.

"How could you, Grandmother?" Valeta scolded with a gesture of disgusted resignation. "How could you invite him over here when you know I can't talk to him?" An edge of impatience crept into her voice and she clipped her words as she continued, "If I'm old enough to be pregnant, I'm old enough to make my own decisions, and I'm not going to talk to Edwin, so you can tell him that the test was positive because that's all he wants to know. Tell him we aren't engaged, so he has no commitment and he can go find another girl, and I will understand. Just tell him that." She glared at Grandmother. "You can tell Daddy and Mom, too, while you're at it, because I don't intend to, and I'm going to sleep now, so please close the door on your way out." She had never meant for it to sound so icily haughty, but it was too late to change it now.

Grandmother laid the cell phone on the computer desk on her way to the door, turned, face wreathed in pity, and then continued out the door, closing it softly behind her.

Valeta spent the rest of the day in her room, and refused to come out, even to eat – especially since Edwin had been invited to dinner. She slept briefly, then went to her computer and surfed the Internet with eyes that craved moisture.

Late that day, she launched *Operation Bitter Fruit*, which, far from being a textbook military operation, was nevertheless good enough to keep her from the battle that was sure to erupt when Daddy and Mom learned that she was pregnant. They would cool down gradually, and then she could venture forth to talk to them rationally.

So she planned her strategy, the estimated outcome – well, the *desired* outcome – of which was that she would survive alone in her room until the war came and went. Kicking her chair, she opened a new computer document file, named it ***Operation Bitter Fruit***, and detailed her plan.

Supplies: Keep room stocked with food, water, and cat food, to eliminate possibility of confrontation. Obtain more fresh cat litter, disposable gloves, and garbage bags.

Allies: Jean Luc – shopping
Grandmother – mediation
Doctor – emergency advice
Leo – companionship

Enemy reactions: Expect frequent door pounding, strong commands, hysterical screams, etc.

Offensive activity: Swear all allies to secrecy, secure doors and windows at all times to avoid enemy raid, and sharpen knowledge and skills for possible conflict.

Defensive activity: Replenish supplies only at night when the enemy is sleeping, and keep cell phone charged at all times.

It was a rough draft, but it would suffice for now, and she would work on it more tomorrow. She looked at the clock. 12:18 AM. Silence roamed the house in dark velvet slippers. It was time for her supply line to move. She crept from her room, laid siege on the kitchen, and strategically selecting what she would need – one leftover Chinese dinner, box of pretzel rods, crackers, cereal, peanut butter, and a case of bottled water – she carried the food to her room, and locked the door. She stored the boxes and jars in the closet, above Leo's inquisitive reach, then made herself comfortable on the bed for a Chinese banquet. The first crunch of cold chow mein changed her mind, and opting to let the food warm to room temperature, she moved it to her desk, told Leo to stay away from it, and went back to work.

"Beginning now, you must learn all you can about having a baby," she told herself, "and about the possibility of abortion." She chose a web site that was dedicated to pregnancy, and scanned a list of subtopics. The multimedia gallery looked interesting. She selected one entitled *prenatal care*. As the brief web cast loaded, Valeta skimmed the written words beside it. *Learning that you are pregnant*, she read, *is exciting*.

"As exciting as a death sentence," she told Leo. She shivered and read on.

>   *After this initial excitement, the mother-to-be must face the enormous responsibility that comes with it.*

Valeta slumped in the slate blue office chair, slender legs stretched beneath the desk and arms dangling at her sides. "Responsibility." Responsibility was not exactly her strongest trait, to which Leo bore witness, and speaking of which, she remembered that she had not fed him.

Date with Responsibility

She paused the web cast just as it began, gave Leo food and fresh water, accepted his condescending thanks, and then sat on the floor to keep him company. Somehow, it made up for neglecting him – or at least, she hoped it did. When he was done, she petted him, rolled him on his back to tickle him, then stood up and took her guilty conscience back to the computer.

The mother-to-be must face the enormous responsibility? Well, if she must, she must, but this baby was Rick's responsibility, not hers. He started it. Why must she be held responsible for something he started?

She watched the prenatal care web cast and another on exercise and pregnancy. Her shoulders moved upward and forward with tension as she began to realize what lay ahead. Carrying a baby involved much more than she had known – far more than she had learned in sex education class. It was not a matter of going about your life for nine months, then giving birth and going about your life again. It certainly was not a matter of carrying a baby around for a while and then laying it in its crib to sleep while you went to a party. It was not like the baby sitting she had done, where parents always returned and took over.

The web cast rolled to its end, promising wonderful memories that remain after pregnancy. "Oh yes, what wonderful memories will remain.

Not! I have to do it, though — have to face the responsibility. The trouble is, I don't even know where to start, so I guess I need to study these health sites later. Of course, an abortion would avoid the whole responsibility thing." People at the church thought abortion was wrong, but if she did get an abortion, it would not be her fault — it would be Rick's.

She shut off the computer, took her food back to the bed, and tried to watch TV as she ate. Lukewarm Chinese food was not as crunchy as cold Chinese food, but it was insipid.

When it was gone, she surveyed her room. "Private Davidson," she told herself, "I estimate that Operation Bitter Fruit will last at least three weeks, so you can start learning responsibility by cleaning up this camp, because these quarters would never pass inspection. Dirty clothes in the hamper! No more procrastination! Hang up your pajamas and robe!" She moved to follow her own orders. "Pick up that magazine that's been lying there for weeks; throw those used tissues in the wastebasket; put those books back on the shelf; and dust this place!" Barking orders to herself lightened the work, and she kept doing it, though she quickly became tired. "What's that surfboard doing in here? Put it on the patio! Get that pizza box out from under your bed — and that snorkeling mask. Put those soggy towels on the towel bars, not on the bathroom floor, and roll that tissue back onto the roll. Put the cap back on that toothpaste, and then clean up that blue gel!"

As she put the squished tube in its holder, she noticed that her toothbrush was missing. "Leo, were you playing with my toothbrush again?" she sighed as she got down on the floor to look for it. If he had been, it was her fault, not his, and if she could not even handle small responsibilities like keeping her own suite clean, how would she handle the *enormous* responsibility of a baby?

The red toothbrush was in a corner, chewed beyond use, and hidden beneath a pair of gray sweat pants. She pulled five dry face cloths and two dry towels from the same corner and threw them in the hamper. Three bottles of shampoo sat open on the side of the tub: ginger flower; kukui nut; and papaya. She replaced their three missing caps, and lined them up on the bottom shelf of the wall cupboard.

Back in the bedroom, she sorted through cosmetics, lingerie, and mangled teen magazines, finding a lipstick that had been missing since Christmas, and an earring that she had worn to Senior Luau – a single earring.

She also found the little lamb key chain, which had been absent only since Edwin brought her home yesterday morning – an eon ago. "I'm sorry, Andrew," she said, and realized that she had not sent him a note of thanks. She tucked the lamb in her pocket as a reminder to write as soon as she completed her cleaning.

Deciding that her camp would pass muster now – well, it would after she vacuumed, cleaned the shower and tub, and mopped the bathroom floor – she sank onto the bed, reached for the TV remote, and wriggling to the head of the bed, fluffed a hillock of pillows for her back. Settling against it, she began to channel surf, and found a preacher. This was not Sunday, and she was in no mood for a sermon, but as she started to move on, she was arrested by one word: *responsibility*.

"Each one of us must take responsibility for his or her actions," said the TV preacher. "The Bible tells us in Romans 14:12 that *'every one of us shall give account of himself to God.'* Everyone of us will take the consequences of our actions. That's responsibility, friends. You don't bow out of it by blaming things on others. You don't say that you *had* to do wrong because the other guy did the wrong thing to you. It doesn't work that way. He bears responsibility for what he did, and you bear responsibility for what you do. He takes the consequences of his actions, and you take the consequences of your actions."

That was a new perspective. Dad and Mom talked at her a lot about responsibility, but never explained it that way. If that preacher was right, Rick would not bear responsibility if she got an abortion. He would bear consequences for his crime, but she would bear the responsibility and consequences for her actions from here on, even if this whole thing was Rick's fault.

The nausea returned, probably because of over-exertion. She closed her eyes, and curled a strand of hair around her finger as she willed her stomach to settle, but a sudden thought popped open her sea blue eyes and ordered them around the room. Where would the baby sleep? It would have to have a crib, although it would be nicer to have a cradle, but either way, the only place big enough for a crib or a cradle was the corner where her computer desk sat. She would have to move the desk out. A rocking chair could replace her wicker chair, but where would she keep the baby's clothing? Her closet was stuffed, thanks to her love of shopping. Well, she was about to be crowned a mother, not a Homecoming Queen, so her clothes could move aside and make room for infant wear. She could fit a dressing table in the bathroom if she removed the vanity and chair, and she would have to buy a toy box for the baby's blocks, teddy bears and dolls – or trucks. She would need a car seat, too, for the white taffeta Accord.

The pretty teen's face glazed with shock. Not only would a baby *change* everything, a baby would demand far more money than she had.

"Bitter fruit," she sighed.

12

Redecorating

Sometime during the night, she had decided that she would initiate the war with Daddy and Mom. She could fall back on the original plan if necessary, but inaction was not her style. She would take Jean Luc into her confidence, and cajole him into serving Thursday's evening meal on the beach back of the house. She would help him plan the menu, and would join them at dinner, breaking the news herself at the most opportune time – after dessert – as they lingered over dark roast Kona coffee.

"Daddy and Mom," she would announce, "I'm pregnant with Rick's child." Simple in the thinking, sitting here in her quiet room, the sun peeping between the slats of her mini blinds. The simplicity of the plan, however, belied its import and the certain consequences – their wrath. They would not blame her, she knew – but that did not mean diminution of the wrath. Mom would launch the nearest object, and spew a geyser of profanity into the air. Dad would curb emotions outwardly, but close his mouth tighter than the shell of a giant *tridacna* clam. For days afterward, he could be expected to move in total, cold silence.

"I wish I wasn't so afraid of them," she mused softly. "Seventeen years old and afraid of my parents. Not really afraid. Apprehensive? Concerned?" She sighed. "Get over it. Remember what that preacher said – responsibility involves taking the consequences of your actions. All right. I'll tell them tomorrow, and take the consequences. This morning, I'll write to Edwin, and take the consequences of that action, too."

The morning was well advanced, the air heavy with ginger by the time she finished the letter. She wrote it by hand, much as she detested her penmanship, and slipped it into a plain white envelope. She showered, and began dressing to take it to the post office, but an attempt to wedge herself into her tightest jeans failed, so she settled for loose denim shorts, and a white tee top adorned with a red hibiscus bloom. The butterfly pendant was lying beside the lamb key chain, and she picked up both, debating. Technically, she still was going with Edwin, so she could allow herself to wear the butterfly.... She donned the dainty pendant and slipped out. She had gotten only as far as the garage, though, and was just lifting the door when a male voice spoke from behind her.

Redecorating

"Hi Valeta. I was hoping I would see you today. Are you going somewhere in a hurry?"

"Edwin! You scared me!" She looked down at her bag, pushing the envelope deep into it. "I was – was going on an errand," she stammered.

"I'll drive for you," he offered.

"I – I guess I really don't have to go now." It would be silly to be caught mailing him a letter when she could so easily hand it to him.

"Let me take you for a walk, then. Come on. We can go down to the beach and talk."

She shied away as he reached for her hand. "I'm sorry, Edwin. It's like you said. You need time to think. I do, too. Things have changed for us now, and I can't hold you to a relationship that has changed so much. I don't know whether I'm going to have the baby or get an abortion, and it isn't fair to you. You didn't plan on a relationship like this. We need time to think." She turned, and as she ran back to her room, her heart insisted that she go back to him, but she did not listen.

* * *

Time, which had sat stone still for over eight weeks, contemplating every second before nibbling it away, suddenly seemed to devour hours in a single gulp. It made its way through Wednesday and Thursday, arriving at dinner time far too soon.

Date with Responsibility

Valeta dressed carefully, in the dress Daddy liked best – a pale green georgette tank with jewel neckline and short sleeves, its flared skirt dotted with lilac orchids and green bamboo. She set it off with small gold hoop earrings, a dangling bracelet, and the green glass turtle pendant from Edwin. Then she created Mom's favorite hair style. She started by pulling her long golden hair up into a bun, which she secured with a handful of pins. Next, she pulled two sections loose on each side of her face and applied the curling iron to form four long ringlets. Finally, she inserted two long, shiny, bamboo chopsticks into the bun itself.

Now for the makeup – a natural, little girl look – to captivate them with the sweetness that had so often bought a reprieve in the past. With a steady hand, she rimmed her top and bottom lash lines with dusky grey eye liner pencil. She made the line on the upper lids thicker than the lower one, being careful to keep both lines sharp and neat, with no smudges. She rummaged through her cosmetic drawer for the perfect pale pink lipstick – one that would appear soft and under-stated. She added a lip liner of the same soft pink. This look was not her personal favorite, and she did not like the hair style with the dress, but her tastes did not matter tonight. Her tastes must bow to a greater goal – hitting the enemy perfectly.

Valeta slipped her tiny bare feet into white plastic zori, each of which boasted three plastic orchids on the straps. She gave Leo a quick hug and whispered, "Wish me luck, little prince," and then left him curled on her pillow as she hurried out to the beach.

The rest of the family was waiting when she arrived, but not impatiently. Grandmother and Daddy relaxed opposite one another at the table, Daddy admiring the sunset's rich colors and the gentleness of the spring waves. Grandmother pointed toward the eastern sky, where a growing cluster of stars twinkled in the clear twilight. Mom, always less placid, chided Jean Luc about his placement of the tiki torches, directing him to move them closer to the table so that they would give more light when the sun was gone. Jean Luc complied, and lit the torches as Valeta slid into her chair. She gave him a quick thumbs-up.

The weather was flawless, and Jean Luc had perfected every detail of her plan, transforming the heavy wrought iron table to a circle of tropical beauty – a white linen cloth strewn with exotic dark green maile leaves – silver napkin rings holding white napkins topped with fragrant red ginger flowers. The perfume of the ginger and maile scented the balmy ocean air.

Over appetizers – shrimp cocktail with a spicy papaya sauce – Daddy smiled and said, "That's the dress I bought you last summer, isn't it? I always liked that one. You look radiant in it."

Date with Responsibility

"Yes," said Mom. "I'm glad you fixed up this evening. You've looked ratty of late, but that hair style is becoming, which reminds me: I must have my hair done before the Kiwanis Officer Banquet."

Valeta gave them a cherubic smile and popped a tangy shrimp into her mouth. Her memory reminded her that spicy food came with a price, but it was too delicious to resist.

Deftly, Jean Luc exchanged empty appetizer plates for an organic Caesar salad garnished with tropical island fruit, and Valeta ate in silence as Daddy told one of his anti-Navy jokes.

A young ensign had nearly completed his first overseas tour of sea duty when he was given an opportunity to display his ability at getting the ship under way. Issuing a stream of crisp commands, he quickly set the decks awash with busy activity. The ship steamed out of the channel and the port faded into the distance.

The ensign's efficiency had been quite remarkable. In fact, crew mates were buzzing with bets that he had set a new record for getting a destroyer under way.

The young ensign, glowing at his own accomplishment, was not surprised when another sailor approached him with a message from the captain. He was a bit surprised, however, when he found that it was a radio message. He was even more surprised when he read: "My personal congratulations upon completing your underway preparation exercise according to the book and with amazing speed. In your haste, however, you overlooked an unwritten rule – always make sure the Captain is aboard before getting under way!"

The joke was old, and not very funny, but this was no time to enlighten poor old Daddy, so she laughed with the others and finished her salad.

The brightening starlight tipped the crests of the waves with pale silver as Jean Luc served the entree: grilled fresh Mahi Mahi topped with Macadamia nut lemon butter; wok style organic vegetables, and a brown rice pilaf.

Valeta affected a caring smile throughout the remainder of the meal, but behind it lurked a worried frown. Her one reprieve was when the air from the ocean freshened and Mom asked her to go in and get a sweater for Grandmother. As she started back to the beach, she paused for five deep, steadying breaths. It would not be long now. She squared her narrow shoulders, and returned to the table as Jean Luc served dessert: Hawaiian coconut custard pie – Mom's favorite – ordered by Valeta to sweeten her for the announcement that was to come. It had seemed perfect when she asked Jean Luc to make it, as had the rest of the menu, but now it offered little more than a small detour on the way to certain disaster.

Valeta ate the custard pie with extreme deliberation – pretending to savor each tiny throat-closing morsel – interspersing each bite with a lingering sip of water.

Daddy finished, and Valeta was still eating. Mom put down her fork, thanking Jean Luc for the pie. Valeta continued to nibble. Grandmother came to the last bit of cream and scraped it from her plate, but Valeta was only halfway through hers. Jean Luc served coffee to the three adults, and Valeta thought she heard him say *cough*. She gulped. Must be *coffee*.

It was her cue – coffee.

Slowly, Valeta placed her fork on the plate, lifted the white linen napkin from her lap to dab at her pink lips, and meticulously spread it across her knees again, removing every wrinkle. She looked at Daddy, at Mom, at Grandmother. Her blue eyes glistened in the light of the tiki torches as she stared across the darkened waves. Her tongue found a sweet crumb from the pie crust and she swallowed it, while atop a smooth napkin, her hands practiced placatory gestures. She cleared her throat, and fixed her gaze on Grandmother.

"I have something to tell you."

It was a soft voice, and it ran headlong into Daddy's as he broached the subject of moving. Valeta cleared her throat again.

"Were you saying something?" Daddy smiled at her, his happy stomach expanding his congeniality.

Valeta slid down in her chair slightly as she nodded.

"Sit up, Valeta," said Mom.

She sat up.

"I have something to tell you," she tried again. But her voice broke.

Every eye was on her now, Grandmother leaning forward in encouragement, and Mom jumping hurdles to the conclusion.

"You're finally going back to school," guessed Mom. "I wondered how long it would take you to...."

"Marjorie, be still and let her talk," Daddy interrupted. "Go ahead, Valeta. What is it?"

"It has to do with her car. She smashed it when she went out yesterday," Mom ventured.

"Marjorie, this isn't twenty questions. Now please!" Daddy's face was stern.

No longer eager to attack an enemy lulled by a signature dinner, Valeta's announcement was beginning to shake and call for retreat. Tempers were heating. Suspicions were arising. Valeta gave Grandmother an imploring half-smile, hoping she would intervene, but Grandmother refused all save a return smile and a quick shake of her head. Mom and Daddy were not so dovish.

"I wish you had taught your son to let me talk," Mom shot at Grandmother.

"I hope Valeta doesn't become a woman who insists on interrupting others," Daddy shot back.

"He thinks I'm just another Marine that he can order around!" Mom shot again.

"You're no Marine," Daddy blasted. "Marines know when to talk and when to shut up."

Mom reloaded and shot back. Daddy returned her fire. Then Mom. Then Daddy.

Before her eyes, Valeta's carefully planned evening spun one hundred eighty degrees off course. There was no hope of rational discussion now. She set her focus on the far end of the beach, and wished for a miracle – anything that would make them stop fighting.

Redecorating

As though in answer, the air suddenly filled with music – an old song – a song from Daddy and Mom's dating days, and Valeta turned to see Jean Luc coming across the beach with his portable CD player. She was sure she detected a wink as he passed the torch near Mom's chair, set the CD player on his serving cart, and bowed to Mom. "May I have this dance, Mrs. Davidson?" He reached to pull back her chair as he asked.

Mom blinked at Jean Luc, opened her mouth to scream at him, but then closed it. She rose to her feet, kicked her sandals at Daddy, and danced away, the tilt of her head indicating that she had called only a temporary treaty.

Daddy turned to Valeta. "What made Jean Luc decide to do that?"

"I don't know," said Grandmother, standing quickly, "but I haven't heard that song for years. Do I have to beg for a dance with my son?"

"Why, of course not," Daddy said with a grin, and he jumped to his mother's side, dancing her down the beach to the edge of the waves.

Valeta looked after them, pushed her plate to the center of the table, and dropped her head on folded arms. "You must tell them," she growled, "and it won't get any easier, because in a few weeks, you'll get a tummy on you and they'll guess, so you simply must do it tonight."

Date with Responsibility

When the music stopped, the dancers returned to the table, and Daddy quickly asked, "Now, Valeta, what did you want to tell us?"

Valeta took a deep breath and blurted out, "I want to redecorate my room."

"Oh. Well, this is not a very good time for that," said Daddy, "since we had to redecorate the whole master suite after the fire."

"I don't need to do major redecorating."

"You never even clean your room," said Mom, "so why redecorate?"

"I just need more room to...."

"Besides, you spend entirely too much time in there. As it is, we only see you at meals – and not at every meal." Mom looked around for more coffee. "If you redecorate, we'll never see you."

Valeta jumped up, glared at Mom, and said, in a voice shivering with ice, "I have to redecorate for the same reason that I've been skipping meals, and not going to school, and spending so much time in my room." She paused, then blurted, "I'm pregnant with Rick's child!"

The next instant, she was gone.

13

Squabbling

In the morning's wee hours, Valeta made a kitchen run of prudence, only to encounter Mom, whose certain questions Valeta preempted with one of her own. "What are you doing up?"

Mom gave a start of surprise. "What? Oh, I needed a glass of water." She turned toward the refrigerator and retrieved a cold bottle, adding, "I didn't think anyone was awake yet."

"Oh, well, I just came out to see what the noise was," Valeta told her, retreating toward the living room, and wishing Mom back to bed.

"Wait a minute," Mom called after her, "and let me have a look at you. You haven't been to bed yet, have you?"

Valeta shrugged. "I guess not."

"You guess not? Don't you mean you *know* you haven't been to bed?"

Valeta bristled. "Well, if it makes you happy, I *know* I haven't slept yet," she said, underlining almost loudly enough to waken everyone.

"Sh! Go and get some sleep so you can think better, and we'll talk later after your father goes to work – about what you're going to do now that you're pregnant. Pregnancy is for adults, and you're a child, with a body that isn't ready for pregnancy."

"Oh my body is very ready, Mother, because I've been doing wonderful childbirth exercises since I was twelve, remember." She hissed the words into the sleepy air. "Five years of exercise ought to count for something, don't you think?"

Mother rejected input, and mused, "Yes, we need to talk as soon as Donovan goes to the Base, and I know both he and I will want you to do what's best – you know what I mean."

"No, I don't know what you mean," said Valeta, "but I'm sure you would like to tell me what you mean, Mother dearest."

"Don't get sassy, young lady. "I mean that you will get an abortion immediately."

"Oh, that's what you mean, is it? Well, that's not what I have in mind at all, thank you very much." Valeta spun on bare feet, leaving Mom staring at the spot where she had been. She dashed away, counseling herself that if Mom voted in favor of abortion, she must vote against it.

Squabbling

Actually, the vote was not easy, since she already had considered abortion, but when she returned to the kitchen at dawn and found Mom still there, sipping coffee, the decision was made.

"Come in here," Mom called sweetly. "You naughty girl, to run out while I was talking to you, and trying to tell you that I'm here for you. If I had known you were pregnant, I never would have harassed you about school, but I had so many things on my mind, with the fire in the master suite and redecorating, and all. You really should have told me, but now that I know, we can take care of the problem, you can return to school, and nobody will be the wiser." She sipped her coffee with peculiar eagerness. "I know five good doctors, two of whom are in the Kailua Women's Club with me, and I've heard them talk about how safe a procedure abortion is, so I will get everything arranged as soon as they open today. I'll make an appointment for this afternoon, and by tomorrow morning, you can go back to school. Of course, if you want a day to just lie on the beach afterward, that's all right, but the sooner you go back, the sooner you can catch up."

"Mom, I am not getting an abortion." Her stomach knotted as she spoke.

"You're too young to know what to do," said Mom, swishing the coffee on her tongue, and smacking her lips.

Date with Responsibility

"Now if you were older, you'd know that this is – this is very good coffee." Mom downed the rest of the beverage and got to her feet, but the feet were not prepared, and she sprawled on the floor.

Valeta looked down at her with disgust. "What was in that cup?"

Mom grinned. "Coffee – very good coffee – and I'm going to have another cup as soon as you help me up from here."

"How much have you had, Mother? You're half drunk." Valeta sniffed at the cup. "That's Irish coffee, isn't it?"

"I'm not drunk. I stumbled." Mom struggled to her feet, a Cheshire cat smile accompanying the words. "I need a little more. It helps me think."

Valeta ran to the coffee pot, scrambling away from Mom's outstretched hand to dump the remaining brew down the sink. She opened the corner cupboard and took out a small box.

"Here. Take these and go to bed." Valeta pressed two red capsules into her mother's hand.

"What are these?"

"Anti-hangover capsules," Valeta said brusquely. "They won't keep you from getting drunk – obviously – but you won't have such a big headache when you wake up." She pushed a glass of water at Mom and watched as she swallowed the capsules. "Now go back to bed and sleep," she said, steering her mother out the door.

As Mom disappeared groggily toward the master bedroom, Valeta hurried to replenish her supplies. This abortion question could make the war drag on, and she wanted to be prepared. She raided the refrigerator for cold cuts, cheese, and two cans of guava juice, added a half loaf of bread, and scurried back to her room.

The next time she left her room was just past lunch time, at Mom's screaming insistence and relentless pounding on the door, signs that the red capsules did not live up to their advertising. "Young lady, I want you out here now!"

The teen topped her shorts with a tee, and stuck out her tongue at the dismal reflection in the mirror. Grandmother's calm voice filtered through the keyhole, telling Mom that Jean Luc was waiting for the shopping list, and would she please go to the kitchen and give it to him.

Valeta allowed Mom time to get to the kitchen, then unlocked her door and walked slowly across the living room, listening to their voices. Poor Jean Luc, having done nothing to deserve a tongue lashing, should be receiving accolades for last night's beach dinner. As she reached the kitchen, she made a mental note to deliver them to him later, but for now, she scowled at Mom, and waited for Jean Luc to depart.

Date with Responsibility

When he did, she began to speak, but Mom interrupted, "Sit down, Valeta. You should be off of your feet."

Valeta positioned her feet firmly, about two feet apart, and set her jaw. "I'm only eight weeks pregnant, Mom. I can be on my feet as much as I want, and I want to be on my feet right now."

"You are almost nine weeks pregnant, and you should not take chances. Sit down." Mom shoved a stool toward her.

Valeta ignored the stool.

"All right, stand then. I can talk to you just as well whether you sit or stand. Now, I've been on the phone to my doctor friends, and I found one who can fit you in this afternoon at two o'clock. I would have waited until tomorrow, but you need to go when everyone else is in school, and if we don't do it today, you will have to wait until Monday. We can go by way of...."

"If you're talking abortion," Valeta planted a hand on each hip, "remember that I told you I'm not getting an abortion."

"It's the only possible way you can go back to normal," Mom said, "and once you get over the abortion, you can forget this ever happened."

"Forget it ever happened? Are you crazy? How can I forget it ever happened? It did happen.

Squabbling

It clearly happened, and abortion is not going to wipe it away. That's ridiculous. Besides, I don't want some doctor cutting me. I don't want to have this particular baby, but I've read about abortion, and I don't want that either."

"Valeta, it isn't that bad."

"How do you know? How many abortions have you had, Mom?"

"Well, I...."

"How many?"

"Well...."

"None. You've never had one abortion."

"Valeta, you have to do it."

"No! I won't have an abortion. Period." Valeta's chin jutted out as she spoke.

"You will if I say you will," spluttered Mom. "You aren't an adult yet, and as long as you live under this roof, you do what your father and I tell you to do."

"Daddy isn't doing the telling. You are. If Daddy agrees with you – – – maybe."

"Your Daddy spoils you, but this time he will say exactly what I'm saying: that you'd better start thinking about somebody besides yourself, and begin to realize what a scandal this is."

"Ah, yes, the scandal is what's really important, isn't it, Mom? You're thinking about those snooty women's clubs that might drop you from their rolls, not about your daughter." Valeta's eyes flashed dangerously, but Mom took no notice.

"I am thinking about you – and about your reputation, which you seem determined to befoul." Mom's face flushed to her red bangs. "From the way you act, in spite of all the times I've talked to you about men and warned you to be careful, one would think I had never taught you a thing. You throw it all aside, go cavorting on a dark beach, and let your family put up with – this!"

"Cavorting? I was not cavorting, and it isn't the family that has to put up with *this*, as you so sweetly refer to my child. I'm the one that has to put up with *this*," she touched her belly, "and I'm not going to abort it because it's half Davidson."

"Watch what you say!" Mom reached to slap her daughter's mouth, but Valeta stepped aside. "That baby has nothing to do with the Davidson family. It's his baby, not yours. His! That criminal's! And I won't have his baby running around my house, so if you're going to keep the child, you're going to leave my home. Just think about that! Think about how you will raise it, with no money, no job, being a high school dropout. The best you can expect is minimum wages, and a shack on the beach where you try to...."

Squabbling

"Mom, stop it!" Valeta stomped her tanned bare foot on the black kitchen tiles. "All you ever do is lecture me! Lecture, lecture, lecture!" She was shouting – had to shout. "You never listen! You never want to know what I think! You think you have all the answers! Always! Well, it's my life! Listen to me for a change! I'm not entirely devoid of intelligence, you know! Stop lecturing! Just stop lecturing!" Her eyes shot blue lightning as she stared intensely at her mother.

Mrs. Davidson paused, but then continued, "Valeta, you're too young to know what's right, and you're in over your head. This isn't a little class play, you know. Now, I think...."

"You think!" Valeta did not wait to hear what Mom thought. She slammed the kitchen door shut behind her, gave it an extra kick, and fled to the beach. "Now, I think...," she fumed. "It's my life, not hers. It's what I think that matters." The petite blonde threw herself to the sand beside the tall coconut palms and tried *not* to think. Why make everything so difficult? Why not tell Mom what she really wanted to do, and let her politely bow out instead of persisting with plans for an abortion? On second thought, Mom bowing out was pretty improbable after seventeen years of her micro-managing her daughter's life.

Valeta became acutely aware of the little lamb key chain digging its nose into her thigh.

181

Date with Responsibility

She pulled it from her shorts pocket and absently stroked its miniature head. No, there was no sense in telling Mom. Not yet. Not until she had decided for sure. Not until the decision was unchangeable.

The midday sun diluted the shimmering blue of the waves, but the blue of her eyes grew intense as she tried to untangle her life.

Eight weeks. Over eight weeks. Had it only been that long since Senior Luau? It seemed a lifetime. She looked down at her tummy. Eight weeks ago, a new life had started.

"If he looks like Rick," she whispered to a passing sea gull, "I think I'll kill myself." She slipped into subconscious thought and continued, "I'm carrying the child of that idiot, with his DNA, which means it might have his white hair – his deep chasm in the chin – his uncouth manners." No, a baby's manners were not a part of DNA. Still....

A small, hairy coconut fell nearby, and made its bed in the soft sand.

"My son," she told the baby coconut. "My son – or my daughter. It's too soon for those words. There are so many other words that should come first – so many ceremonies before a baby's birth." Valeta wrote in the sand with her finger:

> Graduating Class of 2003
> Graduating Class of 2007
> I, Valeta, take you, Edwin, to be my....

Squabbling

No, she definitely was not ready for a baby, and a little girl with Rick's features was out of the question. She *would* have an abortion. She tried the word aloud. "Abortion," she whispered, and trembled. She jumped to her feet and fled from the sound, flying down the beach as she had not done for more than eight weeks. Run. Running may cause a miscarriage – spontaneous abortion. Run! Harder! Faster! Her feet stumbled in the shifting dry sand and she changed course, seeking the harder sand near the waters edge, but she had run only a short distance when her breath came in ragged gasps. Her tiny feet lagged, complaining, and her lungs screamed for oxygen. How could she be out of shape so soon, after only eight weeks of skipping exercise? Why did she feel weak – tired – knees turning to jelly – so – short – of – breath? She stopped, her upper body falling toward her waist in a desperate effort to reach the comfort of the glistening white sand.

Gradually, she caught her breath, brought her body upright, and stared across the eternity of the sea, vaguely aware of the sun's rainbow path across the waves, vaguely aware that it tinted the sand beneath her feet – white sand – sand the color of Rick's hair – possibly the color of her baby's hair. <u>Her</u> baby?

"That's right, it really *is* my baby, not just Rick's. It has my genes and my DNA, too. I told Mom it was half Davidson, but until this moment,

Date with Responsibility

I never fully realized, never stopped to think, that the baby is half Valeta! How could I not see that? My genes might be dominant, and the child will have my blonde hair and tiny nose. It could be short like me, and slim, not chunky. It could have my mouth, and my smooth chin, and be a little girl that looks just like me!"

The breeze tickled her skin, and she inhaled the damp perfume, a smile lifting the corners of her mouth slightly – but the smile soon died. Why get excited about a child she must abort? She was not ready for a child, even if it was half hers and looked exactly like her. She could not support a child – remember? Imagine trying to rock a cradle with her toe while asking, "Would you like fries with that burger?" Abortion was the only answer, just as Mom said, so maybe she should go back to Mom right now and apologize – ask Mom to keep that appointment with her doctor friend – go and end this whole thing. After all, a lot of people on the Internet said it was not a baby yet – only a piece of tissue.

Valeta trudged into the water and walked slowly back toward the house, letting the waves wash and soothe her burning bare feet. By the time she got to the house, she was quite tired of walking, tired of thinking, and tired of living. She did not have the energy to talk to Mom now, so it would have to wait until later. Of course, later she might no longer want an abortion, but so what? She went around the house to her own private patio, kicked the orange exercise ball into a sandy corner, and slipped into her room, locking the patio door behind her. She fell across the bed and closed her weeping eyes.

Immediately, the lamb snuffled its tiny nose against the inside of her pocket, bleating silently until she rolled to her back and extracted it, then rolled to her stomach and perched it high on her pillow. Lambs were so little, so helpless. Wasn't that in the Bible? She remembered hearing some-thing like that in church, about ...*a lamb to the slaughter*. That was the middle of the verse, but what was the beginning – the ending?

She stared at the key chain, her eyes misted with tears, and the lamb wandered into the mist, all helpless, sweet, soft, cuddly – a mere baby. Who could kill a baby, or even consider such a horrific deed? And yet, she was considering it.

Valeta jumped up, tears streaming down pale cheeks, and locked the door into the living room. She was forbidden to lock herself in her room, but from now on, nobody would see her again until she was ready to be seen – or never.

* * *

Friday ended, and Saturday began with a call from Edwin, but, thankfully, the caller ID warned her. She tossed the phone unanswered on the bed, but then, knowing that he would call again, decided to put it out on the patio under the big lounge chair cushion.

Mom, Daddy, and Grandmother Davidson each called her to breakfast, but she refused to answer. They each called her to lunch, and again she refused to answer. Just before dinner time, when Daddy came to the door demanding to know if she was all right, she refused to answer vocally, but ripped a sheet from her binder and scribbled, "I'm fine, so leave me alone, please." She pushed the note under her locked door, waiting for Daddy to leave, and then sat down to eat cereal and fruit, nibble on pretzel rods, and wash it all down with bottled water. Eventually, she went to bed.

On Sunday morning, she nibbled her salty pretzels, sipped her water, then slowly went to check the computer calendar. April 27, 2003. This evening, she would be nine weeks pregnant. She took a shower and dressed in the blue muumuu. She brushed her hair and turned on the TV. Maybe that preacher would be on again – not that she was overly fond of sermons, but today was Sunday – the eighth Sunday she would miss church – she felt guilty – and that preacher's sermon on responsibility made more sense than anything Mom said, for sure, and maybe more sense than Daddy's explanation, too. She clicked the remote, searching the channels until at last, she found him – and he was beginning to speak.

Squabbling

Valeta moved to the bed and scooped the ever-present kitten into her lap. She listened to the whole sermon this time, and jotted the speaker's name and address on a scrap of paper, just in case. She tucked it into her wallet.

* * *

Throughout that week, Valeta hibernated.

Edwin phoned daily, but Valeta refused to take his calls. He came to visit with increasing frequency, but she declined to be visited. He sent her flowers — a shocking bouquet of scarlet anthurium, but she relegated them to the back patio. He patrolled the beach by her house, monitoring her window, guarding her door, pleading for even a brief rendezvous. She watched from behind wispy, white curtains that swayed lightly in the warm spring trade wings – watched, listened, and knew his desires, but denied each one.

The confusion and pain were too great and, although that was not Edwin's fault, it was not her fault either – and Edwin seemed to think it was. His thoughts remained unspoken, of course, but imagination made them seem otherwise.

She retreated into the wicker chair when he glanced toward her window. In a way, you could make a better argument that it was Edwin's fault rather than hers. Had he not chosen to work that evening, life still would be carefree – for both of them. They would be snorkeling, surfing, windsurfing, bodysurfing, and sea kayaking – not worrying.

On Saturday, May 3, Edwin interrupted his usual patrol to stop at the most secluded part of the beach. Curious, Valeta drew aside one curtain and pressed her cheek against the louvered glass to study his actions. Like some creature doomed to participate in a clumsy dance, he bent, swung, rose, and bent again, his feet never straying far from an invisible circle. The dance continued for long intervals, broken only by an occasional rest and single deviation that appeared to be the scrawling of a message. But at last, the awkward movements ceased, he stooped once more, and his finger stabbed the sand. He retraced his steps to the path just below her window, and stopped.

"Read it before high tide, Valeta," he called quietly. Then, he was gone.

14

Riddle in the Sand

The tide would not reach its highest until after 9 PM, but with Daylight Saving Time, it still would be light enough. She would wait until the family was at dinner in the courtyard, and then slip out her patio door unseen.

"Until then," Valeta told Leo, "I'd better start catching up on my school work, since that's part of *Operation Bitter Fruit*."

She pulled an old purple ribbon across the floor and watched the kitten chase it. Laughing quietly, she pulled it up onto the bed, and watched Leo scramble up the mountain of the comforter to conquer his prey.

"I'm glad I have you, little confidante. You keep secrets better than any human," she told him, and then, wrapping the ribbon around his snowy tummy, she pulled him close, moved the ribbon to his neck, and tied it in a royal purple bow.

Date with Responsibility

"Now, you take a nap while I study." Valeta went to the computer and accessed a web site on Hawaii history. History was not the world's most interesting subject so far as she was concerned, but it was important if she intended to stay in Hawaii – which she did. Even if she never got to attend the University of Hawaii, she should know her own state's history. She might even have to help her little girl with homework, if she did not abort her.

She brushed the thought aside and tried to concentrate. "I suppose memorizing this timeline would help keep things in place," she mused. "If only I could set it to cheers. Let's see:

Hey, hey are you ready,
Are you ready to sail away?
Hey, hey are you ready,
On this fifth century day?
To Hawaii, Polynesians, to Hawaii!

Disgusting – and far too time consuming. Maybe she would review climate and topography first. She pulled a binder from her bookshelf, running her hand over the front photo with deep longing: women's surfing championships. She would love to be out shooting the curl right now. She sighed. Later – maybe – if mothers ever went surfing – ever had time for surfing? Or, if she decided in favor of having an abortion, she could surf again. She opened the binder and ran her eyes over her vocabulary notes:

Riddle in the Sand

kona – hot, humid wind from south

leeward – opposite windward side of the island – ergo, Waianae Coast

trade wind – blows almost constantly in one direction: especially one that blows almost continually toward equator from the northeast in belt between northern horse latitudes and doldrums and from the southeast in belt between southern horse latitudes and doldrums

windward – facing the direction from which the wind blows – ergo, Kailua

"Let me see. I suppose a resident of Hawaii should know the nicknames of the seven islands."

Hawaii	The Big Isle
Kauai	The Garden Isle
Lanai	The Pineapple Isle
Maui	The Valley Isle
Molokai	The Friendly Isle
Niihau	The Forbidden Isle
Oahu	The Gathering Place

Valeta fell silent as she turned the pages. This had been boring when she sat captive in a high school classroom, waiting to exchange makeup and gossip with Jennie, but now it was interesting. The Hawaii island group, 2400 miles off the coast of mainland United States, actually included 132 islands and atolls, of which only seven were inhabited and made up the state. She finished reviewing climate and topography and started through the islands' early history.

Date with Responsibility

Settlers arrived 1000 to 1250 years before the *United States Declaration of Independence* was signed. They came on canoes as long as fifty feet, fastening two canoes side by side and building a platform between them to carry as many as one hundred people on each canoe. Masts held sails made of bark cloth, which they called *tapa*. Valeta shivered with delight. She loved cruising waves near shore in an outrigger canoe. It must have been exciting to spend weeks on such a primitive vessel, sailing to an unknown place to make a new home, but it seemed odd that nobody knew why the Polynesians did that. Maybe she could find something on the Internet. She laid the binder to one side and did a quick search.

There are three centers for legends about Hawaiian gods, she read: *New Zealand, Hawaii, and Tahiti.* The people of these islands, separated by thousands of miles, tell the same legends, in almost the same way, with very little variation in names – as if the Polynesians all had lived in the same place when first driven out of Asia. Through the centuries, they did not visit one another. They had no written language, but their physical traits, customs, habits, and speech, as well as traditions and myths, show the three groups to be as closely related as cousins in the USA and Great Britain.

Valeta smiled as she thought of Andrew, among Polynesians in New Zealand while she lived among them in Hawaii.

"Oh, I still haven't written a thank you note for the lamb key chain," she said aloud. "I'll do that right now – while I'm thinking about it."

She swept the binder onto the floor, and rummaged in a drawer for note paper. She did not, after all, intend to write a long letter, and she did not want the note to look lost on a big sheet of paper either. She was sure there was note paper here somewhere. Mom insisted that a girl of her "class" – Mom's word – always write proper thank you notes. She glanced toward the window, saw that she had plenty of time to write before dark, and as she finally found paper, thought to herself that she must get Andrew's e-mail address. Corresponding would be much simpler that way.

"Dear Cous," she began, and stopped. It would really be great if she could tell Andrew about the baby, and ask him what he would do if he was in Edwin's shoes. Would he dump her? Would he continue dating her only if she aborted the baby? Would he marry her now and raise the baby as his own or....

So engrossed was Valeta in the several possibilities that she jumped when she felt soft fur against her bare ankle. "What are you doing awake, Leo?" She looked at the clock. "Wow! Six o'clock already. Chow time. OK. Let's see what we can find." She went to the closet, Leo on an invisible short leash at her side.

Date with Responsibility

"I'll have to call Jean Luc and ask him to put kitten chow on the shopping list." She opened a can and plopped the contents into Leo's bowl. Then she gave him cold water and went back to her thoughts, Andrew's note, and her studies. She would have to wait until seven o'clock to go out, but once she had finished the note, she set the computer's alarm before stepping back into web sites of Hawaii's history.

This time, she stumbled upon a site that included a tongue-in-cheek test as to how well you might fit into the local culture.

You know you are local if...

* *You wear two different color slippers together and you no mind*
* *You drive barefoot*
* *You have a slipper tan line*
* *You let other cars in ahead of you on the freeway*
* *Your best friend's name is Jennifer, Pua, Lani, Lei, Yuki or Emma*
* *You think the four food groups are starch, Spam, fried food, and fruit punch*
* *Your only suit is a bathing suit*

"Hey, Leo," she whispered, "did you realize that I'd become almost one hundred per cent local? If I dyed my hair, maybe I'd really look local." She jumped up and ran to the mirror. Hm. Black hair? With her fair skin, she would look more like death warmed over than a sun-loving local. She paused to study her reflection. If her baby was blonde, she would only raise questions with dark hair, and besides, plenty of Beach Bums were blondes, so....

She swished the golden tresses into a long ponytail and returned to her study. By the time the alarm rang, the missionaries had arrived on the island.

Leo meowed sleepily from the bed, where he had just finished his bath, and did not want to hear an alarm clock.

"Sorry to disturb you, little one, but that means everyone is at dinner, and it's time for me to go see what Edwin wants me to read before high tide." With utmost stealth, Valeta unlocked the door to the living room and pushed it ajar. The French doors stood wide open, everyone was in the courtyard, and Jean Luc was serving dinner. She pulled the door tight, and re-locked it, then dug into the closet for sandals – one green and one white – and slipped out the patio door. A moment's pause to put on the slippers, and she was off to the beach, not running, but making haste slowly.

The evening sun lit the graceful palms from the side, stretching their dark shadows far up the white beach, while the water shone with a rich, deep mosaic of late day blues tinged with reds. Beneath her feet, the dry sand sifted warmly, breathing tiny bubbles as clams stretched their long siphons heavenward. It was the only visible sign of life in this tropical paradise, other than the lush vegetation. Newly blossoming plumeria sprinkled the moist sea air with perfume, and the sea air swept on to a rendezvous with the island's leeward side. Hawaii was wonderful – romantic. Valeta growled at Hawaii, and kicked a large shell with her white left zori. She kicked another with her green right zori. Then she stooped to pick up a third shell and hurl it fiercely into the rolling waves – just to be sure that the ocean knew how rotten she felt about what Edwin wrote – curious, but rotten – so rotten that she stomped sand over the next clam bubble that rose in front of her. She went on stomping sand over bubbles until she reached the secluded spot beneath the coconut palms. Then, she stopped short.

Just above the rushing, scouring waves sat an enchanting castle, its moat full and a draw-bridge of driftwood beckoning one across the moat and past the open gates – if one were a *menehune*.

Valeta stopped to examine the poetic work. How cleverly the architect had blended cylindrical turrets with coned roofs, balanced rectangular stairs and square windows with arched doorways. In ever diminishing size, turret after turret rose from the base, all connected by spiraling sandy stairways and gently inclined walks. Between the palatial structure and the ocean, the sand had been smoothed with a palm frond, then disturbed once more as a finger traced a message that ended with a question mark – a mark with a hole that plumbed the depths of the earth:

> *How would you like to be*
> *buried with my people?*

Valeta recoiled in horror, nearly stumbling over the sandy structure. What a rude thing to write! She glared at the insolent question, a spot of color deepening in each cheek. Her eyes took on a wounded look, then filled with immense tears, whether of anger or hurt, she did not know.

"I'm sorry, Edwin," she whispered. "You must really hate me to write that." She stared through her tears, and the final rays of the sun burned the words into her mind:

> *How would you like to be*
> *buried with my people?*

The message frightened her. She looked around quickly. He was lurking nearby. She felt it. He planned to answer the question for her. He killed Rick, and now he would kill her. As the sun dipped behind the mountains, she shivered, and then scolded, "Edwin would never kill anyone." This could not be Edwin's message – must belong to someone else – but it was Edwin's handwriting, unmistakably Edwin's handwriting. Valeta dashed a hand at the persistent tears and studied the sand for a second message, crawling slowly, tiny shells pressing into her flesh, the daylight fading, the tide rising – but she could find no other writing, so that had to be Edwin's message. She sighed as she stood to her feet, moved to the water's edge to splash sand from her legs, and returned to the castle.

Why would anyone accompany an elegant sand castle with such terrifying words? She looked up and down the deserted beach, then back at the castle, stooping to admire the fragile work that would so soon be gone. She caught her breath. Perched atop a stout, flat turret rested a tiny shell butterfly, iridescent wings spread in the light of the rising moon. Her hand reached for the dainty butterfly, but could not remove it. Against all logic, it appeared to be firmly affixed to the sand.

"Well," she thought, "the tide will destroy the whole castle soon, so it won't hurt if I destroy one turret of the castle. He obviously meant for me to take the butterfly. He wouldn't want it to be lost in the ocean."

With her green zori, she tapped the turret, and a little of the sand fell, but most of it stayed. She tapped again and the turret loosened, but refused to fall. The butterfly, too, remained where it was. The green sandal kicked the turret hard, but it did not break apart, oddly enough. It did topple this time, though, taking the tiny butterfly to the ground with it.

Valeta frowned and reached for the shining insect. Suddenly, her eyes moistened with joy.

"A butterfly ring," she breathed. The ring was affixed to the lid of a sandy jar, which had been the strength of the turret. She removed the ring and held it to the moonlight, lost in the pearly pink iridescence of the butterfly's wings. She stood there alone, caught in the butterfly's spell for a very long time. The incoming tide had dampened the sand and shells beneath her feet, and moved on to conquer her white sandal, then her green sandal, the castle, and everything else in its path.

Finally, the moon went behind a small cloud, and Valeta returned to reality, the tears gone, and a slight smile playing across her lips. She was in water to her ankles, and the tide had eaten both the castle and the message, but she had the ring and the jar. She slipped the ring on her finger, washed the sandy jar in the tide, and moved to higher ground. Then she turned and walked through the darkness back to the house.

In her room, she found that the jar was not empty. It was full of jellybean chocolates in her favorite flavors – and only her favorites: cherry, strawberry, orange, blueberry, green apple, and banana. She must have one right away! She must have that big strawberry one that resided halfway down the side of the jar. In fact, she wanted to eat nothing but strawberry chocolates. She dumped the colorful candy buttons on her bed, and sorted rapidly, pushing aside all but those with deep pink shells.

A folded business card tangled with the candies, but before she could see it, Leo jumped up on the bed, and as she corralled him into her lap, the business card went with him. She never saw it. Finishing her sorting, she sat down beside the strawberry buttons, popped a crunchy pink shell into her mouth, bit it in half, and let the sweet milk chocolate center melt onto her tongue. She closed her eyes to shut out everything but the delicious taste, and as it died away, quickly popped a second button, and closed her eyes again.

Leo wriggled in her lap, batting at the sweet buttons, so she plopped him onto the floor and reached for another jellybean, finally spying the card. She unfolded the pale green note, and read:

I hope you solved the Irish
riddle in the sand.

That message on the beach was not a threat – at least not a clear threat. It was a riddle, and it did belong to Edwin, because the hand-writing on the business card was identical to that of the riddle in the sand. Valeta looked at the bottom of the card. The answer should be written upside down beneath a riddle, but there was none, which made sense when she remembered that the riddle was on the beach, not on the card. She turned the card over. Blank. She gazed at her mental image of the riddle:

> *How would you like to be*
> *buried with my people?*

Absently, Valeta popped another jellybean chocolate in her mouth, her brow furrowed as she puzzled over the riddle. Buried. That meant death, or did it? My people. The Marines? Buried in a military cemetery? Maybe. It could mean French people – Edwin's roots were in France. Be buried in France. The only other use of the term *my people* that she could remember was in church. Edwin might mean that. Buried with the saints? She rubbed a hand over her eyes, and the butterfly flew into the riddle. What part did a butterfly have in a riddle about burial? Buried alive – emerge as something new?

Slowly, she finished the strawberry jelly-bean chocolates, and opened a bottle of water. If the riddle was Irish, Mom might know the answer, but she was not about to ask Mom.

Leo dashed across the room, reminding her again that kittens could reach 31 MPH at full speed, and cover about three times their body length per leap, which made him rather amazing.

The teen turned back to the pile of jelly-beans, and began to sort the candy by color: sour apple green in one pile; tart blueberry in a second pile; banana in a third pile; sweet cherry in a fourth pile…. Suddenly, her hand stopped, and she snatched it back, staring at the candy with eyes topped by startled arches. Poison! That was why Edwin left the candy in the turret. He used the riddle to get her to the beach, the butterfly to catch her attention, and candy containing poison to fulfill the riddle, regardless of her answer – and she already had eaten one sixth of the candy.

She looked down at her stomach, a second thought shoving the first rudely aside as she told herself, "Not poison – abortion pills!" He disguised abortion pills as candy, and she would never know when she ate them – maybe had eaten them among the first sweet bites. Could you hide the taste in chocolate? Would the baby die soon, and, dying, would it feel pain and know that it was dying? "Get a grip," she whispered, "and think who Edwin is. He certainly is not a scoundrel, and you know he wrote the riddle only because you love riddles. The butterfly ring is to go with the glass pendant, and the jar of jellybeans shows that he remembered your favorite candy – nothing more. But if you're going to have a fit over it…."

She scooped the remaining candy back into the apothecary jar, pushed down the lid, set the jar on the desk, and raced to the bathroom where she bent over the open toilet, and stuck a slender middle finger far down her throat.

15

Seventy-two Hours

Exhausted, Valeta threw herself across the bed, intending to get up later and study, but falling fast asleep on top of the comforter instead.

Hours later, the thunder of fists bombarding the door from the living room interrupted a pleasant dream. She moved stiffly, eyes still closed, and tried to go back to sleep, but the fists rained a storm of blows on the door, causing her to squint at the clock with one eye. The eye refused to focus, so she let it return to the charming view on the other side of the lid.

Swinging between wakefulness and sleep as calmly as the pendulum of Dad's grandfather clock, she listened to the storm that continued to beat on her locked door.

At last, she stretched, the blue eyes came to rest on the jellybean jar, and she realized that she was quite alive. Slowly, she sat up.

Date with Responsibility

5:30 AM. The god of the storm could only be Daddy, determined to communicate something to her before leaving for the Marine base.

Valeta swung her feet slowly off the bed and stood, calling sleepily, "It's too early to get up, whoever you are."

The heavy blows continued, and Valeta finally relented, mostly out of pity for Grandmother in a nearby bedroom. She twisted the lock, but did not open the door.

As she shuffled slowly back to her bed, Daddy burst into the room, Colonel face firmly in place. "You certainly took your time, young lady," he said, and added a few choice expletives.

"I was asleep," she replied, daring him to prove otherwise.

"Well, get the sleep out of your brain as fast as you can, and listen closely, because what I am going to say will be said only once, and then I have to get moving." Colonel Daddy glowered briefly, but softened when he looked at the rumpled teen before him. "Your mother and I spent most of the night fighting over the issue of abortion, specifically as it pertains to you, and I have decided to give you seventy-two hours to decide what you are going to do about it. It is now Sunday morning, so you must be prepared with your decision early Wednesday morning. I will arrange to be home for breakfast with the family on Wednesday, at which time you will make the announcement. Do you understand?"

Valeta nodded solemnly and slowly, hoping the rising nausea would wait until he was gone, wishing she had eaten a pretzel before unlocking the door.

If you have not made your decision by then, I will make it for you," Daddy told her, "but I would prefer that you make it for yourself." He glanced at his wristwatch, and did a full about-face, striding rapidly from the room as he fumed about being late for work.

Valeta went to the bathroom and threw up.

Seventy-two hours! How was she supposed to decide a matter as momentous as abortion in a mere seventy-two hours? Seventy-two hours was the sort of time limit you placed on deciding whether you would streak your hair for the next party. Seventy-two hours was hardly enough time to find the perfect dress for the prom – let alone to decide whether to carry a baby or abort it.

Oh well. Daddy was simply in a huff at Mom right now. By evening, he would reconsider.

Valeta sat on the edge of the bed, nibbling a salty pretzel as she considered. If Mom was in that frame of mind, invisibility was the better part of wisdom. She stretched lazily and moved to her computer. Locked doors made her parents angry, but she had no choice in the matter.

She had no choice in the abortion matter either. She intended to carry this baby. It was hers. She was in control here, not Daddy, and certainly not Mom. She might have a fight on her hands, but she did not see how she ever could kill the tiny baby that had taken up residence within. She had read Hawaii's abortion laws, too, which clearly stated that no one, including her parents, could force her to have an abortion. She knew they would be furious. She was prepared for that – at least, she would be by the time the seventy-two hours ended. She would have to be prepared – both for their anger and for becoming a mother.

Accessing the Internet, she typed, "prepare for birth teen pregnancy." Over 10,000 entries appeared, some of them helpful, others a waste of time. She selected a story by a twenty-two year old "good girl" who had become pregnant at age sixteen and decided against abortion.

"Being a parent," the girl wrote, "is the most complicated yet rewarding job there is. All the education in the world cannot prepare you for the ups and downs."

Valeta untwined Leo from her bare leg and plopped him on the lap of her green pajamas as she read on. Admittedly, the girl was right when she said there were no textbooks full of answers on how to be a good parent. There were books on parenting, though. Valeta had seen heaps of them critiqued or advertised on the Internet. As for the absence of tests to pass or fail, which the girl seemed to lament, she would not agree. Maybe no written tests were given, but if the baby developed fever, that was a test of sorts. Diaper rash, colds, Hawaiian sunburn – were those not tests of your parenting ability? Sure, you could only learn through experience, as the writer said, but how difficult could it be? Billions of women had raised children that way since the beginning of time.

The article ended with a simple warning, "Abstinence is the best policy."

"Easy for her to say," Valeta murmured. "She was sexually active. What about people like Edwin and me that do practice abstinence and then some jerk like Rick comes along?"

Leo looked up and mewed softly.

"You won't fit on this lap much longer, Leo," she told him. "Of course, there will be a big ledge up a little higher. You can curl up on it."

The kitten meowed a second question, and Valeta stroked his snowy fur. "Well, when the baby comes, you'll have to take turns on my lap. Sorry about that. You won't be able to sleep with it, either, Leo. You would smother the poor little thing. You can still sleep with me, though."

Date with Responsibility

Leo stretched, batted at her long eyelashes, and then demanded his breakfast, jumping to the floor and hurrying toward his food dish.

Valeta fed the kitten, took a shower, dressed, and then settled at the computer for a morning of serious study – three very different concerns on the docket:

1. Compile list of baby costs, including both prenatal and postnatal items.
2. Make informed decision on abortion, considering parents' position.
3. Complete next section of the Hawaii history course and take the test.

She noted the time, and sighed – 7:18 AM. Grandmother would want to go to church this morning, and soon would be at the door asking for a ride. Well, Grandmother would have to settle for a note of apology and a sermon on TV again. Valeta plucked a deep red pen from an overflowing desk drawer, scribbled her regrets on a torn sheet of yellow paper, and studied it. There was little to say, really. She simply could not go to church yet. Not with Edwin there, and the orchestra members, and everyone who knew her. Still, Grandmother did not like to miss even one Sunday when she was in town, and it was hard to hurt her feelings. Her eyes went from the note to the red pen – burgundy more than red. She turned it in her hand, the stylish, bold black and white letters of the slogan passing before her glazed eyes with little impression.

Get an edge up. Read. That is what it said if you connected the letters – but her blue eyes were not connecting them. Her eyes saw only the pen's dark red barrel, with splashes of white and black distributed at tasteful intervals.

Still staring absently, she finally folded the note, wrote Grandmother's name in large letters on the outside of it, and got to her feet. She quietly attached the yellow paper to the outside of the glossy white living room door, and then locked the door again.

There. She would study until 11 AM, at which time that preacher should be on TV. She would watch him, only because she did not want to enter the week feeling guilty about church. She would eat lunch while she watched. It would give her more time to study afterward.

Valeta opened the jalousie window beside her bed before sitting down again, pausing to breathe the softly scented ocean air. It was already May – perhaps Hawaii's most wonderful month, and a time when she should be out surfing with Edwin instead of hiding from everyone.

She sighed and whispered, "I hate you, Rick!" For the two hundredth time, she reviewed that evening: how she had planned it all; how

Date with Responsibility

Edwin had substituted Rick; how Rick had been such an embarrassment; how she had escaped to the peacefulness of the dark beach, and danced with the coconut palms; how, suddenly, Rick had grabbed her from behind, kissed her, bit her, and raped her; how she had lost consciousness; how, finally, she had awakened to voices fighting.

Valeta caught her breath and her blue eyes widened in the early morning sunlight. She knew! She knew who it was that fought with Rick on the beach! She knew his voice – had heard it almost daily for the seven months preceding the luau. She knew what he said to Rick. She had heard the feet running down the beach. She had heard the gun shot, followed by that deathly scream. Like it or not, she knew exactly what had happened, and she knew that he was guilty – guilty beyond all reasonable doubt – and she was a witness. How could she have forgotten for ten entire weeks?

She dropped down cross-legged on the floor, her head in her hands. She had to tell someone. She should call the attorney. They were on the right track. The remark overheard in the football team's locker room was true. There would be a trial, and she undoubtedly would have to take the witness stand. That would be difficult – not as difficult as facing Rick would have been, had he lived to go to trial for the rape. But everyone in school would show up at the trial, and she would be in maternity clothes, and....

"Well," she sighed to herself, "you can't tell anyone until tomorrow, so let it go for now."

In fact, she thought as she stood and went back to her computer, there really was no reason to reveal this to anyone until after the birth of the baby or the abortion, whichever she selected. It was quite probable that nobody expected her ever to have more information about Rick's murder. It could be her lifelong secret and nobody would be the wiser.

Determined to send the memory back into oblivion, Valeta opened side-by-side windows on the computer screen: Internet access in the first, a word processor document in the second. She titled her document "Baby Costs," clicked the Internet screen, and typed the two words into the search engine. The third entry in response to her quest looked promising, but turned out to be a poem. She read it anyway:

What A Baby Costs
by Edgar Guest

"How much do babies cost?" said he
The other night upon my knee;
And then I said: "They cost a lot;
A lot of watching by a cot,
A lot of sleepless hours and care,
A lot of heart-ache and despair,
A lot of fear and trying dread,
And sometimes many tears are shed
In payment for our babies small,
But every one is worth it all.

Date with Responsibility

"For babies people have to pay
A heavy price from day to day —
There is no way to get one cheap.
Why, sometimes when they're fast asleep
You have to get up in the night
And go and see that they're all right.
But what they cost in constant care
And worry, does not half compare
With what they bring of joy and bliss —
You'd pay much more for just a kiss.

"Who buys a baby has to pay
A portion of the bill each day;
He has to give his time and thought
Unto the little one he's bought.
He has to stand a lot of pain
Inside his heart and not complain;
And pay with lonely days and sad
For all the happy hours he's had.
His smile is worth it all, you bet."

The little poem was from an old book copyrighted in 1916, <u>A Heap o' Livin'</u>. It had little to do with actual financial cost, but she decided to include it in her document before returning to her real purpose.

The next three hours were consumed rapidly as she copied and tried to complete a baby budget work sheet. Prenatal care, with the cost of doctor appointments and prenatal vitamins would be followed by delivery costs. "Pizza delivery is sure a lot less," she whispered. She could not imagine herself going through natural childbirth, so she added the astounding cost of an anesthesiologist to what was already an astronomical sum, telling herself that she was going to need Daddy on her side if she hoped to go through with this. He was a reasonable man. Surely, he would not insist on an abortion when he heard how much she wanted the baby, and saw all of the planning she had done.

She moved to the next category of expenses: health and safety items for the newborn. Of course, she needed a soft baby brush and comb, as well as clippers and a toothbrush, but she had not begun to realize how many other things were needed. The list contained twenty-six items, some of which had to be purchased two or three times every month. She would have to buy a bathtub made especially for newborns, shampoo, soap, towels, washcloths, a faucet guard, baby oil, cotton swabs, diaper rash ointment, mild laundry soap, and a host of other things. She looked up the cost of each item and entered it carefully.

The third category on the baby budget work sheet was labeled "nursery items." These seemed nearly as expensive as the prenatal care if one did not count the delivery costs. She began listing and pricing the required pieces: one crib with crib mattress; two crib pads; four crib sheets; four crib blankets; six receiving blankets; one mobile to hang on the crib; one crib entertainment center; one changing table; one changing table pad; one bassinet; and one sleeping wedge, whatever that happened to be.

Date with Responsibility

The budget work sheet had seven items under the diaper category; three items the new mother would need personally; eight entries just for bottle-feeding; and twenty-one "other" items.

The last category included such things as the vital, but expensive car seat – which had to be replaced as the baby outgrew it; a carrier that she, Valeta, could wear to take baby on shopping trips and still have her own hands free; a doorway swing; a stroller; a play yard; pacifiers, and an amazing assortment of booties, shirts, sweaters, and other clothing, not to mention toys and books.

Certainly, she thought as she entered the final price, her baby should have everything it needed, but where was she to get the money for all of this – and were they necessities? She had to buy maternity clothing, too, which was not on the work sheet, and she knew from frequent shopping that stylish clothing was seldom at bargain prices.

"I wonder if anyone on the Internet has advice about keeping up with clothing trends while you're expecting," she mused.

Her query produced advice from a twenty-five year old who had been in her financial position, though not her physical position. "Quality clothes," she wrote, "are available at the Salvation Army and Goodwill... look for quality – not quantity." Valeta sighed. Salvation Army, huh? Well, she was not buying gowns for a homecoming dance. It would have to be the solution. Doctor appointments alone would exhaust her meager allowance.

Stretching, she glanced at the clock and saw that it was time for the TV church service – and for lunch. She saved her work and went to the closet, returning to her bed with an assortment of cold cuts, lettuce, mayonnaise, bread, guava juice, and bottled water. Her appetite was growing, and she would have to be careful eventually, but for now she just wanted to enjoy her meal, cold though it was.

The TV church service was easier to find this time and, as the congregation finished their song and the preacher began to speak, Valeta turned her attention to her meal, her conscience eased by the fact that she had bothered to turn on the program, but not expecting anything of real interest. After all, there was little chance that he would speak on responsibility again, and the church she had attended with Grandmother had taught her that sermons could be totally boring.

"This morning's message," the preacher began, "is entitled *Unfair to Marjorie*."

Valeta looked up from the freshly-made chicken sandwich and grinned, wondering what that preacher could know about Mom. Maybe he had a wife named Marjorie. Amused, she licked a dollop of mayonnaise from her finger and listened to see where he was headed.

Date with Responsibility

"How many of those listening to me are named Marjorie?" asked the preacher. "Suppose you heard tomorrow that a new law was passed here in Hawaii that made it legal for people to put to death anyone named Marjorie? If that is your name, would you protest? If you have a friend or family member named Marjorie, would you protest? Wouldn't you say it was wrong to make such a law, and wouldn't we all gather to have the law repealed? What if the law was written into the Constitution of our country? Would it be right then, or would it still be wrong?"

The slim hand that held the chicken sandwich stopped in front of the waiting mouth as Valeta anticipated the next sentence.

"We all know that it still would be wrong. Marjories are, as a group, innocent, and it is morally wrong to kill the innocent. If we replace the name Marjorie with the word *Jew*, we have the law of Nazi Germany – and it was wrong. If we replace Marjorie with the word *slave*, and say what the Supreme Court said in 1857 – that these people were not full "persons" and could be treated as property, that law was wrong. Now, I want you to listen carefully. If, here in second millennium Hawaii, we change the name Marjorie to *fetus* or *pre-born baby*, is it right to kill those innocents?"

Slowly, Valeta placed the unfinished chicken sandwich on her plate and leaned forward.

"What," asked the preacher quietly, "do you think of the Marjorie law? If your name is Bill, Mary, Jim, Sally, Jacob, or Matilda, you have no worry. You have a right to life, so why worry about Marjories? Marjories are, like the Jews of Nazi Germany and the slaves of our own country, not really "persons" and not deserving of the same treatment you and I receive. Or are they? Are we not being unfair to Marjorie?"

The preacher paused, looked straight into Valeta's eyes, and continued with intensity, "In 1973, the Supreme Court of the United States of America said that little boys and girls in their mothers' wombs are not considered to be "persons" under the law and may be destroyed by abortion. That, my friend, is as unfair to innocent babies as the Marjorie law is unfair to Marjorie."

The screen swam in mist as the preacher continued, and his voice drowned in the mist.

Valeta's decision was made quite suddenly, and yet not quite suddenly, for she had read so many web sites about abortion that she had known, deep within, that she could never do that to this baby, even if it were to be an exact replica of its criminal father. She cried quietly for the baby that might have been put to death, though it was so completely innocent of any wrong, and made it an unspoken promise that she would fight to her own death to protect it from people like Mom.

When the mist lifted, she focused on the TV again, but the preacher was giving a final prayer. She turned off the set, finished her dry sandwich, washing it down with sweet guava juice, and drifted a little longer in tender thoughts of her baby. It would cost a lot, and not only in cold cash, but that was not the fault of the baby. The baby was innocent of having brought this upon her – innocent of generating financial expenses and innocent of coming between Edwin and her. The baby was innocent, too, of causing the big scandal that Mom so greatly feared. She could not and would not abort it.

Seventy-two hours, Daddy had said. She would wait the full seventy-two hours before making her announcement, but not because she still questioned whether to have the abortion.

Other questions persisted, of course: how she could carry a baby to full term and deliver it; who would support her until she could find work; what Edwin would think of the whole idea.

But there was no longer a question about whether to have an abortion.

16

Casting the Die

Valeta curled up for a nap, the little white Himalayan condescending to join her when she patted a golden seashell on the comforter beside her legs. With the abortion question settled, her mind rested easier, and she fell asleep quickly. She awakened an hour later, refreshed and eager to tackle the Hawaiian study she had scheduled for the afternoon.

Getting up carefully, she retrieved her binder from the shelf and returned to the bed, thankful that the brief journey had not involved nausea.

A glance inside the binder showed that she had come to the end of her class notes. She had no textbook, so her lessons would have to be gleaned from the computer at this point. There were seven major islands out of a total 132 islands and atolls – and not a clue as to where she should begin, but Oahu was her home island, and likely to remain so for the foreseeable future, so she decided to study it first.

Valeta threw a tiny, blue knit shawl over her shoulders, and went to the computer. The shawl had been a gift from Grandmother when she was only three years old, and was much too small for her, but she still kept it on her bed, and wore it now and then when nobody was around, drawing comfort from its soft warmth. Not that she particularly needed comfort at the moment, she thought as she booted the computer. She just felt like wearing it while she studied.

Surprised by the flutter of a sudden gentle image, she ran her hand over the little shawl. "I'll use it for my baby," she whispered.

She began her studies, then, and continued them, interrupted only by frequent calls to the bathroom, until her hunger growls increased in both volume and intensity to the point where she could no longer ignore them.

By that time, she had gained a deeper appreciation for the island of Oahu, the gathering place. To her surprise, even though Oahu had seemed to be the main island, in that it held the state capital, it was only the third largest in size.

Valeta mourned for the imprisoned queen Liliuokalani, as she read of the deposed monarch spending many lonely hours consoling herself by writing music about her islands. Valeta's favorite was *Aloha 'Oe*, a song that some translated to mean Farewell to Thee.

In her growing note binder, Valeta recorded the date that Hawaii officially became a United States territory – 1900 – two short years after annexation. The island was still only a territory when it suffered through the Japanese attack on Pearl Harbor in December of 1941, becoming a full-fledged state on August 21, 1959.

It was at that point in her studies that the growling stomach got the upper hand, and Valeta raided her closet for a meal. Then she studied far into the night, ignoring parental calls and knocks. She began again early Monday morning.

Actually, she did not begin immediately on Monday morning, although she awoke at first light. She could not begin study when the orange-bellied shama thrushes in the neighbors' bamboo grove were extolling the new day, calling eagerly for her to come and join them as they watched for sunrise in the eastern sky. Closer to the patio, papayabirds chirped in the plumeria trees where, she knew, they were keeping one eye on a clutch of greenish-blue speckled eggs. Sitting up with cautious expectancy, Valeta addressed herself to the new morning ritual of salty pretzel and cool water, subtracting three or four minutes in her impatience to join the excited birds.

Date with Responsibility

A strange peacefulness carried her to the window, and she swept the light curtains aside eagerly. Ethereal shades of purple and pink tinted the sand and the waves beyond it. The sky echoed the violet and fuchsia hues, but the graceful palms remained black as night. As she watched, small hands of pale blue sky pushed aside bits of the tinted clouds, and the sun rose white hot from the purple and pink waves, its powerful light parting the colors of the water as it made its way toward the shore. She filled her mind with deep drafts of the unearthly beauty, and then began her day.

It was a good day – a peaceful day, all things considered. Daddy and Mom had decided to leave her alone, it seemed, and only Leo made demands on her. That is, of visible beings, only Leo made demands. The baby within her was growing more importunate by the day, requiring frequent small snacks from the closet, and more frequent trips from the office chair by the computer to the cool blue and white bathroom. She actually paused before going to bed that night to see if there was a visible path in the carpet.

Tuesday began much like Monday. Valeta had no interruptions from beyond the bedroom and, had it not been for the looming deadline, the peacefulness would have been complete. There was a looming deadline, however. The seventy-two hours would soon be done, and she knew that her announcement would not be welcomed.

Casting the Die

"Leo, how would you tell them if you were in my sandals?" she asked the kitten as she laid down for a midday nap. "The outcome is sure to be the same, once they know I intend to carry the baby, but I have three possible ways to break the news, as I see it:

1. Go for the quick kill, dashing in and blurting out my intention.

2. Go for drama, tantalizing them and haughtily stating my intention.

3. Go for respect, acknowledging them and gently revealing my intention.

"Knowing you," she continued, "I suspect you would go for the quick kill, although you do tend toward the dramatic when you're fighting the catnip mouse, but I think I had better just opt for respect."

Getting up, she dug in her drawer for a pen, found a ping-pong ball instead, and tossed it across the room, laughing as Leo pursued it. Digging into the drawer again, she retrieved a pencil and a small notepad, made a brief mental note to take responsibility for the messy drawer, and closed it quickly. There would be time for that later, after she marshaled her thoughts and prepared a gentle speech for tomorrow morning's deadline.

In the midst of writing her speech, she heard the muffled call of the cell phone from beneath the patio chair cushion, and curiosity getting the better of her, hurried out to check the caller ID. Edwin. Again. She decided to answer the call.

"Valeta? I hope you answered because you wanted to, and not just because your caller ID stopped working." His voice filtered quietly through his loneliness as he continued. "I'm on the beach. Would you come out and talk?"

A long silence ensued, and then she said, "I'm on my patio. Come on up."

As he pushed open the arched gate, their hearts reached for one another, but their minds stepped between, allowing nothing more than the exchange of awkward greetings that gave way to awkward conversation: she had received the candy and butterfly ring, thank you; he had heard that the pregnancy was confirmed, and was sorry; she and Mom had fought over abortion; she had been given seventy-two hours to decide what she would do, and had decided to carry the baby.

Forgetting to ask whether she had solved the riddle, Edwin told her, "Honey, I want us to continue dating."

"Even if I don't abort the baby?"

"Somehow, I knew you could not abort it. I would not want you to abort it."

"But its father – and after it's born, what will we do? Will you date an unwed mother?"

Edwin nodded. "I know what its father was, but I know what its mother is, and I will date her, unwed mother or whatever. You might keep the baby or you might decide to adopt it to a loving home, but neither will make me love you less."

Valeta's mind let her heart say what it wanted to say then – that she always would love him – but the mind quickly added an escape clause for him: "I'll understand if you change your mind, and I won't hold you to it. Neither of us can know what's going to happen when I tell Daddy and Mom my decision to carry the baby."

* * *

Wednesday morning dawned as soft and delicate as a lei of maile leaves and rosebuds. The waking thought reminded Valeta that May Day had come and gone without her receiving a single lei. It had been last Thursday – the evening when Jean Luc prepared the beautiful dinner on the beach – the evening when she told Daddy and Mom that she was pregnant with Rick's child.

"May Day is Lei Day," she told a sleepy Leo, "but not when you have to use it to announce a pregnancy resulting from rape."

On May Day of last year, she had spent hours celebrating with her friends, all of whom had exchanged leis until their necks were heavy with the fragrant flower chains, but this year....

Date with Responsibility

Her second waking thought was that she must get ready for breakfast – and ready for the seventy-two hour deadline – both of which would occur in a little less than an hour.

She selected two long, crispy pretzel rods from the box, and began nibbling them, sucking the salt from each bite before grinding it between her teeth. As she nibbled, she thought again about the preacher's sermon, *Unfair to Marjorie*. She would like to tell Daddy and Mom about it, but it might do more harm than good, given their strong opposition to church and preachers. She could tell Grandmother Davidson, though.

When the pretzel routine was done, she walked slowly to the bathroom, showered, and began to dress for breakfast: pale orange under things topped with a long, flowered cotton dress in shades of orange, peach, and yellow. The spaghetti straps of the dress were a deep orange, the same shade as the long ribbon she tied at her waist, and then slid upward four inches. She brushed her hair, pinning back one side with an orange plumeria blossom of silk.

Ten minutes later, the seventeen year old slipped through the doorway to the courtyard and walked quietly to her seat at the round table. She looked around. She stood alone. She walked to the side of the pool and studied the reflection of the morning sky. She looked toward the master suite.

Casting the Die

Though it was past Daddy's appointed time for breakfast, steam oozed from the pores of the new sauna room: Mom had begun the day by steaming her brain into a semblance of tranquility. Valeta's own brain tensed beneath the long golden hair, and she pressed her fingers against the temples as she returned to the table. She stood, tapping her fingers on the back of a chair until she heard Jean Luc's footsteps behind her. Then she turned and, before he could speak, she whispered, "Are my parents in a good mood this morning?"

Jean Luc's eyebrows shot skyward and he shook his head.

"Wait until after breakfast," she sighed. "Their mood will be worse." Little did she suspect how much worse.

Jean Luc was bordering on anxious distress by the time the entire family arrived and was seated, his carefully prepared breakfast hovering between an original delicious and a soon to be barely palatable. He served discreetly and withdrew to the kitchen, though he could have stayed, since no one spoke a word. Even Grandmother, usually the catalyst for cheerful conversation, gave attention solely to the roasted pepper baked eggs.

In fifteen minutes, they had finished. Daddy accepted a second cup of coffee from Jean Luc's bottomless pot and Valeta knew from his expression that he had not reconsidered.

He looked at no one, simply staring into his coffee as he said, "All right, Valeta, it's time to give us your decision regarding abortion."

Mom cleared her throat, and Grandmother reached beneath the tablecloth to give Valeta's hand a quick squeeze of support.

Quietly, her own eyes fixed on the table's centerpiece of hibiscus flowers, Valeta spoke. "I want you to know that I respect you all very highly: Daddy, Mom, and Grandmother – all of you."

"We don't need any of your flattery," Mom interrupted. "We just want to hear you say that you're ready to have an abortion. It will soon be eleven weeks, and you shouldn't wait longer."

Well, Valeta thought as she shifted in her chair, if Mom wanted the quick kill option, there was no reason why she should not get what she wanted. Mom was going to ignore anything Valeta said prior to the actual statement of intention anyway, it seemed, so she might as well blurt it out and be done. She straightened her shoulders, lifted her chin, and looked directly at Mom.

"I am not having an abortion," she said.

The die was cast.

17

Pariah

Once her intention had been stated, there was nothing for Valeta to do but wait – and, as it turned out, there was not a whole lot of that for her to do either.

Never one to mince words, Mom let her have it with both Irish barrels. "You," she spluttered, "most definitely *will* have an abortion, and you will have it today or you will get out of this house!"

Daddy astonished Valeta by agreeing firmly with Mom. "We cannot have an unwanted child in our home, Valeta, and especially not a child that would further entangle us in a criminal case. That baby will not be born – period – full stop."

From some deep, inner well, Valeta drew unknown strength, looked from Mom to Daddy, and calmly asked, "Which of you will ask the baby if he or she wants to be born, or volunteer to take the sentence you just handed to this baby? Does it have no right to live because it will be such an inconvenience to you? And if that is the case," she made a controlled gesture toward Grandmother Davidson, "will Grandmother have no right to live when she cannot care for herself and becomes an inconvenience to you?"

"Watch your tongue!" Daddy shouted. "We are discussing the child of a rapist – a child that will not be brought under this roof."

Grandmother stirred uncomfortably, straightened the collar of her white sweater, and spoke up. "Where would you have her go then, Donovan, since I believe Valeta is determined to carry the child?"

"There are institutions for girls like that." Mom spat out the words.

"Girls like what?" Grandmother sat forward in her chair, gray-blue eyes flashing.

"Rebellious girls!"

"Mom, I thought you would understand," said Valeta. "I thought I could count on support from you and Daddy." She turned to the Colonel. "I thought you, at least, would support me, Daddy."

"I'm sorry," he said, "but we cannot afford a scandal, and that is exactly what this will be the day you begin to look pregnant. You will have the abortion today or leave this house by Saturday."

Pariah

Daddy jumped to his feet, gave her one more silent look, and gestured emphatically as he spun on his heels and crossed the courtyard double-time to his car.

The three women sat in silence for several minutes, and then Grandmother excused herself and walked quietly to her room. Valeta waited, expecting Mom to pursue the issue but, when ten silent minutes had expired, the teen also excused herself and went to her room.

She expected to feel bitter tears well up in her eyes – that vein throb at her left temple – knots of angst form in her stomach – fists convulse with suppressed rage – loathing rise like bile – nostrils flare – face flush with anger. She expected an overpowering urge to hurl belongings around the room – especially any gifts she had received from Daddy or Mom.

She expected all of these, and thought about them as she locked the door behind her, but rather than experience them, she crossed calmly to her closet and took out two large suitcases, opening them side-by-side atop the shell-strewn comforter.

The tears did flow when Leo jumped into one of the suitcases. "I can't take you with me, Leo," she said, plucking him from the luggage and hugging him close to her body. She wiped a tear from his black-tipped ear and set him on the bed. "I'm sure anyone who accepts me and my baby will have their hands full enough. Jean Luc will take care of you, though. He has always loved you, and he has a good heart. I'll write him a note and ask him to take you home. I'll miss you, little one, but maybe someday I can come and get you again. You'll be a big boy then – a king instead of my little prince. And you will be a handsome one. Remember me until then."

She rubbed her eyes with the heels of both hands, but the tears were not that easily dispelled. She stumbled to the closet and surveyed the rows of stylish clothing. Most of the waistlines already felt too tight. Some of her jeans, shorts, and skirts would no longer zip or button at the waist, so there was little sense in taking them with her. She might need a few after the baby was born, but priority must be given to things that would fit for the next few weeks. Unfortunately, her size above the waist had begun to increase, too, so her flattering tee tops and shirts were of little use to her. Even her under clothing was becoming tight. The study she had done said that maternity clothing was not worn until after four months – five and a half weeks from now, so she needed clothing that would look presentable until then, but the closet held few choices.

The misty blue muumuu was light enough that she could wash it by hand and dry it on a hanger overnight, so it was the first thing into the suitcase. Three bathrobes went in next: a pale blue terry cloth, a very old yellow fleece, and the white silk with tear-stained orchids, on which additional tears fell as she folded it. Pajamas were a good choice, she decided, since one could loosen the elastic at the waist and make them suitable for wearing in one's private room – if one had a private room. She added four pairs. At the far end of the closet, she found a green plaid wrap skirt that was hopelessly out of style, but would fit. This, along with two sets of sweat pants and shirts, three cardigans, and a denim jacket, filled the first piece of luggage. She tucked socks and sneakers along the edges and zipped the bag shut.

The second bag took longer to pack, as the silent teen picked up one item after another, only to return most to their places with quavering sighs. Those that went into the luggage included a music box doll she had received when she was a baby; a small white teddy bear whose nose had been all but eradicated by her wet baby kisses; pink and white booties that she removed carefully from a thick scrapbook; a handful of old photos from her childhood; a framed photo of Edwin; and the soft blue knit shawl that she loved so much.

She filled the corners of the second bag with smaller bags containing a few carefully chosen cosmetics and other grooming necessities; several pairs of sandals; and a small pillow with a cover of spring-green satin – looked around the room carefully, and then zipped the big bag.

Date with Responsibility

She squeezed Edwin's friendship bracelet onto a wrist that had retained too much water, draped the butterfly pendant around her neck, and slipped the butterfly ring onto the pinkie finger of her right hand, which finger also was a bit thicker than usual. Finally, she draped her head and shoulders with a long white scarf, letting the fringed ends trail to her waist.

Before she put on the scarf, however, she removed the silk plumeria flower, brushed her golden hair, and pulled it back to achieve the most mature appearance she could manage.

This done, she sat down at her desk and wrote four pithy letters: one that told Daddy and Mom she was leaving; one that told Grandmother how much she loved her, and wished her a good trip back to Colorado; one that asked Jean Luc to please take Leo home and keep him for her; and one very difficult one that explained her sudden departure to Edwin, and promised to be in touch.

A car engine roared at the other side of the house, announcing Mom's departure for one of her women's club meetings – an unexpected godsend.

Valeta placed the notes in envelopes, sealed them, scratched a name on each and, in Edwin's case, an address. She laid the pen on the desk, but the act reminded her that she should have a few books and writing supplies. Quickly, she retrieved her backpack from the closet and stuffed it to capacity with the most important items and, on impulse, two of her childhood books for her baby: one about a cat who learned the meaning of character, and the other about a skunk who lacked self-control. She tucked her cell phone into the backpack's side pocket.

It was difficult to know for certain that Mom had gone, but the teen decided to take her chances. Opening the door to the living room, she listened carefully, then stepped out to deliver the notes: one on the floor in front of Grandmother's door; one on the seat of Daddy's leather recliner; and one placed carefully in the top of the deep kitchen utensil drawer that no one but Jean Luc ever opened. Back in her room, she exchanged sandals for brown ballet style shoes, carefully lifted the first bag from the bed, and wheeled it through the living room, across the courtyard, and out to the garage, where she lifted it cautiously into the white Accord's deep trunk. She did the same with the second piece of luggage, and then returned for the backpack and her brown leather hobo bag.

But before she shouldered them, she picked up the little white Himalayan kitten one last time, snuggled his soft fur against a wet cheek and poured out a myriad of whispered promises that she might never be able to keep. He seemed to understand, as he forgivingly licked the salty tears, first from her pale cheeks, and then from his own damp fur.

Date with Responsibility

She put him down, gave him fresh food and water, and closed the door behind her so that no one would think of him until Jean Luc had taken him home.

There was something strangely foreign about the house, now that she was leaving it. It breathed out curses against her as she moved through its interior one final time – flung more curses onto the breeze to accompany her across the courtyard.

She hurried away from the house, kicking at the confinement of the long orange-flowered dress to lengthen her stride, leaving Daddy and Mom to their precious house and their carefully protected reputations.

She hurried toward the car, throwing the backpack into its warm interior, and sliding into the driver's seat; fastening her seat belt with a vow to the tiny, unborn child that from now on, she would drive very carefully for its sake.

Backing from the garage, Valeta permitted herself one final look toward the house, and saw Grandmother with tear-bright eyes, waving. She returned the wave briefly, and departed. Without conscious decision, she followed her favorite route, winding slowly past the lush gardens of beachfront properties until she found herself almost at the gate of Kaneohe Marine Base. She pulled to the side of the road and stopped, trembling.

Pariah

"You can't go to Edwin," she told herself, "no matter how much you want to be with him. You still don't know what that Irish riddle means, and even though he said this didn't change his love for you, it could. Besides, you don't want the entire Marine Corps to know that you're carrying Rick's child, so where do you intend to go?"

She had been so eager to leave after Daddy and Mom gave their ultimatum that she had not stopped to consider where she should go. It was one thing to decide that carrying the baby was vital enough to give up your home, but entirely another thing to find a new home for you and the unborn child. Mom had mentioned institutions for girls like her. How did one find such a place? It would be listed in a phonebook, but she had no phonebook in the car, and even if she called for directory assistance, what would she ask? What did you call such institutions?

A black car pulled up beside her and a young Marine officer opened the window to ask if she needed help. Valeta declined, thanked him, and waited for him to leave, smiling briefly when he saluted her.

Well, whatever she did, she could at least get away from the base and away from this side of the island, she decided, and see what she could find in Honolulu. It was mid-morning, and she had forgotten to bring snacks, so the Pali might be the best route, since there would be stores. Still, the Pali was more likely to bring on nausea. She settled for the interstate – a strange term for a road that could become interstate only if someone constructed a very long bridge to California.

She drove for a long time, looking at the scenery, listening to her thoughts, trying to find the slightest glimmer of an idea as to where she might find shelter. It was not until she left the freeway near Honolulu, however, and was slowly wending her way through the busy streets toward Waikiki Beach, that the needed idea surfaced.

Valeta stopped abruptly at a red traffic light, and dug into her handbag. "That TV preacher lives around here somewhere," she thought, "and he is sure to know of a place where I can stay while I wait." She found the small scrap of paper on which she had written his address, and considered it for a moment.

When the light turned green, she put the paper on the seat, made a left turn, and followed the road into Palolo Valley.

18

Tiny Feet

The preacher was thinner than he appeared on television, sunburned, possessed of a quiet smile beneath knowing brown eyes, and much more approachable in khaki shorts and flowered Hawaiian shirt than he would have been in his suit and tie. The three children crowded around his knees, each smiling shyly at the blond teen, softened the picture further, and built enough courage in her for a short request.

"I'm sorry to come without an appointment, but I heard you speak on TV, and I thought you could help me," she said.

As Valeta watched, the preacher gestured vaguely down the long hallway and the children scampered away. Then he opened a door to his right, and ushered her into a small, plain room, which was filled from floor to ceiling with books. At his invitation, she moved to a dark green chair by the window, and perched on its edge, curling the long orange ribbon of her dress around nervous fingers.

The preacher sat down, fully relaxed, and looked at her in silence for a long minute. Then he smiled and asked, "How can I be of help?"

It was difficult to begin, he being a total stranger, but in a very few minutes, Valeta was pouring the entire story into his receptive ears.

When she stopped, and the preacher handed her a box of tissues for her streaming eyes, she wondered why she had said so much. "I'm sorry. I didn't mean to take up all of your time," she apologized, "but I need a place to stay since my parents have made me leave, and I thought you might know of such a place. Do you?"

"I do," he replied. "You may stay with us, but only temporarily. You have seen three of our children – there is a baby as well – but we can make room temporarily – until you find a more permanent solution."

It was settled so quickly that she almost thought it was a dream. Within minutes, the preacher had introduced her to his wife, the three children she had seen earlier, and the baby, who was having an afternoon nap, but seemed able to sleep through any amount of noise. He told her where to park her car, and carried in her bags.

Tiny Feet

Then he set up a rollaway bed in the baby's room, which seemed to be the only room with a space large enough to accommodate it. His wife provided linens, and Valeta was left alone to make up her bed and unpack a few things.

At first, she did neither, being mesmerized totally by the sleeping baby. He was only two months old, they had said, and adopted, as were their other three children. His little head sported two tiny patches of peach fuzz, one on either side of the soft spot on top. She had read about the soft spot of a baby, but seeing one for the first time, and watching the pulse beat in a tiny skull was disconcerting.

She reached out a tentative hand and touched the filmy white blanket that covered the little boy. His tiny eyelashes moved slightly, and his little chest rose a fraction of an inch higher, but there was no other indication that he had felt the touch. She left the hand where it was, feeling the almost imperceptible breathing, and trembling at the thought that her baby would be like this. Whether boy or girl, it would be tiny – perhaps even tinier than this boy if it inherited the "size genes" from her. Of course, Daddy was very tall, so even her genes could produce a long baby. She studied the little face, its lips like a Cupid's bow, cheekbones slightly higher than expected, and a round little chin. How could any one not love such a baby – give it up for adoption and go through life without it – regardless of the circumstances that surrounded its conception?

Valeta withdrew her hand, and raised her eyes. On the wall above the crib, three photos shared a triplex frame. On the left, a beautiful Hawaiian sunrise was inscribed with the words: *Children are a gift of the Lord; the fruit of the womb is a reward.* On the right was a newborn, the boy that lay in the crib below. The central photo was black and white, and difficult to understand at first glance. Two tiny feet protruded from between what might have been large folds of flesh. The caption, however, informed her that these were the feet of an unborn baby just ten weeks old, and were held between the fingers of an adult.

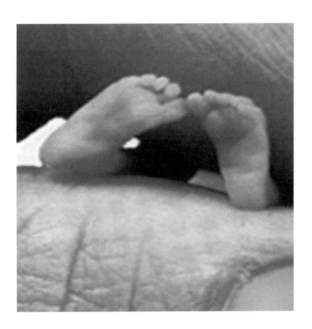

Tiny Feet

Valeta looked down at her own stomach and thought of the unborn child she carried. Her baby was just ten and a half weeks old, but it already had tiny feet. She held a thumb and finger before her face, imagining such miniature feet nestled between the two. The feet could not be much larger than a fingernail, could they? She studied the photo more closely and saw that, indeed, a small bit of the adult's thumbnail showed in the lower right hand corner.

Without warning, she began to cry softly, and the baby in the crib joined her. He did not open his eyes, but he cried faintly, as though he understood what she was thinking and wanted to share her burden.

She stilled her own crying, lest she waken him, and set to work making up the bed, then hanging up a few pieces of clothing that she could wear for the next day or so. The preacher had not said how long she might stay, and *temporarily* was no more a measurement of time than *sometime* was, so she should be prepared to leave soon. It would be best, she thought, if she could move on before Sunday when they would have their church services and the television broadcast.

The door to the room opened a crack and the preacher's wife peeked in. "Would you like to come down for lunch, dear?" she asked. "You're probably hungry after such a trying morning."

Valeta nodded, smoothed her hair, and murmured her thanks as she followed the woman down the stairs.

After lunch, the three little ones were sent to play quietly in their room, and the preacher took Valeta to his office again.

"Have you let your family know where you are," he began, "or do you still need to do that?"

She shifted in her seat and ran a finger over the tiny flowers of the orange dress. "I don't think they care, really," she said.

"Perhaps they care more than you know," he suggested. "If you aren't ready to call them, is there someone else you can call who will let them know that you are safe?"

"I can call my grandmother. She winters with us – them – and will be there until Sunday. She returns to her home in Colorado on Sunday." Her face flushed as she tried to choose the right pronouns.

"You may use my phone," he said, gesturing to the desk instrument, "and let me know when you are done. Then we can take the next step." He left the room, and she heard his footsteps retire to a discreetly distant place.

Suddenly, the former cheerleader knew an apprehension greater than she had ever known.

Tiny Feet

Grandmother's room had a phone in it, to be sure, but she answered only when no one else was at home. If Mom was there, she would answer first, and Valeta would have to ask for Grandmother. Mom would know her daughter's voice instantly and might begin yelling at her or, worse yet, hang up without letting her speak to Grandmother.

Her voice would have to be disguised if Mom answered, she thought as she lifted the receiver, and she would have to disguise it well. She dialed the number and counted the rings: one, two, three, four, five. That was a good sign, since Mom had a rule that phones must be answered by the third ring. Patiently continuing to count, Valeta had reached nine when Grandmother answered.

"Hi Grandmother. This is Valeta, and I can't talk long because I'm calling from a preacher's phone, but I wanted to tell you that I am safe," she said quickly, "and you can tell Daddy and Mom that I found someone to help me. I don't think I should tell them where I am, but the preacher and his family have invited me to stay for a few days, and he's going to help me decide what to do next." She paused, listening to her grandmother's response before adding, "I hope you got the note with my bon voyage wishes, and I hope you have a nice trip back to Colorado on Sunday. I have to go now. Good-bye." She hung up quickly, and reached for the box of tissues, wiping uninvited tears away just as the preacher knocked on the door.

Date with Responsibility

After that, Valeta had her first counseling session, listening to the preacher explain many things, and answering his questions, including whether she had considered giving up the baby for adoption when it was born. She really had not, but promised to give it serious thought.

When she was certain he could not possibly have any more to ask her, Valeta smiled shyly and suggested that she get better acquainted with the little ones while he did the work that she had interrupted. She could even give his wife some time to herself by baby-sitting all four children.

"That's very generous of you, Valeta," he said, "but you and I have one more essential item to address. We need to find a home for you – a place where you can live until the baby is born, and a few months after that, if necessary. Now, I don't know your family situation, aside from what you've told me today, but I noticed that you seem fairly close to your grandmother. Is that correct?"

Valeta nodded, but said nothing.

"And you mentioned that your grandmother is leaving Hawaii in a few days – was it Sunday?"

"That's right," said Valeta cautiously, "but I don't follow you."

"Would there be a possibility," he suggested quietly, "of you flying to your grandmother's home with her and staying there until the baby is born?"

Valeta looked up, strong hope fighting with despair in her wide eyes. "I never thought of it. She couldn't take care of me. She doesn't drive, and doesn't own a car. She has a large enough home, though, so it might be possible. I just don't know whether she would want the responsibility..." Her voice trailed off on the last word and she smiled at the preacher. "The first time I heard you preach, you were talking about *responsibility*," she said, "and you explained it better than I ever heard it explained before or since. My parents harp on responsibility, but they never explain it well. I memorized part of what you said."

She stood and recited like a schoolgirl, "Each one of us must take responsibility for his or her actions. You don't bow out of it by blaming things on others. You don't say that you had to do wrong because the other guy did the wrong thing to you. He bears responsibility for what he did, and you bear responsibility for what you do. He takes the consequences of his actions, and you take the consequences of your actions." She sat down, blushing a bit at her performance.

"And did you hear my entire sermon?"

"No. I tuned in late – by accident, really."

"Then remind me to give you a little book on responsibility before you leave us," he said, and made a memo of it himself, adding the sticky green note to a multitude of similar notes on his desk.

Date with Responsibility

The preacher returned to the subject of Valeta living with Grandmother Davidson, and offered to place a second call to Grandmother, handing the phone to Valeta only after he was sure it was Grandmother that was on the line.

Valeta gave him the number, and fidgeted as she waited, counting imaginary rings in her head until there must surely have been five or six, and then breathing easier. The preacher took only a moment to establish that he was speaking to Grandmother Davidson, and not simply Mrs. Davidson, which would be Mom. Then he handed the phone to Valeta, and remained in his chair as she tried to convey his idea to Grandmother.

Grandmother listened to her. She asked a question now and then, voice guarded, and seemed to accept the idea. She was willing to have Valeta in her home through the summer, but called her attention to the fact that the baby would not be delivered until after Colorado's cold weather had arrived. Grandmother normally would be back in Hawaii by then, and although Valeta was more than welcome to house-sit for her, there would be no one to take her to doctor appointments, or to get her to the hospital when the time came.

"That's on the one hand," said Grandmother, "but on the other hand, I could endure one more Colorado winter if I had my granddaughter and my first great grandchild to keep me company. In fact, it's exciting just to think about it. We could spend the holidays together and snuggle around the fireplace to stay warm."

There was no turning back. Grandmother would make it happen, and do so without telling Valeta's parents until she had reached Colorado.

With Grandmother still on the line, Valeta gave the preacher one glance that let him know the call was successful, watched as he left the room, and then began making plans. She agreed to sell her car to Grandmother, using the money for air fare and, once in Colorado, for maternity and baby needs. Grandmother would deed the car over to Edwin, who would be going to the airport to see her off, asking him to take care of it while she was gone, and use it to take her to church when she returned. He already had his own set of keys, so Valeta simply needed to sign the papers in the glove compartment. Valeta would leave the car at the airport early Sunday morning, and take the flight just prior to Grandmother's, assuring that she was on her way before Daddy and Mom reached the departure gate. When she reached Denver, she would wait for Grandmother in the airport, and then share the final leg of the journey to Colorado Springs.

When it came to the question of how Valeta could buy a ticket, since she had so little cash, Grandmother suggested that she go to the airport ticket counter, order the ticket, and then have the ticket agent call Grandmother for authorization on her credit card.

Valeta thanked her grandmother and, just before she hung up, had one more request. "I left so quickly that I forgot my clarinet, and I really want to have it with me. Would you have room to hide it in your luggage?" Grandmother agreed, and promised, also, to be sure Jean Luc took Leo.

Valeta hung up, then, and reported the plan to the preacher, thanking him for his counsel, and excusing herself to go to the airport and make the reservations.

By bedtime, a ticket to Colorado Springs resided in her handbag, and peace resided in her heart.

"Dear baby," she whispered to the one with whom she shared the room, "we will have only a few days together, but I will remember you and your family forever."

Her eyes returned to the triplex of photos and she stared at the center one for a moment before turning out the light, and then, as she drifted toward sleep, she told her unborn baby, "My little one, I can hardly believe that you already have two tiny feet."

19

Acute Mountain Sickness

The same stars that adorned the vast skies over Hawaii twinkled above Colorado Springs, but the air at 9:30 PM on May 11 was a chilly 39 degrees rather than the perfect 73 degrees that had seen them off in Honolulu. Valeta's 7 AM flight made an extra stop at San Francisco, meeting Grandmother's 8 AM flight in Los Angeles rather than Denver, and giving them a leisurely hour together in the Los Angeles airport, followed by two hours and fifteen minutes together on the flight to Colorado Springs.

Despite Grandmother's reminder that this was not an adventure trip, and the rending of her heart as she left Edwin behind, Valeta could not dispel the excitement that insisted on fluttering around her, whether she strolled slowly down bright airport concourses, or sat buckled in a seat high above dark clouds. This was her maiden flight without her parents, and her maiden flight *as a* parent, and those two facts alone accounted for a great deal of the excitement. Of course, no one around her knew that she was a parent and, technically, she supposed she was not a parent yet, but she was going to be a parent, and she began to revel in the knowledge.

She had expected to be plagued with nausea for the entire ten and a half hours from Honolulu to Colorado Springs, but to her surprise and delight, she felt better than she had in weeks.

"I think my baby likes to travel," she told Grandmother. "It must have my gypsy blood."

"Either gypsy blood or Marine brat blood," said Grandmother, which was, for her, very strong language indeed.

Valeta giggled, and went back to what she had been doing for hours – imagining life with just Grandmother, in her beautiful ranch style house. "You know," she told the older woman, "if I use the back bedroom with the shower, I won't have to waken you when I get up at night. I can be quiet as a mouse, and you will never hear me."

"I will use the back bedroom and you will use the larger room," said Grandmother. "By the time you get a crib in there with a changing table and rocker beside the queen bed, you will be plenty crowded." She patted Valeta's arm and added, "We're going to have a lively time, I can see that."

"Oh, we will! And I will help you with the housework. You must let me because I need to learn responsibility, and I don't know a better way than being responsible for things around the house. We will not have Jean Luc, so I will learn how to cook. I need to learn. I will have to cook for my baby and me, and I will have to learn to do my laundry. Can you imagine Mom never teaching me to do laundry? She wanted to live like a wealthy woman, I suppose, and I must admit it was nice to send out the laundry, but now I will have to watch my pennies, and doing my own laundry will help. Oh, but I will stay out of your way. I promise. And I won't be this excited every day, you know, but it is so wonderful that you are letting me live with you! It seems as though I have been sad forever and now, at last, my fairy god-mother has rescued me from despair." Valeta's flushed face radiated happiness as she chattered.

The contagion of her excitement overtook Grandmother long before they reached Colorado Springs and, tired though she was from the long trip, the older woman smiled merrily as she tipped a skycap to get their luggage and load it in a taxi. "It will never do to have you lifting and carrying those heavy bags," she told Valeta. "I worried about you taking them to the airport at Honolulu."

"Now, you must not baby me," Valeta said, giving Grandmother a crooked grin. "And don't remind me that I am tired. I want to get all settled as soon as we reach the house, and if you remind me of how tired I am, I will fall asleep on the floor just inside your front door."

"That would be a dusty bed," Grandmother observed, "since the house has been closed since last autumn. In fact, everything will be a bit forlorn looking. It always does when I first get back. It's late, though, and we both *are* tired, no matter how excited you are, so we will just throw some fresh linens on the beds and get to sleep. You will have plenty of time to unpack and get settled in the morning."

The taxi made good progress through the quiet, late evening streets, and in ten minutes, deposited them at Grandmother's home, the driver kindly carrying their array of luggage all the way into the house for them, and earning a generous tip for his efforts.

"Now, Valeta, before you get involved," said Grandmother, "We both will get into our pajamas and have a cup of warm tea. I'm sorry I have no cookies for my guest, but we will shop tomorrow, and then we will start cooking – and you will start eating for two."

Demurring to Grandmother's wishes, Valeta found her way to the larger bedroom she was to share with the baby, gratefully changed from her tight clothing into pajamas and a robe, and joined Grandmother for tea. Then they slept.

Acute Mountain Sickness

On Monday morning, chilly rays of sunlight slipped between the slats of the shutters and awakened Valeta early. She shivered and pulled the heavy blankets around her shoulders. "We're not in Hawaii anymore, Baby," she whispered, "and I am cold. Lucky you – to be in a snug, warm place all the time. I wish you would behave, though, so I didn't have to go across the hall so often. I must have made three trips last night, and I need to go again now – but I'm so cold!" It was no use. Cold or not, she had to go. She crawled out of bed and crossed the hall, then hurried back to bed to wait for Grandmother to get up.

She had a dreadful headache this morning, and she was not prone to headaches. She was having trouble breathing, too – as though she had just climbed a long, steep flight of stairs. Maybe the recycled air in the plane's cabin had affected her. She hoped it had not distributed a virus.

She slipped under the blankets again, and tried to go back to sleep, but neither the headache nor her excitement would permit it. So, with a reminder that she must be very quiet so as not to waken Grandmother, she got up and began to unpack. She placed the music box doll and the white teddy bear in the rocking chair, tucking the little blue shawl around their legs.

She lifted Edwin's photo from her luggage, its golden frame echoing his uniform's bright brass buttons, placed it on the small desk under the high window, and stopped. It was the one sad thing about coming to Grandmother's house – being so far away from Edwin. She was no farther from him than she had been in Kailua, measured in emotional miles, but in Kailua there had always been potential for a break-through – the possibility that he would come to visit, take her in his strong arms, demand that she marry him immediately, and move both of them into a new little home near the beach where they would wait together for the baby's arrival, with him supporting her every step of the way. He had tried to talk to her so often, but – how foolish she had been, refusing to make time for a long, serious talk with Edwin. If only she had known....

Sadly, she kissed her fingertips and placed them on the smiling lips of Edwin's photo. She always had planned to talk to him more, to mend the wall that Rick had built – *sometime* – that indefinite date that was on no calendar in the universe – and now they were separated by more than 3,000 miles, and any possibility of visiting had died. Of course, she did have her cell phone with her, and there was nothing to stop her from calling him right now.

She took the cell phone from her backpack, but remembering Grandmother sleeping in the next room, she sighed, placed it on the desk beside the photo, and went back to her unpacking.

Acute Mountain Sickness

She opened the mirror-fronted closet doors then, to hang up her limited wardrobe, but found the closet quite full of Grandmother's clothing, hung in neat array, dust covers over every dress, blouse, skirt, and pants. It was clothing for cooler weather, and Grandmother probably had used little of it since Grandfather died four years ago. She had become a snowbird after his death, and rarely used winter clothing. Yet here it hung – a closet full. Well, Grandmother would need it this year, for sure. Valeta decided to save the rest of her unpacking until later when she could carry the clothing to another closet.

She sat on the edge of the bed, rubbing her temples and breathing deeply. It seemed she could not get a sufficient breath, no matter how hard she tried. Her lungs seemed to be working harder, but taking in less oxygen, and although she had no nausea, the headache and general malaise felt as though she was getting the flu – real flu, not morning sickness. That was the bad news. The good news was that, even with no pretzels this morning, she felt no nausea whatsoever, so maybe she was beyond morning sickness at last.

Feeling chilly, she decided to dress, and rummaged through her suitcase for something comfortable and warm enough. There was, of course, the blue muumuu, but it was light cotton, and had short sleeves. Besides, people here did not wear muumuus. Well, she could change later.

Date with Responsibility

She really did not want to wear anything tight this morning. She slipped into the muumuu and added the warmth of a long white cardigan. Then, although it definitely would be declared a fashion disaster, she donned white ankle socks and denim sneakers. She laughed softly at her reflection in the mirrors on the closet doors, but she was warm, and for now, that counted more than style.

She got out her brush, and began to brush her hair, but bending over to brush the back set her nose to bleeding. She grabbed up a handful of tissues and, hearing Grandmother go down the hall to the kitchen, followed, dabbing at her nose.

"Good morning, Grandmother," she said through a wad of tissue. "Did you sleep well?"

"I slept like a log, and I feel so much better this morning. How about you?" Grandmother's head was in the pantry.

"I slept pretty well, aside from trips across the hall, but I don't feel well this morning. I woke up with a headache and breathing trouble, and now my nose is bleeding. I hope it isn't a virus I picked up during the flight."

Grandmother backed out of the pantry and turned to look at her granddaughter. "It sounds to me as though you have altitude sickness, dear," she said. "It probably is only the mild form, though: *acute mountain sickness*. You have lived at sea level so long that your body doesn't know how to handle our thin air. Colorado Springs' altitude is only a little above 6,000 feet, which is fine for most people, but your sea level life plus the pregnancy may make you more sensitive. Here, get yourself a drink of water." She handed Valeta a glass. "It's important to drink plenty of fluids – and move slowly for a couple of days. You'll feel better if you keep your exercise to a minimum, too, and we have plenty of time to get settled."

Valeta's nose stopped bleeding, and she sat down with a tall glass of water, adding dizziness to her list of symptoms. "How long does this acute mountain sickness last? I can't take care of a baby if I'm going to feel like this all of the time."

"Oh, it doesn't last long. Most people are over it by their fourth day."

"Do I need to see a doctor – for the sake of the baby, I mean? Will this hurt the baby?" Valeta rubbed her head with her fingertips as she asked.

"You just be sure you drink a lot and take deep breaths so your blood has plenty of oxygen for the baby. You'll be fine." Grandmother opened a box of shelf milk and set it on the table, then opened a large tote bag she had carried on the plane, producing individual boxes of cereal, two bananas, and sugar packets. Refusing Valeta's help, she set out dishes and utensils, and they had a quick breakfast.

Date with Responsibility

After breakfast, Grandmother decreed that Valeta would rest and adjust to the altitude while Grandmother cleared away the dishes and went grocery shopping. She called a taxi, strictly warned Valeta to do no cleaning or unpacking, and was on her way within fifteen minutes.

Valeta sat down in Grandmother's orange recliner, her eyes smiling in spite of the mountain sickness. She felt at home – peaceful – in control for the first time since Senior Luau. Daddy and Mom had done her an immense favor by kicking her out of their house. If they had allowed her to stay, she would still be in Hawaii with all of the terrible memories, and Mom's constant lectures, and her old friends that she did not want to see, and other people taking her responsibilities, and little Leo – of whom she must not think unless she wanted a worse headache – and Edwin. She could not stop thinking about Edwin: wondering how he really viewed the pregnancy – in his heart of hearts; hoping there was still a chance of being married someday; wishing she could call him.

Grandmother was out now, and Valeta would bother no one if she called, but she had to wait until this dreadful headache subsided and she could think straight, or she might say something that she would regret. She was tired, too, and that was not a good time to make such an important call. She reclined the chair, and closed her eyes.

"Valeta!" The voice broke through a happy dream in which she, flyer on a college cheerleader squad, was spinning to dizzying heights while thousands of spectators cheered.

"Valeta?" The questioning voice seemed very close to her ear.

"In a minute," she murmured, reaching for the evaporating dream, and then added softly, "Oh dear, it's gone." She opened her eyes.

Grandmother stood there, as genteel and stylish as ever, short silver hair lifting the almost imperceptible wrinkles away from her eyes. "That must have been a lovely thought," she said.

Valeta smiled dreamily, but only said, "I didn't expect you back so soon."

"So soon?" Grandmother pointed at the clock on the mantel. "It's nearly lunch time! I never intended to stay out so long, but I met a friend, and took time for a cup of coffee. You must be hungry."

"Not really," she said, and stretched. "My head still feels as though some cruel giant is hammering a wedge into each side of it."

"I have just what the doctor would order, if you asked him," said Grandmother. "You stay right there and I'll cook something your mother, Marjorie never would dream of cooking."

"Oh, that reminds me." Valeta returned the chair to an upright position. "You should have heard the sermon I heard last week. It was called *Unfair to Marjorie*." She followed Grandmother to the kitchen, sinking onto a stool by the counter and re-telling the sermon while Grandmother made plain, ordinary macaroni and cheese and added a quick deli garden salad.

Grandmother liked the story, just as Valeta had known she would, and called it a "poignant reminder of moral values." They took their food to the table when it was ready and, as they ate, talked about all the things they must do in the months until the baby came. Grandmother told Valeta what the value of her car had been, and said that, with wise planning, it would pay all of her expenses, including delivery of the baby.

"We will stick close to home until your acute mountain sickness disappears," she told Valeta, sprinkling oil and vinegar on her salad, "but then, we will shop until we drop!"

"That means by the end of the week, I can get some clothing that fits!" The anticipation alone made her feel better.

20

Change of Plans

The first week in Colorado was history, and Valeta wished the same could be said for the acute mountain sickness, but it could not. She had so totally sated herself with liquids that she dared not venture far from a toilet; she had avoided all exercise as though it were a plague, spending her days in the recliner with her feet up and her eyes closed; and Grandmother had stuffed her with the recommended high-carbohydrate, low-fat foods. They even had visited Grandmother's doctor, only to hear that, for some people, the sole solution was to return to a lower altitude.

"But I can't go to a lower altitude," Valeta reminded her grandmother, "unless I go home, and I'm certainly not welcome there."

"That may not be the only option," said the older woman, taking a pan of chocolate chip cookies from the oven. "Delaware is a coastal state and, if

Date with Responsibility

I remember my geography correctly, the altitude in Wilmington should be about 100 feet – not much different from Kailua."

"Do you mean Uncle William and Aunt Margaret's home?" Valeta looked out over her toes with wide eyes, considering what it would be like to live with her Delaware cousins.

"You have to go somewhere, and it certainly would give your mother her comeuppance if her sister took you in, not to mention the fact that you could thank Andrew in person for the little lamb keychain."

The two shared a conspiratorial smile, and Valeta agreed.

"I'll call Margaret as soon as I get these cookies into the cookie jar," said Grandmother. She opened a large bear-shaped crock and carefully layered her fresh cookies into its belly, but before she replaced the lid, she lifted two cookies onto a small white plate and carried them to Valeta's reclined chair. "I'll get you a glass of milk," she said, and then, leaning close to Valeta's stomach, she added, "These chocolate chip cookies are for you, Baby, from your great grandmother. I'll bake more for you when you come back from Delaware." She got the milk, loaded the dishwasher, and then went to the phone.

* * *

Change of Plans

It all had been so amazingly simple. Aunt Margaret, just home from her midweek writers' club meeting, was delighted to settle a very long-standing grudge by taking in her niece and the unborn baby. The cousins were sure to be excited at the thought of a long visit from Valeta, and their involvement in preparations for her baby. Uncle William agreed to meet Valeta's flight at the Philadelphia airport, and then drive her to Wilmington. They should give him a call as soon as they had arrival times.

Such great news put a smile on Valeta's lips, then sadness as Grandmother dialed her travel bureau to make flight arrangements, and then a second smile, a little smaller, when she learned that the most economical flight would be next Tuesday evening – nearly a week away. It did seem a shame, Grandmother said when she hung up, to be limited to a red eye and have to spend your entire night in either an airplane or an airport, but this was just a part of financial responsibility, which Valeta wanted to learn.

"Actually," she told Valeta, "Uncle William is the best one to teach you financial responsibility, since he's an accountant." She stood up, and then sat down again, saying, "I need to wire him your money, too, so he can help you set up a budget. I guess I should arrange that when I call with your arrival time." She jotted a note on a pad of paper by the phone, and then stood again.

Date with Responsibility

At that moment, the front door bell rang, and in the afternoon sunlight that danced in when Grandmother opened it, stood a small boy with a quiveringly tiny kitten in his arms. "I found your kitty," he said, pushing the little gray thing into Grandmother's apron pocket. And then, as though caught up by an invisible hand, the child vanished. The kitten popped its head out of the pocket, but only for an instant before returning to the decidedly safer warmth and darkness.

"Who was it?" Valeta asked, raising the orange recliner a few inches, and peering toward the front door.

"I really don't know," said Grandmother, a bemused look in her eyes. She walked gently to the living room and, crablike, approached Valeta's chair with the pocket wiggling at her side. "He put something in my apron pocket. Would you take it out, please?"

Valeta reached toward the pocket, curious, but cautious. Cradling the pocket with her left hand, she inserted the right hand and drew out the tiny kitten.

"Oh!" It was all she needed to say.

"I'll get some broth from our chicken soup," said Grandmother, and she hurried to the kitchen.

Valeta called out to ask her whose kitten it was, but the older woman ignored the question.

Change of Plans

The look on Valeta's face had told her that the kitten was sent for a reason, which Grandmother believed was true of everything. There would be time to find the owner later.

While the kitten licked up the chicken broth, Grandmother found an old kitty litter box in her garage, and Valeta patiently shredded old newspapers into it. They gave it a temporary place beside the recliner so that Valeta could be sure the kitten appropriated it when necessary, and put him – or her – into it the moment the broth was gone. After that, Valeta and the kitten spent the rest of the day in the recliner, parting only when one or the other had to make a quick trip. Much of the time, Valeta slept, but when she was awake, her hands were constantly fondling the tiny ball of fur.

The kitten did nothing, actually, to relieve the symptoms of acute mountain sickness, but it did take her mind off of them, and the next few days passed in relative happiness.

Grandmother secretly placed a classified ad to locate the kitten's owner, but no one responded, and so, when the day came for Valeta to leave Colorado, they named her, for it was a female. "Let's call her Shadow," said Valeta, "because she follows one or the other of us everywhere we go."

"No," said Grandmother, "I'm going to call her Velvet. The *V* will remind me of you, and there could be no more descriptive name than Velvet for a kitten so soft and cuddly in both personality and appearance."

So the kitten had a new name and a new home – and after an early dinner, Valeta slowly packed for the trip to *her* new home.

It was wretched to be departing at 8:30 PM and arriving at 6:05 AM – she would see nothing other than the inside of the planes – two different ones – and the inside of the Las Vegas airport.

"I won't complain, because I know this is saving me money," Valeta told Grandmother, "but do you realize that I have to fly west when I want to go east? You would think they could schedule a flight to go part of the way east, and then have a layover if they don't want to reach Philadelphia too early in the day."

Grandmother smiled as she folded Valeta's orange flowered dress, carefully rolling the long ribbon belt so that it would not crease. "As many times as I've flown, I've never learned the secret of their odd scheduling," she said, "but cheer up. You can sleep on both legs of the journey, since neither of the flights will continue beyond your destination. I wouldn't sleep in the airport, though, unless you are in a well-lighted spot with people around you." As she placed the orange dress in the luggage, she saw a cloud drift across the teen's face and a single tear drop from the cloud. Her own eyes dimmed suddenly, and she reached in her pocket for a tissue. Then she left the room, and came back with a beautifully-wrapped box.

"What's that – or do I have to wait and open it in Delaware?" Valeta smiled brightly at her grandmother, the clouds having moved on.

"You must open it now," said Grandmother, while I finish your packing. "Sit down there on the bed and stay out of my way."

She placed the large box, which looked like a suit box, on the bed and gently pushed Valeta down beside it. Then she made a show of busily packing, all the while keeping her eyes and ears keenly attuned to the opening of the gift.

"Oh, how beautiful!" Valeta exclaimed.

"I wanted to be the one to buy your first maternity clothing – an outfit to wear on the plane," Grandmother said, seeming too busy to look, but watching with joy the success of her most recent shopping trip.

Valeta took out a scoop neckline burgundy top with a touch of pink around the neck, a wide pink sash that tied above the waist, and long sleeves that ended in wide pink bands. Beneath the top was a pair of soft, stretchy pants striped in burgundy, pink, beige, brown, black, and white. "These are absolutely perfect!" Valeta jumped up. "I'm going to give you a fashion show right now."

Date with Responsibility

"Aren't you going to look at the second outfit?" Grandmother tucked the tiny blue shawl into a suitcase as she asked, and turned to sit down beside Valeta.

"Oh! There are two outfits?" Valeta lifted out a pale green short-sleeved chiffon top with a hint of darker green flowers scattered across it, a slimming elastic forming a high waistline. Instead of pants, this outfit had a soft, flowing long skirt of the darker green. "Your taste is absolutely exquisite, Grandmother. I will feel pretty in this even if I get as big as a barn. Thank you so much! And now – now you *will* have a fashion show, like it or not, but you will have to sit in the living room so that I can make a grand entrance."

The older woman looked around and, seeing that the packing was done, bowed to her granddaughter's wishes and went to the living room.

It was strange to be putting on maternity clothing, especially when she did not have much of a tummy to show, but new clothing was always fun to Valeta, maternity or not, and it would be much nicer to travel in this than in her tighter clothes. She slipped into the striped pants first, noting with pleasure that the vertical stripes would have a slimming effect, even in October and November when she became ever so much bigger. The top might be a bit dark for summer, she thought as she slipped it over her head, but it had long sleeves and would show the dirt less than a lighter top, and both were important factors for a chilly overnight trip to Delaware.

"Drum roll, please," she called, tying the top's pink sash behind her back, and sashaying down the hall to the living room. She posed, twirled, and posed again, asking, "Isn't it perfect?"

"Does it fit? I didn't know for sure what size you were," Grandmother worried.

"It fits perfectly, and I'm only going to take it off long enough to show you the other one. Then I'm going to put this one back on and wear it all night – on one plane – in Las Vegas airport – on a second plane – when I greet Uncle William – and when I greet Aunt Margaret and my four cousins. I will feel so good in this, Grandmother, and I will think of you with love every time I wear it." Valeta put a little skip in her step on the way back to the bedroom – the greatest exercise she had done since reaching this altitude.

When she had changed into the dressier top and skirt, she took time to admire herself in the mirror, swept her hair on top of her head, and then waltzed back to the living room, holding the hair with her left hand. She smiled coquettishly as Grandmother whistled, thanked her again, and then returned to her room to change back into the striped pants and burgundy top.

Date with Responsibility

Suddenly, it was time to leave. Oh, there was still an hour and a half until the plane would lift off, but she had to check in early. Carefully laying the skirt outfit in the top of her larger bag, Valeta zipped it shut, put on the pant outfit again, and then surveyed the room to be sure she had packed everything. The rocking chair looked so empty – so sad with no toys and no promise of a baby to soothe with its gentle motion and its tiny squeaking song.

She hurried out of the room, asking if Grandmother had called for a taxi, and if it would be all right for the driver to go in the bedroom to get her bags so that she would not have to carry them. She gave Velvet a farewell kiss, all the time trying not to think of Leo, and then, as the taxi driver rang the bell, she gave Grandmother a kiss.

"You stay here with Velvet and keep her from crying," she told Grandmother. "It will keep me from crying at the airport, too."

They hugged each other fiercely, and then she was gone – to yet another home.

21

Turret Room

Valeta stood alone at the towering window of Philadelphia's airport, staring at the last fluffy pieces of sunrise clouds, their rosy pink now paled, and their silver linings gone. From time to time, she glanced down at her luggage, counted the pieces, and then stared at the clouds again, lost in the vastness of the early morning universe.

Uncle William found her there, a small, tired waif in travel-wrinkled pants and top that gave no hint of pregnancy, thanks to her recently tied sash. He negotiated a waiting crowd, and reaching her side, quietly asked, "Are you Valeta?"

"Uncle William?"

"You can't be the little girl that crawled on my knees a few years ago begging for pony rides, can you? Why, you are a stunning young woman!" He stepped around her, his eyes running from blonde head to dainty slippered feet.

Date with Responsibility

Valeta gave him a self-conscious smile and, because he was her uncle, a brief hug that betrayed the same self-consciousness.

"This isn't your entire luggage, is it?" Uncle William flashed a grin. "Your four cousins each would require twice this much or, in Alicia's case, three times this much." He threw her backpack onto one shoulder and, reaching for the two large bags, set them on their wheels and led the way toward a distant exit.

Valeta trailed him, jostling through a steadily growing crowd of business commuters. His mention of Alicia by name was reassuring, since she otherwise could not be certain that this was Uncle William, it had been so many years since she last saw him.

At the arrival curb, the tall uncle insisted solicitously that she wait with the luggage while he went for the car, and leaving her by a dirty concrete bench, he jogged toward the parking lot.

Everything within her wanted to sit down on that bench, hard as it looked, but that one small part of the brain that was trying to be responsible reminded her that she needed to take care of the new maternity outfit, and the fewer times she had to launder it, the longer it would look good. So she stood, and watched the parade of individual men, women, and children, each bustling along in a cocoon of anonymity.

The drive to Wilmington was less than an hour, the Interstate highway journeying southwest along the ever-widening Delaware River, which soon would flow into the Atlantic Ocean.

Uncle William kept the conversation alive as they drove, at least the part of it that proceeded from his side of the car. Valeta was so weary from travel and lack of sleep that she supplied mostly monosyllables, with only an occasional spark of involvement.

"Once I get some rest, I will probably talk your head off, Uncle William," she warned at one point, "but it's been nearly twelve hours since I left my grandmother's house, and I can't seem to think now. I'm not even sure what day it is."

"Wednesday, May 21," said Uncle William.

"May 21?" An alarm brought Valeta bolt upright in her seat. "Oh groan. I scheduled a doctor's appointment for today and ran off without canceling it. Now I suppose they will charge me for it, and I have no way to let them know."

"You can call Colorado Springs when we get home, and cancel it. There is a two hour time difference between here and there, so they aren't even in their office yet."

"Oh, but it isn't in Colorado Springs. It's in Honolulu, and I know there's an even greater time difference, but the cell phone charges will kill me."

Date with Responsibility

"First call is on me," said Uncle William, "but you're on your own after that."

Valeta sat back again, gradually returning to uninspired conversation, and soon falling fast asleep, not stirring until Uncle William turned slowly up a broad driveway to a beautiful old mansion. Then she sat up drowsily to ask, "Who lives here?"

"This is your new home," he replied with a smile, "and the room in that turret on the corner of the house is for you and the baby."

The car had crept slowly to the end of the brown cobblestone driveway, passing between rows of dogwood trees dressed in fresh spring gowns, and now it stopped in front of a wide gray stairway that led up and up to the manor's big oak door. Rich green box elders flanked the stairs, allowing small azaleas to peek from between them, flaunting vivid blossoms in varied hues of pink.

Valeta had never seen the McKean family homestead, and was instantly enthralled, asking her uncle to tell her all about it, including when and why they moved here.

Uncle William answered her questions as he helped her from the vehicle and removed her luggage from the back, continued answering as they climbed the fifteen broad steps to the porch, but stopped when he opened the door and called out, "Margaret, I found a little homeless girl at the airport. Have you room in your house for her?"

Like a scene out of a book, Aunt Margaret appeared at the top of a curved stairway, a pile of auburn hair atop her head sporting a blue pencil in back, and a pair of dark-rimmed glasses in front. Valeta could see that she was every inch Mom's sister in physical appearance, but Mom never had a smile like that for anyone, let alone a waif who was, in a sense, forced upon her.

"I have room in my house," Aunt Margaret said, "and room in my heart, too." She took two steps down the beautiful staircase and then, with a wink at Valeta, hopped lightly to the banister and rode the smooth wooden curve to its bottom.

Valeta giggled, and took an instant liking to this wonderful aunt, whose heart floated out to her niece as readily as she floated down the railing.

"The first thing you want to do is see where you will be living," said Aunt Margaret, wiping invisible dust from the seat of her navy slacks and giving Valeta a warm hug, "so let's go right up. The stairs aren't a problem, are they? Of course they aren't," she answered her own question. "You're a cheerleader and a surfer and goodness knows what else."

She led the way, then, and opened the door to a room far more wonderful than Valeta could have dared to imagine – actually two rooms, with the smaller one incorporating the circular turret.

The larger room held a vintage double bed covered with a red floral comforter, and flanked by twin antique chests. Two side chairs crowded close to a round table at the far side of the room, their deep red seat pads drawing inspiration from the bed's comforter. An old armoire along the wall opposite the foot of the bed had been converted to hold a small TV set. Three large windows streamed with morning sunlight filtered through white lace curtains.

As Aunt Margaret gestured Valeta into the smaller room, the teen caught her breath, and then let out a squeal of delight, for next to a loveseat, snug in its own quiet corner, sat a small cradle of glowing, carved oak. The room also contained a baby's changing table, and a small oak chest, which Aunt Margaret promised to help Valeta fill with baby clothing.

The turret room had a private bath, and a door that opened onto a small balcony at the front of the house. The only thing it did not have, it seemed, was its own kitchen.

"Are you sure this is all right? I mean, this room and this furniture and all?" Valeta asked.

"This was a guest room when William's parents had the house," said Margaret, "but this house has so many rooms, and we always put our guests in the extra bedrooms downstairs, so this one has been used by Alicia as a romantic hideout. I'm afraid the furniture is terribly old."

"The furniture is marvelous," said Valeta. "but I don't want to take her hideaway."

"Ah, but you see," said Uncle William, "you are part of Alicia's romantic daydreams, and she is the one who suggested giving you the turret rooms. She would be crushed if you did not stay here." He lifted the two suitcases to the double bed for her and told her to let him know anytime she needed to have something heavy moved. "I'll immediately send Andrew to help you," he said.

"The furniture in both of these rooms," said Aunt Margaret, "was William's parents' or even grandparents' furniture. William slept in the cradle, as did each of your four cousins: Andrew, Alicia, Catherine, and Caleb." She turned to her husband to add, "We should let Valeta freshen up for breakfast. She must be starved." She took his arm then, and let him lead her from the room.

When they were gone, Valeta stepped back into the small turret room and sat down on the floor beside the cradle, legs crossed and hands holding the smooth, carved side rail. Gently, she swayed the small bed, humming a classical lullaby, and sensing that at last she had found a home for herself and the unborn child.

Date with Responsibility

It was her last quiet moment until late that evening, but she took from it the strength she needed to begin her new life in Wilmington – and to renew her acquaintance with cousins who had changed as much as she had in the past few years.

22

Four McKeans

Gaining two brothers and two sisters in one brief day delighted Valeta, but depleted every ounce of energy that remained after the red eye flight of the night before. They were not, of course, true brothers and sisters, but the teen who had until that day been an only child, and pampered to a great degree, now found herself sharing time and attention with the four McKean cousins, and found it not entirely unpleasant.

Catherine and Caleb, the first two she met, arrived around noon, having an early dismissal school day, filled with plans to go shopping – and to take their newly arrived cousin with them.

"Next Tuesday is Andrew's birthday," said Catherine, hanging on Valeta's arm and donning her most fetching smile to enhance the papaya curls that framed her round adolescent face. "We need your help to find the prefect gift for him, and you can shop 'til you pop!" Catherine said, totally oblivious to the injury she dealt the quote. "The Shipyard Shops have everything imaginable, and they all are factory outlet stores. Did you have factory outlet stores in Kailua?"

"Not in Kailua, but – listen, you live with Andrew every day, and you know him far better than I do," said Valeta, "so what help would I be?"

"You're his age," Caleb explained carefully, "at least the physical age that he will achieve next Tuesday – cognitive age aside – and you are thereby better qualified to know what a matriculating high school senior would appreciate. Come on. We'll persuade Dad to let you chauffeur us so we won't have to take public transportation. You have enough expertise to operate a mini van, don't you?"

Valeta grinned at the choice vocabulary of the carrot top, but declined their invitation, which meant that when Alicia arrived home from high school, the two girls could get acquainted without the younger McKeans' presence.

Alicia was everything Valeta ever wanted in a younger sister, although very different in her likes and dislikes. Whereas Valeta loved water sports, horseback riding, cheerleading, and her clarinet, fifteen year old Alicia preferred ballet, baseball, reading, and her kaleidoscopes. Common to both, however, were their romantic dreams, and it took Valeta few minutes to realize it.

"Thank you for giving up your romantic hideaway for my baby and me," she told Alicia soon after they met. "Are you sure you're all right with that – because if you aren't, I can move my things to another empty room. Your mother says you have several unused rooms."

"Oh, Valeta, I *want* you and the baby to use the turret room," Alicia answered, impatiently pushing strawberry red bangs out of her eyes and adding, "I can't stand having these in my eyes."

The conversation went from long bangs to music, from music to school, from dogs to cats as Schnauzie, the gray miniature schnauzer trotted in to introduce himself – Pierrot, the black and white cat was nowhere to be found.

By the time Aunt Margaret asked the two girls to set the table for the evening meal, only one big topic remained. Alicia was handing down a stack of plates from the kitchen cupboard when she asked, "How did you get pregnant?"

Valeta fought to hold the tottering stack, and pretended she had not heard.

But Aunt Margaret interrupted, "Valeta, would you place those plates at the near end of the table, and Alicia, you chop vegetables."

"Yes, Aunt Margaret," said Valeta. "I'll put on napkins and silverware, too." She fled to the dining room and deposited the stack of plates, and then clung to the back of a chair as she took five deep breaths. Her face flushed and then paled. When she felt steadier, she began setting out silverware, wondering as she did so how much Aunt Margaret had told the cousins. Then she wondered how much Grandmother had told Aunt Margaret and Uncle William. After that first phone call, Grandmother Davidson had written a letter in which, she told Valeta, she explained everything so that Valeta would not have that burden, but how much did she explain?

Valeta stood there with a handful of white napkins pressed against her cheek, her eyes tightly shut as she pondered what to do. She did not want to explain, did not know how to explain to teen and pre-teen cousins that a man had raped her; that he then had been shot to death by – the name and face of the murderer appeared again, and she trembled.

"She's here," said a deepening male voice, "and me looking like this! A guy can't even sneak into his own home anymore."

Valeta opened her eyes slightly. She could see a figure – male – young – tall – an athletic body – topped by rich copper hair. The figure was clad in dirty blue jeans, a dirty gray tee shirt, and a bright orange vest.

"Hi. I'm Andrew," he said, "and I promise not to touch your hand until I get cleaned up, but it's good to see you again." He grinned, gesturing toward the napkins. "Serviettes."

Valeta came to life, and opened her eyes fully, looking at the paper napkins as she asked, "What did you say?"

"Serviettes. If you ever take a trip to New Zealand, call them anything but napkins. They use that word for baby diapers, which I learned the hard way."

"Thanks for the tip!" She distributed the napkins around the table, asking as she did so if he always dressed so nicely.

Andrew gave her an ironic smile, and the short version of why he spent every afternoon in this orange vest, picking up trash in the public parks and otherwise being humiliated as a part of his punishment for being accomplice to a felony. "I've been doing it since the end of February," he said. "Three months volunteering with Wilmington's Department of Public Works is the community service portion of my penalty. Every year, our city has *Operation Clean Sweep*, but this is the first and only time they will have me, if I can help it. I'll tell you more about it later, but I'd better get cleaned up for dinner, or Mom will have my copper head."

As the dinner hour arrived, so did every member of the busy family, seating themselves in their accustomed places, and giving Valeta the seat at Uncle William's right hand. It was odd to have a family dinner without Jean Luc's discreet service, and Valeta watched as her uncle dished wild rice pilaf onto each plate, topped it with grilled chicken breast in a sweet sauce, and piled steamed vegetables beside it. Aunt Margaret, unlike Mom, obviously had learned to cook well and provide abundantly for the teen appetites that surrounded her table. Conversation centered mainly around the events of the day, and Valeta, too weary to do more than let it swirl pleasantly around her, ate in silence.

After dinner, Caleb, Catherine, and Alicia were placed on kitchen duty, and Andrew invited Valeta out onto the wide front porch to talk. The evening was mild, and the sun surrounded by a wide golden aura on the western horizon. They sat on faded green cushions in wooden chairs, not directly facing each other, but on either side of a small wooden table, twisting sideways in their chairs as they kicked aside awkward icebreakers and plunged into spirited conversation.

What felony had Andrew committed, Valeta wanted to know, that resulted in him being pressed into community service, and what other penalty did he get besides the trash collection?

Personally, he had done almost nothing, he replied, except bow to peer pressure. A couple of guys in choir had decided to wreak vengeance on the school coach for an imagined discrimination, and had posted flyers – printed on Andrew's color printer – stating that the coach had molested a girl after gym class. The whole thing was invented with absolutely no grounds, but the school believed it and fired the coach – best one they ever had. Then, adding insult to injury, Andrew learned that the girl for whom he had just fallen head over heels was the coach's daughter. So, in essence, he had been responsible to a degree for making his girlfriend's dad get fired and stand trial for a crime he never committed.

Was that before he went to New Zealand, or after, she pursued, and what happened between him and the coach's daughter – her name was...?

Andrew gave her a lopsided grin as he said, "It happened before I went to New Zealand. I was desperate because they caught the other guys, though none of them fingered me, and the trial date was fast approaching, so when I learned that my grandfather had put in an exchange student application for me just before he died, I thought it was my passport to freedom. Believe me, I couldn't get away fast enough! Penny – she's the coach's daughter – was the one thing that made me want to stay, but not once she found out what I had done. I wrote to her the whole time I was over there, but she never answered any of my e-mail. That, and the fact that I was sure I'd get sent to prison made me decide to stay in New Zealand. Well, to make a long story short, I ran away from my sponsor family, and my real family ended up going over there to get me. Then when I came back, I contacted the judge that tried the case and confessed my part. Talk about a speedy trial! Within a week, he had me assigned to three months of community service, four days a week, and a fine of $300, which Dad paid, but I have to work off as soon as I get done cleaning up trash. I guess I'll get a fast food job for the summer. The other guys each got five months of community service and a fine of $500, but since I played a lesser role, I got a lighter sentence."

"So, when you got back, did you talk to the coach's daughter – Penny – and explain to her, or did she find out from someone else?" Valeta was too tired to sit forward, but her voice conveyed the eagerness that her body lacked.

"Penny," he said cheerily, "now wears a pink paua ring from New Zealand. I can fill you in on the details later, but believe me, it took every ounce of courage I could dredge up to call and ask if she would see me. She agreed, but only if we met at her home, with her parents present in the room. Talk about a trial! Someone had dropped a hint that I might be involved in her dad's dismissal, and Penny wanted the truth from my own mouth. I explained – apologized to them all – and learned that she had never gotten any of my e-mail. Then they sent me home. I was sure it was over between us, but she called the next day and said she and her parents all were willing to forgive, since I had tried to resist the guys' idea. It was her dad, I guess, that told her to return good for evil."

Valeta shook her head slowly. "I think I can understand some of what he must have felt," she said, but when Andrew asked for clarification, she told him she was too tired – maybe later.

The sky was dark now, as the breeze grew cooler and the moon slid up the eastern side of the velvet sky. Valeta got to her feet slowly, and looked out over the curving drive. "I think I'll go to my room," she said. "I can barely keep my eyes open. I should find your mom and tell her that I'm going to bed."

Andrew watched her as she shuffled across the porch, and then jumped up to open the heavy door for her. "I'll tell Mom for you," he said. "Sleep well, Cous."

Valeta nodded vaguely and climbed the steps to the turret room. It greeted her with a soft welcoming scent of fresh potpourri – a bowl of it sat on one chest, with a sweet note from Alicia. Valeta smiled, and got ready for bed, pausing only to brush her long hair.

She had just put the brush away when she heard a knock at the door, and thought, "Edwin!"

Date with Responsibility

She did not know why she thought Edwin, and it was not Edwin – it was Aunt Margaret who had come, she said, to decide together how much of Valeta's story to tell the four cousins. Valeta invited her in, and they talked for a half hour, sorting out the minimal elements necessary to explain discreetly why Valeta was pregnant.

"I'll tell them only what they must know," Aunt Margaret said, "and I'll tell them tonight so that you won't face more questions tomorrow. I think they only need to know that the pregnancy is not your fault and that it was important for you to leave the islands for a while, so I invited you here. Then, if you're in agreement, we can get them involved in baby preparations – change the focus from past to future."

"Thank you," Valeta whispered, "for that and everything you've done for me."

Aunt Margaret left then, and Valeta turned out the lamp beside the bed, emptying her mind of cousins – filling it with Edwin.

23

Unexpected Proposal

The sun that heated Wilmington's summer watched as the popular little teen who knew so little about responsibility gradually blossomed into a responsible mother-to-be.

The first two weeks, she read and re-read the little book, <u>Responsibility</u>, which had been given to her by the preacher in Hawaii, noting in her binder that responsibility involved:

> *knowing and doing what people expect of me without needing someone to remind me and to check up on me.*

She made a growing list of synonyms for the word:

accountability	*conscientiousness*
maturity	*answerability*
liability	*dependability*
reliability	*trustworthiness*

She drafted her own definition in those first weeks, but it was rough.

At the end of the second week, on a quiet Saturday morning when all four cousins were studying for final exams, Valeta sat on the porch, talking with Aunt Margaret. It was the hottest day since her arrival in Delaware, and the most bothersome so far as her physical state. She fanned her face with a magazine she had been reading, and asked guardedly, "Aunt Margaret, you're Irish, right?"

"About as Irish as they come."

"I have an Irish riddle that I need to solve, and I thought you might be able to help. Someone gave it to me in Hawaii, and it's very short, but no matter how much I study it, I can't come up with the answer. It was *How would you like to be buried with my people?*"

"Oh my goodness!" Aunt Margaret laughed merrily. "I hope it was Edwin that gave it to you."

"It was, but what made you say that?"

"It's a marriage proposal, my dear – an old Irish marriage proposal. When did Edwin ask, and is he still waiting for an answer?"

"He didn't ask," said Valeta. "He wrote it in the sand by a beautiful castle he built for me, and I haven't answered because I didn't know."

Unexpected Proposal

Aunt Margaret's eyes twinkled as she said, "If I were you, I'd send him a telegram saying, 'November is the time to wed, the harvest's in and it's cold in bed.' That's a very Irish response."

Valeta laughed, but knowing that she had no right to say any word that might be construed as agreement to a marriage proposal, she changed the subject and did not return to it.

Her third week, in addition to going for the first prenatal visit in Delaware, she asked Uncle William to teach her financial responsibility, since she now had free access to her money.

"I'm glad you want to do this," he said when they sat down for their first lesson. "A lot of teenagers not only don't *know* how to be financially responsible, but also do not want to *learn* how."

He made notes on a pad as he explained his *Six Lessons of Financial Responsibility*:

1. *Financial freedom is not a pipe dream.*
2. *Credit card debts are wolves.*
3. *Baby foxes are as bad as wolves.*
4. *Regular investing creates millionaires.*
5. *College need not be expensive.*
6. *Spreadsheets are our friends.*

The first day, he discussed only financial freedom. "I always tell accounting clients," he said, "that this is the biggest lesson they can learn." He sketched a pair of handcuffs as he continued, "You have to picture debt this way. The bigger the debt, the less the freedom. I once heard a preacher say that the borrower is the slave of the lender, so I found the Bible proverb he gave and printed it on cards to give to new clients." Uncle William handed Valeta a business card inscribed:

> *The rich rules over the poor, and the*
> *borrower becomes the lender's slave.*

> Proverbs 22:7

"Right now," he told her, "you have a sum of money that looks large, but that will disappear quickly. You may be tempted to borrow for college or other things, but if you do borrow, you become the slave of the lender. I'll talk about specific debt later, but the most important thing to remember is that the best debt is no debt, just as the best handcuffs are no handcuffs. As soon as you owe people money, you work for them – to pay them. They charge interest, the price of your purchase keeps increasing, and you keep working for them. The money you earn is no longer yours to spend as you wish, because you have become a slave to the lender, and your financial freedom is gone. Many adults think that financial freedom is a pipe dream, but it is very possible to avoid debt, and if you avoid it in the beginning, and make a habit of avoiding it, you will find that it is not that difficult to be financially free. That's the first and most important lesson of financial responsibility."

Valeta tested that lesson the next day when she went to the mall with Alicia and Catherine, purposing to buy nothing more than two or three maternity tops and pants for her changing figure.

"Oh, look!" Alicia gestured toward a display of designer diaper bags. "Those diaper bags don't scream frumpy mom. You should get one."

Valeta looked at the price tag and flinched, although she never would have before. "They are stylish, but I can't afford that."

"We will be happy to set up payments for you," said a clerk, appearing as though by magic, "and the interest rate is very reasonable."

Suddenly, the clerk was dangling before her eyes an enormous pair of shiny metal handcuffs. Valeta smiled graciously and declined the clerk's offer, laughing inwardly at the vivid image.

"Come on, girls. Let's get back to looking at maternity wear," she told her cousins. Of course, that was only the first skirmish, and victory in it did not guarantee that she would win the war, but it strengthened her resolve – until Catherine hauled her off to see "the sweetest sheep mobile for your baby's crib." On the mobile, four fleecy lambs surrounded a sleepy moon sitting on a cloud. When Alicia discovered that the mobile played *Brahms' Lullaby* for six full minutes, Valeta could not resist. She bought the mobile.

Date with Responsibility

On the afternoon of June 15, Valeta received a surprise call from Edwin, and talked with him for the first time in many weeks, beginning with meaningless drivel, straining to find cautious words as they continued, extending her sixth sense to feel the meaning behind his words.

Jean Luc loved Leo, he told her, and was taking good care of him – Edwin seldom met her daddy or mom now, but the last time they did meet, Mom told him that Valeta was somewhere on Oahu, so they were still in the dark.

Valeta told him about Wilmington, assured him that she was well, and happy to be past both morning sickness and mountain sickness.

"The police detained the star quarterback and charged him with both Rick's murder and the fire at your home," Edwin said then, and Valeta gasped. "Actually, he turned himself in because he couldn't live with the guilt," Edwin continued, "but they had been hot on his trail. It seems he was determined to take the homecoming queen to Senior Luau, and so angry when you turned him down that he watched every move you and Rick made. When Rick followed you to the beach, he listened, and then he heard you scream. He waited for you to return, but when neither of you did by the time the buses were loading, he went to find you. That's when he saw what Rick had done. He fought with Rick, chased him far down the beach, and avenged you by shooting him with his own gun. When he realized that Rick was dead, he ran even farther down the beach and threw the gun in the ocean. Then he got a bus to Kailua and set your sauna on fire to implicate Rick in his own murder. They matched his shoe prints and tire marks that the arson investigators had, and it looks like an open and shut case now."

Valeta expressed relief, withholding the fact that she had known who did it, and then she waited for Edwin to speak again.

After a pause, he asked quietly, "Did you ever solve the riddle in the sand?"

"No, not until I got here and asked Aunt Margaret. She told me what it means," Valeta said.

"And did your heart tell you the answer?"

"My heart is very confused, as is my head. I know you said that this would not make you love me less, but I thought you would have changed your mind by now. You might rather have me be buried anywhere *but* with your people."

"The baby can be mine," he said, taking her by surprise. "I can adopt the baby."

"You would do that? You would adopt Rick's baby after what he did to me, and live with that little boy or girl reminding us every day?" Valeta looked at Edwin's photo beside the bed, her eyes suddenly moist.

Date with Responsibility

"Valeta, nothing has changed between you and me. Not really. I love you as much as I ever did – no, more than I ever did before. When I see the way you are taking responsibility for all of this, even though it was not your fault, I wonder if I am even worthy to marry you now, but I want to marry you – I want to more than ever. Do you feel at all that way?"

Valeta had been standing in the middle of her bedroom, but now she moved into the smaller turret room and sank onto the love seat. "I do," she said. "I wanted to stay with you, or to fly back to you, but I had to take care of the baby, too, and I just wasn't sure what you thought – which was my fault, because I never gave you much chance to tell me what you thought. Not really."

"Listen," Edwin said, "I have more that I want to say, but I have to hang up now. Promise that you will think about my proposal. You may need time to make a decision, and I understand that, but promise you will at least consider it."

She made the promise, and hung up, but her mind continued the conversation unhindered. Did he mean what he said – that he was willing to marry her – willing to adopt this baby that was not his? He did say it. She had always trusted him. Surely, she could trust him in this, too. There was no reason to doubt him. He sounded sincere. Impatiently, she pushed aside her long hair and hugged the cell phone to her ear, expecting to hear his voice, so real was the imaginary conversation, but he was not in the cell phone.

That entire week, she expected Edwin to call, although she knew he had work, and the time zones would make it difficult for him to call when she was not asleep. Nevertheless, she waited with increasing expectancy and increasing eagerness.

Uncle William corralled her for a session on why credit card debt was a wolf at her door, and she dutifully listened, but she had not been offered a credit card yet, and would not be until she turned eighteen, as he himself admitted. Granted, it was frightening to consider the high amount of interest one paid on credit cards, and she resolved always to pay her bill in full when it was due, but the point was moot for now.

It was the following Sunday before Edwin was able to call again at a convenient time of day. She knew the call was from him, even before she saw the caller ID. Her premonition had told her he would call on Sunday, so she excused herself as quickly as possible after helping wash the lunch dishes, telling the family that she expected a call from Edwin and would take it in her room. She was feeling heavier today – her tummy had suddenly begun to bulge – and she took her time climbing the wide stairway, walking down the hall, and preparing herself for his call.

Date with Responsibility

She sat on the love seat in the turret room when she was ready, but only after moving Edwin's framed photo to the top of the baby's oak clothing chest so that she could look at him as well as talk to him. She wound the tiny music box of the lamb mobile, which now hung above the baby's cradle, and while it played its lullaby, she carefully tucked around an imaginary baby a light blanket of the softest possible plush, its wide satin border fencing three white fluffy lambs in its pale green pasture. She plumped the tiny green satin pillow she had brought from home, and then settled into the love seat to await her call. When it came, she answered quickly.

"Is this Madame Butterfly?" asked a deep voice from thousands of miles away.

Valeta laughed, and asked who wanted to know, followed quickly by, "That was a long week."

"Too long," Edwin agreed. "Did you think about what we discussed last week?"

"Yes...." She stretched the word, and then said, "The Irish answer to your Irish riddle is this: 'November is the time to wed, the harvest's in and it's cold in bed.'"

Edwin laughed gently, and then said, "*That* was very unexpected!"

"You mean you didn't expect me to answer the proposal?"

"I mean I didn't expect that kind of answer," he said, "but I like it. I like it very much."

"It came straight out of Aunt Margaret's store of Irish lore. The trouble is, I don't think November will work, actually, since I can't fly back to Hawaii in my last month of pregnancy, and you can't leave Hawaii then, not to mention the fact that wedding gowns, although they do come in maternity sizes, look a whole lot better when they are cut in more flattering lines. You should see me now. I'm beginning to pop in front."

Edwin laughed teasingly and told her to be careful she did not pop too much too soon. "I wish I *could* see you now," he said, "but if you promise to marry me, I will watch you carry the next baby."

"I promise," she said.

"You mean it?" Edwin's voice vibrated with joy. "Is that a definite yes?"

"It is," she said, and went on to tell him in tones and words why her answer was yes.

They talked for two hours, Valeta excusing herself twice for quick breaks, and finally hung up reluctantly, Edwin promising to call again as soon as possible – which might not be for a week.

It was a week between calls, but a very busy week. There was another doctor's appointment; shopping with Margaret and the girls for baby clothing; and a third lesson with Uncle William.

Date with Responsibility

This lesson, aiming much more at her present need for financial responsibility, and about little foxes being as bad as wolves, dealt with her every day purchases, which, her uncle told her, can largely determine a person's financial success. If she had a large need, like an infant car seat, she would certainly shop carefully and compare prices to be sure she used her money carefully. Most people did. However, if she went to the mall for three packages of diapers and, while there, bought a large candle for $20, a novel for $20, a latte for a couple of dollars, and then a sweater for $60, she was letting the little foxes help themselves to her grapes. Do that every week and, at the end of the month, she would find that the little foxes had unwittingly cost her as much as a good TV set.

Valeta vowed that she would be careful of little foxes, and, by the end of June, when she and Uncle William finished his lessons, she had done so well at it that he offered congratulations on her progress.

He was just telling her, "We won't go and celebrate at a restaurant, since they all have dens of little foxes, but I'll take you out to get the best infant seat available...," when her cell phone rang.

It was Edwin.

24

Cherity

"November is the time to wed, the harvest's in and it's cold in bed," were Edwin's first words when she answered, while hurrying to her room.

"Oh, Edwin. You must have thought I was being horribly forward when I said that. I didn't mean to press you to get married *this* November. I know we have to wait until after I finish college."

Edwin laughed across the miles, telling her that he knew it was just an Irish saying, and that even if it wasn't, he liked her being forward on occasion, since it made him feel as though she wanted to get married as much as he did.

"Oh, I do want to get married," she said, "but I'm willing to wait, especially considering the pregnancy and all."

"Do you mean," he asked, "that you would not marry me in November after all?"

"November is a wonderful month to get married," she replied, "but I don't expect you to make it *this* November."

"What would you say if I told you that we *can* get married this November?"

"I would say that you're teasing me, because I already told you that I can't fly to Hawaii that late in my pregnancy. Also, Uncle William has me seeing a counselor, and she said I should not get married until you and I have more time together to discuss this whole thing, and maybe not until after the baby is born, just to be sure you aren't marrying me because of the baby. If we have to spend more time together before we get married, and we wanted to get married this November, that would mean I'd have to fly to Hawaii for that, and since Mom and Daddy threw me out...."

Edwin interrupted her worried chatter by saying, "Listen, Honey, even if you tried to fly to Hawaii to spend time with me, it wouldn't work. I just received orders to leave Hawaii."

"Oh, Edwin. You're being deployed?"

"No, I'm being sent on a five month tour of duty to Dover Air Force Base – about an hour down the road from you – and I leave tomorrow night. I'll have every weekend free from now through the end of November, so we can have as many discussions as your counselor recommends."

Cherity

Excitement played across her blue eyes as she said, "You're teasing me! Dover Air Force Base? Oh Edwin, if you leave tomorrow night, that means you...." She paused, and then added suddenly, "Oh! The baby just moved! I wondered a few days ago, but this time I'm sure. It must be as excited about your coming as I am!"

"You mean you can feel it already?"

She put her hand on her belly and laughed as she told him, "It feels like a butterfly in there, but it has to be the baby moving. It just happened again. Wait. I'll put the phone to my belly and you can talk to it."

What Edwin said, she could not tell, but the baby stopped moving, so she returned the phone to her ear. "You must have told it to go to sleep," she said.

Edwin laughed. "Actually, I told it that I plan to be on your doorstep very early Saturday morning, so it had to let you get a lot of rest in the next three days. I also let it in on another little secret. Would you like to know what that is?"

"Well, I certainly don't want you and this baby keeping secrets from me," she said, tossing her head as though he could see her.

"I told it that my thirty-day vacation is to be tacked on to the end of my time at Dover, so I will be there to welcome it, even if it's late."

Date with Responsibility

Valeta popped out of the loveseat, her eyes wide and her full lips parted in a moment of speechless breath before stammering excitedly, "You don't have to go back until January?"

"That's right," he said. "I will be pestering you for six straight months, and you have only three days to get used to the idea." He paused, and then said, "I can't take time to talk longer today, but I'll see you Saturday morning."

They said quick good-byes, and Valeta sat down again, dreamily closing the phone. Only three days. She would see Edwin again and, this time, she could find out every tiny thing he had been thinking for the past four months plus. She could tell him all that she had been thinking, too: how she had longed to confide in him from the first day; how she had hoped he really could still love her; how she wanted to keep this baby – and did not want to give it up for adoption, although her counselor had been urging that. She wanted to tell him how hard she was working to become a responsible person.

The thought jerked her back to her feet. Nobody had to tell her that she had a lot to do in the next three days. She knew that she did! And the first thing she needed to do was to get Aunt Margaret and Uncle William's permission to use one of the downstairs guest rooms for Edwin – to use it every weekend for six months!

Cherity

* * *

Valeta awakened very early that Saturday. The sun was still wrapped in its nightshirt, and only the rounded top of its orange cap showed that it was stirring in its damp eastern bed, ears still ringing from yesterday's fireworks that celebrated Independence Day. Valeta had gone to the parade with the McKean family early in the day, after which Andrew and Penny had spirited her away to the park for an impromptu picnic. Penny, nearly the same age as Valeta, was rapidly becoming a replacement for Jennie and others left behind in Hawaii, with one difference. Penny knew all about Rick, but based her friendship on who Valeta was, not on what she had experienced, whereas the friendships in Hawaii, including Jennie's, might easily have been based solely on Valeta's high school celebrity profile and popularity.

But, today was not a day to dwell on that! Edwin was coming – might already be on his way! She had told herself, but nobody else, that she would surprise him by cooking his breakfast and, while she was at it, cooking for the whole family.

As her toes touched the floor, the unborn baby fluttered inside her, and she smiled down at her belly. "Nineteen weeks tomorrow, baby," she said, "and Edwin won't believe how big you and I are." She hurried to the mirror, and stood sideways, her right hand above the protruding middle and her left hand below it. She could accentuate this with those shorts that she barely buttoned below her belly, or hide it with her new maternity outfit. She decided on the latter, since Edwin had not seen her in so long, and hurried to dress: stretch panel stone colored shorts, a sleeveless top scattered with tiny blue flowers, trimmed above and below with blue piping, and a matching long blue ribbon, which she tied high above her waist. She decided to remain barefoot, but took time to slip on the friendship bracelet, the butterfly ring, and finally, the glass butterfly pendant, the blue universe of which matched her ribbon perfectly.

At the top of the stairs, as she did several times a day, she fought a strong desire to sail down the railing the way Aunt Margaret had done on that first day, reminding herself that responsible mothers-to-be did not risk injury to themselves or their babies by sliding down banisters. Instead, she walked quickly and quietly to the bottom, and proceeded to the kitchen.

Valeta could not begin to cook the way Jean Luc did, of course, but she hoped to serve better food than Edwin would get in the mess hall. With an eye on the clock, and wondering when Edwin would arrive, she got out a large fry pan with lid, a large griddle, two big stainless steel bowls, two loaves of unsliced French bread, sliced strawberries, eggs, and an assortment of other items. She broke eighteen eggs into one bowl, added cream and butter, but then decided to set the table before she cooked them. When the bright yellow placemats held eight neatly-set places, she hurried back to the eggs and had the bowl over the fry pan, the eggs about to slip from it when she realized that they would be done too soon if she started them now. She set the bowl aside once more, and began slicing bread for French toast, cutting a side pocket in each two-inch thick slice.

She was mixing strawberries with cream cheese and pecans preparatory to spreading the mixture inside the bread pockets, and had just splashed a bit of strawberry juice on her nose, when someone knocked on the backdoor. Hoping it was Penny, who had said she might get over to help her, Valeta dashed across the kitchen and opened the door, but there was no one in sight. She was about to close the door when she noticed a small pet carrier on the back step.

"How odd," she murmured as she bent down to look in it. "A cat. A big Himalayan cat. You know, you are one huge kitty!"

"One huge kitty named Leo," said Edwin. He stepped from behind a bush, took her in his arms, and kissed the strawberry juice from her nose.

"Edwin! I didn't expect you for at least thirty minutes yet!" Her voice pretended to scold, but her eyes, her lips, and everything else about her welcomed him with pure ecstasy.

Date with Responsibility

"If you want, I can go away," he said.

Valeta laughed, and then turned shy in his presence, realizing that the last time she had seen him had been the day before that final ultimatum that made her leave her home in Kailua. Even that had been only a brief meeting on her patio.

"You are beautiful," Edwin said, at which her shyness left as quickly as it had come.

She affected bashfulness, nonetheless, as she replied, "Why Edwin Laroque. How can you lie that way?" She smiled coyly.

"Well, you are a bit pudgy," he said, grinning down at her – reminding her of how tall he was. He kissed her nose again, pretended disappointment that it no longer had strawberry juice on it, and asked if she had eaten breakfast.

"Oh, my breakfast! I'm cooking breakfast," she told him, "for you and the whole family. It's a good thing I hadn't put anything over the heat yet, but I'd better get back to it or we'll all starve."

"Shall I bring Leo in or leave him out here?"

"It's really Leo?" Valeta bent down again, and the kitten purred loudly. "It *is* you, Leo! Oh Edwin, how did you ever get him here?"

"Bribed Jean Luc and a few more people, but it was worth it to see that big smile," said Edwin. "Besides, he needed you."

Cherity

They took Leo into the house, but left him in the crate until the resident cat could be cajoled into accepting him. Edwin sat on a stool and watched breakfast preparations, which were made infinitely more difficult by having an audience, but infinitely more enjoyable also. He offered to scramble the eggs for her, and she did let him stir them after they were in the pan, but other than that, she took full responsibility for the entire meal. When it was ready to set on the table, or nearly so, she dashed to the bottom of the stairs and called the family to "hurry down" for a big surprise, thinking to herself that she had at least three surprises: Edwin, Leo, and breakfast.

From that moment until late the next evening, Valeta knew nothing in particular, but a great happiness in general – happiness that filled everything that she and Edwin did, every topic they discussed, and every look they shared.

"Aside from my belly," she whispered once, "it seems as though nothing has changed since that Sunday morning before Senior Luau."

* * *

Neither of them expected the weekends that followed to be as wonderful as that first one, and none was the same as it, but every hour they spent together made it increasingly clear that they would get married. Even difficult topics like the rape served only to strengthen their bond.

Date with Responsibility

When they discussed the baby, they tried to consider factors suggested by Valeta's counselor: how Valeta would feel raising a child that was connected with such trauma; how Edwin would feel raising a child that was connected with such trauma; what support the child would need when it learned about its conception; what effect it would have on both of them if the baby looked like Rick; whether Edwin would marry Valeta only to avoid the stigma of an unwed mother; whether Edwin would be willing to adopt the baby; and a host of other potentially devastating problems. Valeta took their answers all back to the counselor, and was encouraged by her response.

When they discussed the baby's mother, they considered factors suggested by Valeta's doctor: how natural childbirth worked; how valuable a birth plan would be; her need for support and help after the baby's birth; and how useful others could be for everything but breastfeeding the baby.

"A baby really does change everything, doesn't it?" Edwin admitted at the end of July. "I've gained a new appreciation for how able you are to handle everything."

"That's because I was so irresponsible back in Hawaii," Valeta answered. "My main goal since coming here has been to learn responsibility, and it's been a tough goal for someone that always had things done for her, but I think I am learning."

Cherity

The last weekend in August, Edwin went to the doctor with her and, for the first time, Valeta agreed to look at the ultrasound, having resisted the doctor's previous coaxing, but now excited to share it with Edwin.

"Hello, baby," said the doctor, pointing to a tiny body on the ultrasound screen. "I see you're sucking your thumb today."

"Oh, it is!" Valeta exclaimed. "Look at how clear it is! You can see its whole body – little legs, little arms, tiny hands and feet." She pulled Edwin's head close to her own, pointing.

The doctor smiled and asked, "Would you like to know whether it's a boy or girl?"

Valeta turned her head to look at Edwin, her smile trembling. "What do you think?"

"I think you would like to know, wouldn't you? It would help you buy the right clothing, and you could begin thinking about its name." He smiled and squeezed her hand.

"All right," she told the doctor, "you may tell us. Is it a boy or a girl?"

"Well, you have a beautiful, petite baby girl, so you can think of a girl's name."

Valeta's eyes filled with radiant tears, and she looked at the monitor again. "I already know what her name is," she said. "It's Cherity."

"What a pretty name," said the doctor. "I don't believe I've heard that one before."

"I created it especially for her," said Valeta, "if it was a girl. I had another for a boy. Cherity is a combination of the French word *cher*, meaning dear, and the word *charity*, which incorporates love and generosity. That's the kind of person I want to be for her – and the kind I hope she will become when she gets older."

She turned to Edwin. "Do you like it?"

"It's perfect," he said, "and she's a lucky little girl to have you for her mother." He looked back at the monitor and added, "Although I can't see it, the doctor says you are beautiful, so we'll take her word for it. You get big and strong, and hurry out to join us, Cherity."

25

Sparkling Grape Juice

Cherity grew rapidly from that day onward, and Valeta's figure grew with her, amazing both Valeta and Edwin as it expanded. Valeta's schedule expanded, also, with more frequent doctor visits, childbirth classes, baby showers, and every weekend with Edwin. It would be nearly three months yet before the baby was born, but Valeta began to feel as though she would run out of time, there was so much to be done.

On the morning of September 27, the weather having turned cold, and it being Valeta's eighteenth birthday, Edwin took her for a drive in the countryside west of Wilmington, to a place where hundreds of maple trees of varied species paraded their autumn colors – brilliant red, pale yellow with red to pink accents, bright yellow, and orange. He followed a narrow, but paved side road that tunneled beneath giant maples, parked by a picnic table that sat under a canopy of golden leaves, and helped her out of the car. As though she were made of eggshells, he walked her gently to the picnic table, and gestured to the bench.

"Now, I want you to relax," he said. "You've been trying to do too much, and you need a day to just be lazy."

The spot was secluded, and the autumn colors so beautiful that Valeta began gathering some of the best leaves, telling Edwin that she wanted to take them home and see how long they would last. He laughed at her efforts to bend, but began helping her, adding his leaves to the pile she started on the table. After a few minutes, he caught her around the waist and, leading her back to the table, pulled her down on the seat with him as he reached for an especially large golden leaf.

"These really are beautiful," he said, "but they aren't as beautiful as you are." He held the large leaf beside her smiling face, then pulled off its broken stem and curled it around her thin pinkie finger. "That's not a very good fit, is it?" He laughed as the stem fell off.

Valeta reached for the stem of another leaf, but he pulled her hand back. "Maybe it will fit this finger," he said, but instead of a stem, he slipped a sparkling engagement ring onto the third finger of her left hand, getting down on one knee and asking, "Valeta Davidson, will you marry me as soon as your baby is born?"

"Oh!" It was all she could say until she caught her breath, and then she added, "Yes! Yes! Yes! I will marry you as soon as my baby is born."

Without warning, Edwin pulled her into his arms, and for the first time in the long months since they had met, he kissed her full on her lips. He thanked her for being willing to marry him, and she protested that she should be thanking him, and then they kissed again – on the lips.

"I told your father that you would," he said. "I called last night and asked for his blessing, which he readily gave." Edwin pulled a cell phone from his jacket pocket and handed it to her. "Why don't you call him while I get something out of the car," he said. "Let him be the first to hear our news. He promised to be at the base, even though it is the wee hours of Sunday morning. I programmed the number for you."

As he turned and went to the car, Valeta looked at the phone, and then looked down at the beautiful diamond, on either side of which sat a tiny coral flower – a memory forever of where they had met, and of the countless hours they had spent snorkeling the coral reefs. She looked at the phone again, remembering the last time she had spoken to Daddy and he to her. She pressed the speed dial button, and looked again at the ring, waiting for Daddy to answer. When he did, she opened her mouth, but could barely speak.

Date with Responsibility

"Is that you, Valeta?"

"Yes, Daddy. How are you?"

From the phone came the husky sobs of a crusty Marine colonel.

"Daddy, are you all right?" She realized that she never before had heard him cry.

"I'm all right, but I'm so sorry for sending you away, Valeta." She never had heard him sound so tender before either, and he continued to speak tenderly as he congratulated her and Edwin, and assured her that they both were welcome in his home anytime that they wanted to come. He and Mom had talked after Edwin's call yesterday, and Mom, too, had been persuaded to forgive. He asked about Valeta's health, and about the baby's health, and told her that he liked the name she created for the baby. He made her promise to stay in touch so that he would know how she was, and then, still husky but tender, he wished her a happy birthday, and sent her back to Edwin.

She told Daddy good-bye and hung up, turning to see on the table a stunning bouquet of red roses intertwined with white baby's breath and fern fronds. Edwin set a champagne bottle beside the roses, but told her it was only sparkling white grape juice, since she ought not to be drinking alcohol. He had found jellybean chocolates, too, a big jar of strawberry jellybean chocolates. He sat down beside her on the bench, but instead of opening either the grape juice or the candy, he put his arm around her and kissed her again.

Finally, he reached for a small cardboard box and produced two beautiful crystal goblets, each etched with five delicate symbols. "Happy birthday," he said, "and welcome to the adult world, Eighteen Year Old." He uncorked the juice, filled each goblet, and lifted his in the air. "Let's use these five toast symbols and drink to us," he said, and pointed to the delicate symbols on the goblets as he named them, one by one:

- Heart of love
- Dove of peace
- Bowknot of happiness
- Wheat sheaf of prosperity
- Sun of health

"I wish all of that and more for you, Honey, but whatever life brings us, I always will be glad that I can spend the rest of it with you."

They drank all of the sparkling grape juice, then, and nibbled on jellybean chocolates as they eagerly planned the near future: marriage at the end of November; a brief honeymoon trip – if Aunt Margaret would baby-sit Cherity; a merry month in the turret room with the baby; holidays with the McKeans; a return flight to Hawaii January 1 or 2, a move into Kaneohe Base housing, and then – then Edwin would adopt Cherity.

Date with Responsibility

Their news, announced late that Saturday, sparked a flurry of activity in the home, from Uncle William and Aunt Margaret to Andrew, Alicia, Catherine, and Caleb.

Before the weekend was over, Alicia had the latest bridal magazine, and right after school Monday, had to show Valeta every page of it. Valeta was telling her that she would require an enormous size gown even after the baby's birth, so why dream about romantic? Even if she could squeeze into a small gown, she must be careful of her finances, and it was much more responsible to buy a simple dress – with a belt that she could pull in once she got her figure back.

Aunt Margaret, coming to the door of the turret room and overhearing this conversation, declared that there was no reason for Valeta not to wear a wedding gown. Her own mother's gown was in storage, and since her mother was also Valeta's grandmother, Valeta should wear the gown. "Don't worry about it not fitting your tummy, either. It may even be much too large for you," she said, "since Mother was not a small woman, but I think we can nip it in here and there so that it fits you well enough. I'll get it out of storage at the end of the week."

"Mother, where do you think they should have the wedding – and the reception?"

"Alicia!" Aunt Margaret laughed merrily. "This isn't your wedding, dear, and although I know you wish it were, you have to let Valeta and Edwin do their own planning."

"But look, Mom," said Alicia. "Look at this beautiful old church. Wouldn't that make a great place for a formal wedding?"

"Alicia," Mom warned, "I'll write it into a book for you if you love it so, but bow out."

"Oh, I know! They could get married at the Historic Little Wedding Chapel across the border in Maryland. A lot of famous people have gotten married there."

"I appreciate your help, Alicia," Valeta said then, "but I know just where I want to get married if Edwin agrees. When we got engaged Saturday, he took me to a forest of beautiful maple trees, and there was a very old church there. It was tiny, and crumbling, but if we can use it, I would love to get married out there in the country."

Aunt Margaret cast her vote in favor of the old country church, and then told Alicia that she must let Valeta rest before dinner.

They left the room, and Valeta did rest for an hour or so, but then she called Grandmother Davidson to share the good news. She knew that Grandmother usually left Colorado sometime in October, but she begged her either to leave after the wedding, or to come back from Hawaii for the wedding. "We simply must have you with us that day, Grandmother," she pleaded, "since you were the one that brought us together."

"I did no such thing," protested the older woman, "or if I did, I don't remember it. How did I bring you and Edwin together?"

"Don't you remember? You insisted on going to church, and to a church that was off the bus line, so Daddy made me drive you, and that's where I met Edwin. If you hadn't chosen that church, I certainly wouldn't be getting married!"

Grandmother remembered then, and they chatted about all that was happening, even though Valeta faithfully wrote to her every week.

The bridal magazine came to the dinner table that evening, but after dinner, Valeta was rescued again from Alicia's impossible dreams. This time, it was Andrew and his girlfriend Penny who snatched her away.

"I know you haven't gotten acquainted with a lot of people here in Wilmington," Penny said as she led Valeta to the living room, where Andrew was adjusting logs in the fireplace. "I mean, the baby showers were great, and it was kind of the church women and Mrs. McKeans writers' club to throw showers for a stranger, but – okay – what would you think of a bridal shower of just high school girls? I'd have a blast arranging it, and I know the girls would love to meet you, but I wouldn't want you to feel uncomfortable."

"What a great idea!" Valeta said, her eyes sparkling with renewed energy. "I'd get to make more friends that way – and I could use some young friends. I never realized," she added ruefully, "how fast pregnancy can take you from carefree teen to weighed down mother, if you know what I mean. It's as though you go to bed with visions of parties dancing in your head, and wake up with four strange walls closing in on you, and not a friend in sight – and it isn't just because I had to leave home. Even in Hawaii, I knew that the minute my friends found out I was pregnant, my name on party lists would appear in invisible ink. I watched that happen to two other girls in high school and – well – I miss parties."

"Then it's settled," Penny said, helping Valeta into a recliner, and curling her own feet under her as she sat down on the couch.

Andrew joined Penny, his fire burning brightly now, and grinned at the girls. "I hope I have some say in this party," he said, "besides the permission you need from my parents to hold it here. I assume that's what you intend."

"Oh, would that be possible?" Penny asked, pretending the idea was new, and leaning closer to Andrew. "Would you mind terribly?"

He shook his head resignedly, but grinned. "I'll do it on one condition," he said, "since I don't want to miss any parties, either. It has to be a mixed shower – not bridal. You have to invite both genders, and you have to include Edwin."

Valeta laughed. "I'm not sure Edwin would agree to attend a shower," she said.

"Sure he will," Andrew promised, "because he won't know what it is until he gets here."

"And how do you propose keeping such a secret, with him spending every minute of every weekend in Valeta's presence? Did you ever think of that?" Penny punched his arm good-naturedly as she asked.

"I propose that we combine it with a late birthday party for Valeta since, according to a little mouse that's been running around the turret room, she secretly turned eighteen the same day she got engaged – September 27. For a girl who claims to like parties so much, you would think she'd have thrown a confetti storm of hints around, but now that we know, let's have a birthday party shower."

Valeta demurred, but not convincingly, so Penny and Andrew began to make plans, telling Valeta, "We hate to excuse the life of the party, but would you mind going to your room?"

"If you'll help me out of this chair," said Valeta, and laughed as they jumped to her side.

Sparkling Grape Juice

Upstairs, Valeta sat in a rocking chair in the turret room, looking at the piles of baby gifts and calculating when Cherity might be born while Leo, now happily ensconced as monarch of the turret suite, sat at her feet.

"In a way, Leo, I'm luckier than most any other mother-to-be," she told the cat, "since I know exactly what day Cherity was conceived, and since the average length of pregnancy is 266 days from conception," she looked at the calendar in her lap, "she should be born on or about November 15, which would give two weeks to adjust, and still have a December 1 wedding."

Leo did not deign to acknowledge this news, simply watching the rocker warily to be sure it posed no danger to his very long whiskers.

Valeta patted the cat, and said, "Well, this conversation is going nowhere, so if you'll excuse me, I think I'll work on my spreadsheet. Uncle William says the responsible handling of money includes listing every penny I spend, which is pure drudgery, but now that I know it's important, I'd be my old irresponsible self if I didn't do it. I must write thank you notes for all of these baby gifts, too. Oh, and follow through on my commitment to Caleb – practice my clarinet in exchange for his promise to play the piano at our wedding." She hurried to the table in the larger room, and worked much later than usual before dropping into bed.

Date with Responsibility

* * *

The party, set for October 18, was a great success, including Edwin's obvious surprise, but gracious acceptance of the fact that he had been tricked into attending a shower. Andrew and Penny had happily accepted help from Alicia, Catherine, and Caleb, and what decorations and games one or the other of the four redheads did not create, dark-haired Penny did. Contracting for the entire downstairs, the four McKeans virtually sold the next two Saturdays to their parents, but it was worth every concession they made.

When the party ended, and the hosts chased the guests of honor away from the after party, known as "eat what's left while you clean up the mess," Edwin held up the long skirt of the dressy green maternity outfit, which now was perfect for both her size and the weather, and helped Valeta climb the stairs. Then the two stood outside the door to the turret room and said goodnight.

Edwin pretended difficulty in getting close enough to kiss her, teasingly saying that something had come between them – and it was growing!

"She won't seem big in a few weeks," Valeta told him, and then, eyes suddenly widening, she exclaimed, "Oh Edwin, something's wrong! Help me lie down!"

26

The Old Church

Something was wrong. Something was very wrong. Edwin got Valeta to the bed quickly, but she would not lie down when she got there.

"I think I'm having contractions," she told him, "but it's too early. It's much too early."

"Let's get you to the hospital," Edwin said.

"But Edwin, I don't want Cherity to come too early. She needs more time to get ready."

"She may have a different strategy, Honey, and I don't want to take chances with her. More importantly, I don't want to take chances with you." Edwin got Valeta's coat and draped it over her shoulders. "Do you think you can make it down the stairs?"

"Not yet. My stomach hurts so." She leaned against him until the pain eased, and then let him help her slowly down the long, long stairway.

Date with Responsibility

Edwin drove rapidly to the hospital, where Valeta was taken from him immediately for an emergency ultrasound, placed in a birthing room, and hooked to a variety of monitoring machines, all of which terrified her. Edwin, after identifying himself as her fiancé, was allowed into the room, and waited with her for the doctor to arrive, but Valeta continued to have sharp pains – never close together – not at all regular – but frightening.

The doctor came, and diagnosed Braxton Hicks – false labor pains. "I'm glad you came, though," she said. "Better safe than sorry, since you're young and this is your first child. I think we will keep you here for a few hours, just to be sure all is well." She watched the monitor another minute and then asked, "Would you like to hear your baby deal with hiccups?" The doctor placed a small probe against Valeta's middle and moved it until all three of them heard the distinct sound of tiny hiccups. After that, noticing how pale the tall Marine was, the doctor suggested that he go home. But Edwin refused, and stayed at Valeta's side until, as the window beside the bed hinted at first light, she awoke and, smiling at him, rang for the nurse. Within minutes, she had talked briefly with her doctor, and they were free to go.

The sun seemed to hit the snooze button that morning, but as they drove home along the banks of the Delaware River, it finally stretched its bright wands into the crisp October sky, and filled the grayness with wispy pink clouds lined in both gold and silver – promises of an absolutely perfect Sunday – harbingers of happiness.

At first, it was hard to tell whether Edwin was listening when Valeta suggested that they drive out to the old church before going home, but an improvised smile gradually gave way to the genuine article, and he agreed. "Only if you let me grab some donuts to take with us, though," he said. "I'm starved."

They had found the donut shop several weeks before, and Edwin drove directly to it now, purchasing two strawberry jelly donuts with chocolate frosting for her, and two enormous bear's claws for himself. With these, a large carton of milk, and two plastic cups, he returned to the car and headed out the country road to the church.

"It's older than I realized," Edwin said as the church came into view. It was the first they had been back to the church since the day of their engagement, when it had been only one more part of an idyllic autumn scene. Today, however, it was the potential site of their wedding, and their eyes were more critical.

On either side of the structure, tall trees, which before had been clothed in glorious autumn gowns, had dropped those gowns at their feet, and now stood naked, staring drearily down at the dusty, crackly brown piles. The walls of the church, nearly as naked as the trees, had lost much of the gray-white substance that once had hidden their rough rocks and crumbling bricks.

"Pretty old, isn't it?" Edwin said, as he parked the car near the little old church.

"Let's look inside anyway," Valeta urged, "after we finish this breakfast." She unbuckled her seatbelt, and tried to find a more comfortable sitting position, at the same time trying not to spill the milk Edwin was pouring. A moment later, she was still trying not to spill the milk, which was now in her left hand, as she tried not to squirt the red strawberry jelly from her donut anywhere other than in her mouth.

Edwin had a much easier time, of course, his front encumbered only by a steering wheel rather than a belly that looked like a beach ball. Each time she dropped a bite of donut, which was fairly often, he teased her about trying to feed the baby through her tummy by osmosis.

"One more bite and I quit," Valeta said at last, sticking out her tongue as far as possible in an attempt to lick chocolate from the tip of her nose. "I don't think I have enough coordination left to eat in the car – and without a bib."

At that moment, the front door of the old church opened slowly, and a trembling voice called to them, "Did you young people need something?"

The Old Church

Edwin rolled down his window and asked, "May we look around inside?"

The janitor – he was the janitor – was very willing, and ushered them through the front door into a quaint chapel, clean and full of beauty inside its decaying outer shell.

"This is perfect!" Valeta said, squeezing Edwin's arm. "It will require hardly any flowers or decoration to look beautiful, with those white pews and white altar rail – no pew will hold more than four people either – it will look as though we have a nice crowd. Our tiny group would get lost in a big church, but not here." To the janitor, she said, "Is this church available for weddings?"

"Depends on when a person wants it," he wheezed, and coughed repeatedly.

"Well, we aren't sure yet," Edwin told him, "but probably late November or early December. You see, we have to wait until the baby is born."

The janitor had been eyeing Valeta's middle in a rather surreptitious manner before, but now he stared pointedly at the place where the coat buttons refused to join the buttonholes, and a frown deepened the furrows in his old face. "Seems to me you got the cart before the horse," he grunted. "Not that it's any of my business, but used to be a man waited until he bought the cow before he tried to steal the milk."

331

Valeta blushed and turned away, knowing that Edwin's honor and her own were at stake, but not knowing how to answer such a comment.

"Sir," Edwin said, gesturing strongly, "we both are as guiltless as the dove hanging from the canopy of that pulpit. I won't embarrass this woman by explaining to you, but suffice it to say that one who wishes to judge fairly must first gather all of the facts." He put his arm around Valeta and softened his voice as he continued, "How far in advance must the church be reserved?"

The janitor, duly chastened within if not without, looked toward a window as he mumbled, "Four, maybe five days. Just call the preacher." He moved to a small table by the door and picked up a card. "Preacher's phone number," he said. "You folks look around, and – well, I'm sorry." He reached for a dust mop and pushed it across the wooden floor, leaving them alone.

There was little for them to do, but they lingered, discussing how Edwin would come out of the door behind the pulpit, which undoubtedly led from a small room. He would stand at the front there, just to the right of the big white table. "Is there someone at the Air Force Base that can be your best man?" Valeta asked.

"I'm hoping Andrew will be my best man," he answered, and laughed at the look of joy on her face. "I'm guessing that Alicia will be your maid of honor, or will it be Penny? I suppose if Andrew is my best man, he would rather escort Penny than his younger sister."

Valeta giggled at the thought and said that, yes, Penny should be asked to be maid of honor. The church was so small that they really needed no other bridesmaids or groomsmen, and Alicia could be consoled by having her take care of Cherity during the ceremony. "I'm glad that stained glass window is at the front of the church," she said then. "The lamb will divert attention away from the big bridal ewe."

"Honey," he said, "you will be my ewe – all mine – and nothing will divert my attention." He looked at the janitor, squeezed her hand three times, and whispered that it was a secret kiss – a signal that they used often in the coming weeks.

* * *

When Edwin left Sunday evening, Valeta closed the front door and walked slowly toward the stairs, only to be intercepted by her aunt. "Wouldn't you rather sleep down here until the baby comes? You could use Edwin's room when he isn't here," said Aunt Margaret. "You worried us last night, and I hate to think of you going up and down those stairs."

"I'm always careful," Valeta said, "clinging to the rail and stepping firmly. I'll make it."

Date with Responsibility

"Well, if you're sure, but there's no reason for you to go up and down so much. Why don't you plan to bring things with you when you come down to breakfast in the morning. You can sit in the living room and write notes or read. Then you won't have to make so many trips on the stairs."

It was a good idea, and Valeta promised to consider it, but she knew she would not change. Leo was upstairs, and the turret suite was home, with the baby's treasure of toys and clothing as well as the pile of wedding gifts. She told her aunt goodnight and mounted the stairs.

Carefully donning disposable gloves, she washed Leo's twin bowls, filled one with fresh water and the other with dry food, and then cleaned his litter box meticulously, throwing the tightly closed plastic garbage bag and used gloves in the lidded waste can.

She spent the next six minutes beside the cradle, listening to the lamb mobile's lullaby, and gently rocking the bed with one hand, the other hand on her tummy to feel Cherity's early evening activity. The baby was very active this evening, having slept well after last night's emergency trip to the hospital. Valeta closed her eyes and tried, for what must have been the millionth time, to imagine how Cherity looked. Oh, she had seen the ultrasound photos, but she was getting eager to meet the little girl in person.

Leo's sudden thump into her lap effectively canceled the daydream, and her eyes flew open. "Hi puss. Did you enjoy your meal?"

The big Himalayan gave a huge yawn, and settled down to take a bath, but then he stood, and looked inquisitively at her middle.

"You just can't figure me out, can you?" Valeta laughed at him. "You used to know every move I made, but the little alien in there keeps you guessing. Well, you need to bathe on the floor anyway. I want to finish perfecting my definition of responsibility before the real labor arrives." She lifted the cat to the floor and stood up.

In the larger room, she sat down heavily at the small table, and opening her notebook, began to review key phrases that might help her. There probably was, somewhere, an excellent definition of the term, but she had not found it in any book, though Caleb had brought dozens of them from the library for her. She felt handicapped without her computer; unable to do the study she had so firmly purposed to do; unable to finish those last few months of high school. Not that there were no computers in the house, but Uncle William's was in his office, and constantly in use – Aunt Margaret's was in her office, where she spent much of every day writing her novel – and the third, although free when the four cousins were at school, seemed too public for storage of her own files.

However, she was determined to conquer at least this one topic before her baby arrived. It seemed, somehow, the one thing that could delay Cherity's arrival, and thus the wedding.

Responsibility

She wrote the word in the center of a clean sheet of paper – as she did every time she applied herself to this task. Then she began the definition: "Responsibility is" and stopped.

"What is responsibility?" she said aloud. "Responsibility is me fulfilling the commitment I made to myself to learn what responsibility is." She shivered, and putting the pen down again, got up and retrieved a sweater, which had not a chance of buttoning, but would keep her arms and shoulders warmer. She made a quick trip to the bathroom to be sure Cherity would not demand it as soon as she sat down, and then, for the next hour, she neither spoke nor left her chair.

At the end of the hour, she put down her pen and read her definition aloud.

> *Responsibility is a character trait that, accepting no excuses, makes an effort to know what obligations you have, and takes action to perform those obligations in the best manner possible, at personal sacrifice, and taking the consequences if you fail.*

The Old Church

There! It was done. It would take an entire book – like the book the preacher in Hawaii gave her – to cover every facet of responsibility, but the definition would help her remember all that she had read, and put action to her knowledge.

As she dressed for bed, and arranged all of her pillows to attract the greatest comfort and the longest possible sleep, Valeta talked to Cherity, telling her all that was in her heart. She talked to God that night, too, as best she could, asking Him to please keep her from having false labor again. Then she slept, off and on, until morning, and went to breakfast with an enormous appetite.

The next night was the same, as was every night for the next three weeks. The days between the nights were relaxed now, with her study done, thank you notes written, and few expenditures to record, since she spent most of her time in the house and paid only for things such as visits to the doctor and an occasional craving, which one of the cousins was always willing to fetch for her. The craving that set them all to laughing was the one that popped into her head the evening of November 9, just after Edwin had driven slowly down the drive, returning to Dover Air Force Base, and counting the three weeks that remained in his tour of duty there.

"I have a craving," Valeta said as she and the McKeans gathered in front of the fireplace.

"Uh-oh. Get out the car," Andrew said, laughing at his pretty, but no longer slim cousin.

"Nobody has to go to the store this time," Valeta said, "but could someone go out back and get me a little cup of dirt from the garden? I've just got to have some dirt."

Catherine giggled, and Alicia's eyes popped, but Caleb and Andrew rolled on the floor, holding their sides and laughing uproariously.

She really did crave dirt, but nobody would get it, and Aunt Margaret warned her that such cravings, though real, must not be fulfilled.

Valeta craved dirt the rest of that week, but steeled her will to refuse it and, when Edwin came on Saturday, November 15, was able to describe it as a craving that no longer bothered her.

"What does bother me," she told him that Saturday morning, "is how dirty the turret room is. I simply must give it a thorough cleaning from top to bottom. Will you help me?"

Edwin's protests were many and rational, including the fact that she was near her due date, but Valeta insisted, and they spent the entire morning scrubbing, sweeping, and polishing.

Just before noon, as she bent over to straighten the baby's blanket before going down to lunch, it happened.

27

The Best Gift

Early on Sunday, November 16, Edwin sent telegrams to the still-sleeping world of relatives:

Cherity Mara Davidson (Laroque)
November 16, 2003 at 12:58 AM
6 pounds 10 ounces (or 3 kilograms)
18 inches (or 45.72 centimeters)
Length of labor: 13 hours
Painful? Not for me (Late night humor!)
Beautiful Baby's health: Excellent
Beautiful Mom's health: Excellent
Adoptive Dad-to-be's health: Overwhelmed

Valeta had declined pain medication for the first twelve hours of labor, telling Edwin and Aunt Margaret that the pain was surprisingly bearable, and less than she had been led to expect, judging from books and TV sitcoms. The anticipation of pain was far worse than the real thing, which seemed to be a matter of enduring sixty to ninety seconds and then resting for a few minutes. She did not scream at anyone around her, nor did she feel like screaming at them, but she did come close to profanity several times when she loudly voiced her opinion of Rick and his part in her discomfort.

The last hour was more intense, making her request medication, and resulting in Baby Cherity receiving an unplanned middle name: Mara instead of Marie.

"Marie means *the perfect one*," Valeta told Edwin, tears streaming down her cheeks as the baby delivered, "and that's what I thought she would be, but now I know that no matter how hard we try, she always will be a bitter reminder, and Mara means *bitter*."

Neither bitterness nor tears could suppress joy though, when a moment later, tiny Cherity was swaddled in a pure white blanket, and being placed in Valeta's outstretched arms, ceased her crying, and looked right into the sea blue eyes of her mother. Edwin, strong Marine that he was, cried at the sight, but Valeta was too tired to cry. She simply fell in love with Cherity, hugged her close, and let her nurse. Then, she gently handed the little girl to the big man that soon would be her father, watching with a smile as he counted fingers, and observing that the baby's abundant hair was not white, but quite dark.

Aunt Margaret caught the whole thing on camera, hurrying to the waiting room to share the digital photos with the rest of the family, and then inviting them, at Valeta's request, to meet Cherity in person.

"She's so beautiful!" Alicia exclaimed. "She's bigger than I thought she would be, too. Was she hard to deliver, Valeta?"

The new mother looked up with a soft smile and said, "It was difficult at times, but I guess my mother actually knew what she was doing when she made me exercise to prepare for childbirth, because it was nowhere near as difficult as I had been led to believe." She winked as she added, "So, I give you fair warning – I may set up an exercise plan for my two favorite female cousins as soon as I get out of here."

Penny, who had accompanied them to the hospital, glanced quickly at Andrew before saying that she would not mind being included, although she did not, emphasis on the *not*, plan to become a mother as early in life as Valeta had.

Even though it was the middle of the night, Valeta had not eaten for more than twelve hours, aside from a cherry Popsicle for energy, and she now was ravenous. A nurse supplied a tray, and placed Baby Cherity in a crib beside Valeta, but when she returned twenty minutes later, the visitors – except Edwin, asleep in a chair – had gone, Cherity was back in Valeta's arms, and both mother and child slept peacefully.

Date with Responsibility

The hospital stay was to be twenty-four hours, but when the examining doctor heard that Edwin must return to Dover by early Monday morning, and considered the excellent health of both Valeta and Cherity, she released them late Sunday afternoon, extracting a promise from Valeta to call immediately if a problem developed.

A quick SOS to Uncle William brought the infant seat for Edwin's rented car, mother and baby were taken to the door in a wheelchair, and by the time Edwin left for Dover, both were settled in the turret room, the cradle placed beside the bed to save steps for Valeta, since the baby would nurse every two hours. Alicia received permission to spend the night on the smaller room's love seat, which made into a bed, so that she could get help if Valeta needed it.

"I wish you could stay," Valeta told Edwin as he bent over her for a kiss.

"In two weeks, I will," he promised, "and two weeks is not long. Besides, I'll be back early Saturday morning, and you will be so busy taking care of that little bundle over there that you will never miss me."

Although not at all right about not missing him, Edwin was right about being busy. The two hour intervals between feedings seemed much more like fifteen-minute intervals – and perhaps they were, since every feeding involved getting up to wash, changing the baby, feeding the baby, burping the baby, and frequently, changing her again. By the time all of that was done and Valeta fell asleep, it was nearly time to begin again.

She was very tired, and a little on the cranky side Tuesday when she said, "You know, Cherity, it would be a lot easier to get formula for you and give up this breast-feeding business. Then I could hire Alicia and Catherine to take turns feeding you while I got some rest." The words were hardly out of her mouth, however, when a big yawn from the tiny bundle in her arms made her sorry she had spoken them.

"You're right, Angel," she told the bundle. "Breast-feeding is a part of my responsibility to you, and the doctor said it's very important to your good health, so I promise to do it for your first full year of life, even though I have to sacrifice sleep." The decision did not make it much easier to go through the feeding and changing process every two hours, and definitely did not make her more rested, but it was reassuring to know that she was beginning to practice responsibility, even when it cost something as precious as a night filled with sweet dreams. "Besides, Cherity," she said, "a child is only a moment – I think Grandmother used to sing a song like that – your great grandmother. A child is the best gift you can get, but it is only for a moment and you have to hold onto the moment, because it never comes again.

Date with Responsibility

By Wednesday, the ritual had begun to be routine, and Valeta was regaining her strength so, during Cherity's naps, she completed her baby's birth announcements, which Aunt Margaret had created and printed from the computer, each with that first newborn photo on the front. After much thought, she decided to send them to a few of her best friends back in Hawaii, and with each of these, she included a brief note explaining the pregnancy and her decision to carry the baby. She did not mention the upcoming wedding, though, because there were wedding announcements to be sent soon – right after the wedding.

"I should get the wedding announcements ready now, too," she told Cherity, and seeing Leo eyeing her, realized for the first time that she was leaving him out of conversations that once had been exclusively his. Oh well. She supposed he would have to get used to it, but this once she repeated for him, looking directly into his rich blue eyes. The cat forgave her, and jumped onto the bed, still watching her with one eye as he licked his left paw to commence his bath.

She certainly was not sending out wedding announcements to get gifts, she told herself, even though the replacement of invitations with announcements might appear to be a request for *presents but not presence*. Friends in Hawaii and distant relatives certainly should understand her reasoning when the card read:

The Best Gift

Valeta Davidson
and
Edwin Laroque
are pleased to announce
that they were united in marriage
November 30, 2003
Wilmington, Delaware

She worked at the cards and notes off and on throughout the week, and by the time Edwin returned, had them all done, ready for mailing.

* * *

That last weekend before the wedding sent the entire household into a flurry of preparation: flowers, clothing, blood tests, reservations....

Aunt Margaret brought the wedding gown to the turret room and, although the gown was quite long on Valeta, the full skirt allowed ample room for her still protruding tummy. A few stitches here and there made it fit perfectly above the waist, and the fact that it was long was, as Aunt Margaret put it, "charming," so it was whisked away to be dry-cleaned and pressed.

Penny and Alicia returned from the florist shop with photos, from which they helped Valeta choose ivory rose boutonnieres for the two men, a long-stemmed ivory rose for Penny, and for Valeta, a large, cascading bridal bouquet of ivory roses and white Australian daisies interspersed with red pepper berries, greens, and baby's breath.

Date with Responsibility

"With that in front of me, I might even look thin," Valeta said, smiling at the florist's photo.

Edwin and Andrew had reserved tuxedoes two weeks earlier, and Penny had purchased a long gown in light burgundy that would serve well both for the wedding and for next spring's prom.

Valeta's parents were flying in from Hawaii with Grandmother Davidson, Edwin's parents would drive down from upstate New York, and the local branch of the McKean family would attend. There were a few people from the wedding shower who were invited, too, although Edwin and Valeta had met them only that once. They would help fill the little old church, and they had given gifts, so it seemed only right to invite them.

Late Saturday evening, when they were alone at last, Edwin told Valeta, "We can have a normal honeymoon next year when Cherity is done nursing and can be left behind for a few days, but we need a few days of peace away from everyone, so I reserved a room for all three of us at a resort in the Pocono Mountains."

"And when we come back," she said, "we will move you into the turret suite with Cherity and me – and Leo."

Cherity cried, then, and Valeta took her from her bed, showing Edwin how good she had become at changing and feeding the little one.

The Best Gift

Sunday morning, Edwin and Valeta placed Cherity in her infant car seat, and drove to the little old church in the country. They arrived at what should have been service time, but a single car sat under the bare trees, looking as though it was there from habit and did not expect company.

"You wait here with Cherity, and I'll see what time the service begins," Edwin said, as he opened the car door. He walked briskly to the church and, within two minutes, returned with the news that the church no longer had services, because the people had gone to newer churches. "The preacher was there, and agreed to marry us next Sunday afternoon," he said, "but who knows why he comes when nobody else does?"

"Who knows why you love me when nobody else does?" Valeta said, giving him a coy smile.

"That's my secret," he said, "but I do love you. I love you so much that next Sunday, I am going to say good-bye once and for all to every other girl on the face of the earth, and be completely faithful to you for the rest of my life."

He reached into the back seat of the car and, retrieving a small envelope, held it unopened in his hand as he said, "The other day, I was in the library on Base and found some wedding vows that I think you might like, but if you don't, please say so, and we can just use whatever the preacher has, the way we planned." He opened the envelope, withdrew a single sheet of plain paper, and read the vows, first the one he would say, and then the one she would say:

> *I, Edwin, take you, Valeta, to be my wedded wife, and with deepest joy, I receive you into my life that together we may be one. I will be to you a loving husband. I will be a faithful husband. I promise you my deepest love, my fullest devotion, my tenderest care. And so throughout life, no matter what may lie ahead of us, I pledge to you my entire life as a loving and faithful husband.*

> *I, Valeta, take you, Edwin, to be my wedded husband, and with deepest joy, I come into my new life with you. As you have pledged to me your life and love, so I too give you my life, loving you, obeying you, caring for you, ever seeking to please you. And no matter what may be ahead of us, I pledge to you my entire life as an obedient and faithful wife.*

Edwin put the paper back in the envelope before looking at Valeta's face, but when he did, he read full acceptance.

"I like them both," she said simply.

One week from today, they would make those vows in the little church over there, and they would mean every word of them.

"Well," he said, and smiled at her. "Since we aren't going to church here today, and we are too late to attend anywhere else, I suppose we should get you two beautiful girls home so that you can rest. Would you like to eat out or join the family's midday meal?"

"If I were not so tired, I would love to eat out, if we did not have an infant who might catch something from other people in the restaurant," she teased. "Would you mind terribly if we ate at home today?"

"Of course not," he answered. "Your Aunt Margaret is a good cook, and eating in crowds is a daily occurrence for me on Base, so it's nice when I get to eat at home. Besides Cherity is sleeping."

Cherity was sleeping, and continued to sleep the entire time they were out, until Edwin slowed the car to make the ride over the drive's cobblestones as smooth as possible. Then she awoke, crying as he came to a stop in front of the McKean home – and continuing to cry as they lifted her from the car seat and carried her into the house. Aunt Margaret teased them, accusing them of pinching her, while Alicia cooed for the baby, dancing along beside Edwin as he carried her, and begging to be allowed to hold her.

Date with Responsibility

"I know what you need, little girl," Valeta said, and excused herself to go upstairs to change and feed her. When she had done both of these and Cherity continued to cry, however, Valeta became concerned. Thinking back to the things she had been taught in childbirth classes, she checked carefully to be sure there was not a pin pricking the baby, or a fresh case of diaper rash. She felt the baby's skin, and it was neither too hot nor chilly. She held the baby close to her, and tried to sing a lullaby, but Cherity continued to cry. She rocked the baby. She talked to her. She rubbed her back. She burped her again. Still, Cherity cried.

Valeta herself was about ready to cry when Edwin stepped into the room, wondering what was wrong and whether she had done this before.

"She's never done it before," Valeta said, a frown shadowing her features. "I'm afraid she's sick, Edwin. I think we should call a doctor."

28

I'll Be There

"Colic." Aunt Margaret was certain, though they had barely entered the dining room with the crying baby.

"Colic?" Valeta's alarmed look deepened. "She's in such pain, Aunt Margaret! Look at how she pulls her legs up to her tummy. I try to give her a pacifier, and she just spits it out."

Edwin stood close beside Valeta, holding the rejected pacifier by its pink ribbon, concern etched as deeply in his face as in hers – a picture that made Aunt Margaret smile, knowing that in his heart, Edwin already was the baby's father.

"Let me take her," she said, "and you sit down and eat."

"Don't you think a doctor should see her?" Valeta tentatively placed Cherity in Aunt Margaret's arms as she asked. "I know we would have to go to the hospital, since it's Sunday, but I'm worried. I'd feel terrible if...."

The tiny girl in the bundle of soft green pasture and fluffy white lambs stopped crying, and closing her eyes, began to fall asleep on Aunt Margaret's shoulder.

"Oh, thank you. She must have had one more bubble. I'll take her now," Valeta said, but as soon as she did, Cherity began to scream. Valeta held her tightly, staring at the baby with aching, intense helplessness written across her features.

"Let me try," Edwin said quietly. "He took little Cherity into his big, strong arms, and put her little tummy against his steady broad chest. In a moment, the crying stopped. Cherity took her pacifier when Edwin offered it, and peace returned.

But only to others. Valeta felt none of the peace, as she realized that two people who bore no direct genetic connection could quickly soothe the baby who had needed only her for nine long months, for whom she had suffered thirteen hours of labor, and whom she loved with every ounce of her being. For the first time, after all that she had given up, after all that she had done, and all that she had allowed to be done, Valeta had failed Cherity. She had failed in her responsibility to keep her baby comfortable, and the consequences of her failure were written in body language that needed no interpretation.

I'll Be There

Aunt Margaret slipped an arm around Valeta, and guided her toward the dining room, telling her that colic was that way. The sudden end of the car ride probably startled the baby, and when Valeta tensed because she saw no cause for the crying, Cherity picked up on her tension. "Just relax, and let her feel through your body and voice that Mother is not afraid," said Aunt Margaret.

Plausible, but Valeta would ask the doctor at Cherity's first check-up, which, unfortunately, would be delayed until after the wedding, but they would manage until then – somehow. Valeta ate, watching Cherity sleep against Edwin's shoulder, despite the fact that he, too, was eating. Edwin's ability to quiet the baby should have comforted the young mother, but only served to emphasize the fact that she had failed, so she stopped eating, relaxed every muscle, and taking Cherity into her arms, carried her to the turret room alone. There, finding in memory a soothing sound from her own infancy, she whispered its title, *"I'll be There,"* and rocked the baby as she crooned softly:

> *"Sure as rainbows end, my forever friend,*
> *I can promise you, I'll be there."*

"I promise that I'll always be there for you, Cherity," she said, and softly continued:

> *"A kiss and a smile, then dream for a while,*
> *You'll wake up, and I'll be there."*

She kissed the baby and put her in the cradle.

Date with Responsibility

The end of that first episode of what Aunt Margaret called *colic* was not the end of all episodes, and throughout that week, Cherity cried for hours on end, defying Valeta to find a solution. If she had a car at her disposal, or if Edwin were there instead of an hour away, she would have taken Cherity to a doctor the moment she resumed her crying on Monday. One did not, however, seek a ride from drivers who labeled a doctor's visit an unnecessary, and – could it be – irresponsible use of one's money.

So, while Cherity slept only off and on, Valeta slept not at all, not for the entire week. Wedding preparations demanded her attention, with the florist calling to change the Australian daisies to white dendrobium, whatever those were; Daddy calling to say that he did not want to give a speech at the reception, because he knew he would be too choked up to do so; and the bakery calling to say that the new shipment of caketop ornaments did not include the one Valeta wanted. But worse than those was the Thursday afternoon call from the photographer they had retained for the wedding, who "just realized" that he double-booked the day, and would not be able personally to make it to their wedding, but would supply a substitute who did work for him from time to time, with whom he was sure they would be happy.

"In other words," Valeta fumed, "someone came along with a more profitable offer, so he's pawning us off on his flunky. How could so many things possibly go wrong at the last minute?" It was outrageous.

Aunt Margaret pleaded with her to lie down and take a nap, offering to keep Cherity downstairs so that Valeta could sleep, but Valeta refused. Cherity was her responsibility, and only hers. She would take care of her.

Just after noon on Friday, with Cherity in the midst of a crying marathon, a bright yellow taxi crawled up the long curving drive, and stopped at the foot of the manor's wide stairway. A man and two women stepped from the cab. The man paid the driver, who took three large pieces of luggage from the trunk. The taxi left, and the three people climbed the fifteen gray steps to the porch. The younger of the two women fussed with her red hair, and shivered in the unaccustomed cold, her mouth forming words of complaint as the man knocked at the big oak door. It was opened at once by Aunt Margaret, who had watched the arrival of the taxi from her office window, but before she could speak, the younger woman said harshly, "I don't see why my daughter chose to come here, of all places, with your litter of children and your wretchedly cold, damp weather."

"It's good to see you, too, Marjorie," said Aunt Margaret, her smile as angelic as that of the proverbial cat that ate the canary. "Come in." She took their coats and led them to the two guest rooms where they would be staying.

"I don't believe you look one day older, Colonel," she told the man as she gestured toward the door of the first guest room, "and it must be at least five years since I last saw you. You must let William drink from your fountain."

Colonel Davidson grinned and his height increased by an inch as he told her that, although he looked the same, he felt a lot older now that he had become a grandfather, to which Marjorie replied that *he* might be a grandfather, but *she* was not a grandmother, especially if that awful screaming that was echoing through the house was the "grand" child.

"You two put your weapons away before I call Valeta," Aunt Margaret said briskly. "The poor child is beside herself caring for a colicky baby, and the last thing she needs is to jump back into the same fray she left last spring." She turned to Grandmother Davidson, gesturing across the hallway to a second guest room. "Let me know if you need anything," she continued, "and when you all are settled, come out to the living room and I'll let Valeta know you have arrived." She turned to her sister then, and said pointedly, "Marjorie, try to make your daughter's wedding memorably happy, and afterward, I promise to let you fight with me to your heart's most wicked delight."

Twenty minutes later, as the three visitors sat near a cozy fire in the living room, entertained by Uncle William and warmed by mulled spiced cider, the sister with the auburn hair and the sweet smile walked softly down the hall to Valeta's turret suite and knocked on the door.

"Your parents and your grandmother are here," she whispered, noting that Cherity had at last fallen asleep. "I'll sit here with Cherity while you go down and greet them. They can meet her later when she's awake and can capture their hearts with a sweet smile."

"Thank you, Aunt Margaret, but she's my responsibility," said Valeta, sighing. "I hate to awaken her when I just got her to sleep, but I can't leave her up here alone, and you shouldn't have to take care of her."

"Valeta, come into the hall a minute," said the aunt, gently leading her, and closing the door softly. "You are an extremely responsible young mother, but you are an extremely tired young mother, and if you continue to be so tired, your ability to be responsible will suffer. You see, dear, responsibility does not have to mean doing it all yourself. None of us is made to handle everything that comes along. Sometimes, we need to ask for help, and this seems a very good time for you to ask someone whom you trust to care for your baby long enough for you to have a brief conversation with your grandmother and your parents, and then get some rest so that you don't spend your wedding day in a hospital bed. I would like to be the one you ask, but if it's your grandmother or your mother, that is fine with me. Just take your responsibility a step further, and get some rest."

Aunt Margaret placed a hand on the young mother's weary shoulder as she added, "*A stitch in time saves nine*, or to put it another way, a little preventive maintenance eliminates the need for major repairs later – in your health as well as in Cherity's. Think about it."

The aunt dropped her hand, then, and turned to go downstairs, but had gotten only as far as the top of the long stairway, having no thought of sliding down the railing with that sister present, when a quiet voice called her back.

"Would you please sit with Cherity for a few minutes while I go down? She's just been fed, so she should sleep."

"I would be happy to sit with her."

"Oh, and I hate to ask, but would you stay when I get back so I can take a nap? You were right. I am frazzled. I'll explain to the others before I come up."

For the rest of the afternoon, Valeta slept and, surprisingly, Baby Cherity also slept, not awakening for her usual afternoon feeding. Valeta wondered at that when she finished her nap, but never knew that Aunt Margaret had given the baby a small bottle of sugar water.

* * *

Edwin, the bridegroom arrived very early on Saturday morning, and sat on the turret room love seat holding Cherity on his lap, tummy down, while Valeta changed clothes in the bathroom.

"My parents are eager to meet you, Honey," he called to her, "and I can hardly wait to make the introductions. They know you're beautiful from the photos I sent, but photos can never capture your real beauty."

Valeta was looking in the mirror when he said it, eyeing the belly that still refused to return to Homecoming Queen size. She had imagined this first meeting with Mr. and Mrs. Laroque many times, but with her looking her absolute best, and making a fantastic first impression. Well, you had to work with what you had, she thought, stepping into the long striped pants, and pulling the pink trimmed burgundy top over her head. This was comfortable, anyway, and would complement the pink dress Cherity wore today. Besides, when she wore her wedding gown tomorrow, the cascading bouquet covering her tummy, maybe they would forget how she had looked today. She tied the glass butterfly pendant around her neck, brushed her hair, and returned to the baby's room.

Edwin smiled, turning Cherity so that she was looking at her mother, and said, "You have a beautiful mommy, don't you?"

Valeta gave him a small thank you kiss, and glanced at the clock. She was ready on time.

"Do you feel all right?" Edwin asked her. "You look very pale."

"Oh, it's just this dark burgundy," she told him. "I'll put a little blusher on my cheeks." The blusher was of little help, of course, seeming to sit in two clown spots on the white canvas of her skin, try as she might to blend it.

The decision to wash it off and start over was already traveling from brain to hands when her aunt called, "Your parents have arrived, Edwin."

"Okay, Baby Cherity," he said, a big smile in his voice, "it's time to meet another grandma and granddad. Tell your mommy to come." He got to his feet, and straightened the little pink dress.

"Don't you want me to carry her?" Valeta felt a stab of guilt and another of jealousy.

"Oh, she's so content right now, let's not risk changing a thing," he said, which Valeta right away interpreted as meaning that she could not keep her own baby content, but then decided was not meant that way at all, and willingly let him carry the baby to meet its adoptive grandparents.

Meeting Edwin's father and mother was even more nerve-wracking than her first date with Edwin had been, especially when Valeta's own mother made a whispered comment about her daughter being an unwed mother. Mrs. Laroque never missed a beat, though, and took Cherity into her ample arms in a moment, smiling at her, cooing, smoothing a wrinkle from the little pink dress, welcoming her into the family, and turning to tell the unwed mother, "We've loved you from the moment Edwin first spoke of you, dear, and your selfless decisions regarding Cherity have only made you more lovable to us."

Mr. Laroque teased that it was unfair to hug only one of Edwin's women, and although he refrained from hugging, gave Valeta a quick wink, and promised to kiss the bride the next afternoon. He took his turn at holding Cherity, giving her Valeta's hug as well as her own. Valeta thought when they handed Cherity to her that since the baby had not cried for them, she must be having a good day and would not cry for Valeta, but alas.

"She's a bit colicky," Edwin told his parents, and snuggled Cherity against his warm navy blue sweater as he walked toward the fireplace and sank into a deep chair.

"Poor thing," said Mrs. Laroque. "She must have inherited from you – oh." She laughed. "See how completely I've made her my granddaughter!

What I meant was that you were colicky, too, as a baby, and worried me nearly to death."

"It's almost time for the baby's lunch," Valeta interrupted, "so I should take her upstairs, Edwin. You stay here and talk to your parents."

She crossed the room to take the little girl, but as she did, the tall strong walls that glowed with rosy firelight suddenly turned to misty gray and melted toward her from every direction. She blinked, and reached a trembling hand toward the back of the couch to steady herself, but the couch inched away, and she tumbled in an unconscious heap at its side.

29

November 30

Uncle William joked that this day belonged to Andrew, since November 30 was St. Andrew's Day in Scotland, McKean homeland. Andrew teased that the day belonged to Thomas McKean, signer of the *Declaration of Independence*, because a preliminary peace treaty signed on this day in 1782 led to the end of America's Revolutionary War. Caleb quipped that it was the birth date of composer Carl Loewe; Alicia said it was Desi Arnaz and Lucille Ball's 63rd wedding anniversary; and Catherine, coming to breakfast with papaya red pigtails, said that comedian Al Sherman would have been 79 years old today. When reminded by Valeta that it was her wedding day, all but Aunt Margaret feigned surprise.

At sunrise, Valeta had awakened with a smile on her perfectly rounded lips. Her sea blue eyes had sparkled as a prying sun ray lifted their lids, and she had stretched in eager anticipation.

Date with Responsibility

"Edwin's marrying me this afternoon," she had whispered to herself.

A tiny sound at her side had reminded her that she had kept the baby in bed with her all night – at the advice of Edwin's mother – who had given such sweet advice after Valeta had regained consciousness, finding herself lying on the couch with Edwin on his knees beside her.

"Baby can sleep in her own bed after you're married, dear, but you need rest if you're going to be a bride tomorrow," Mother Laroque had said. "You need to sleep with baby beside you and, when she's hungry, pull her close to feed, and then go back to sleep."

Then, Edwin carrying Valeta, Mother Laroque carrying Cherity, they had climbed the long stairway to the turret room, where both Valeta and Cherity were told to sleep all of Saturday and Saturday night. Alicia had taken up occupancy in the baby's room, with a thick novel, a stack of clean diapers, and a promise that when Cherity did awaken, she would change her for Valeta. Edwin had gone to a hotel with his parents, since the downstairs guest rooms were now full, and the others had busied themselves with last minute details of the wedding. Valeta had slept.

The grandfather clock chimed eight times now, and the bride's side of the family gathered for breakfast, teasing the little bride.

"I think Edwin escaped," said Daddy, with a grin at his only daughter. "He pretended he was taking his parents to a hotel, but I think he just came to his senses. He's AWOL – cut and ran."

"Daddy, he's not supposed to see the bride the day of the wedding," Valeta said, fastening the baby into her infant seat, and then sitting down to breakfast.

Even Mom entered into the teasing, having called a one-day truce with both Valeta and Aunt Margaret, and asking, "Do you know what the difference is between a boyfriend and a husband?" When all answers failed, she said, "About thirty pounds."

After breakfast, Valeta showered, bathed and fed the baby, and then said. "Only four hours, Cherity. Only four hours."

Four hours to wait, and nothing to do. She had decided to wear her hair simply, so it required no attention. She was doing her own makeup, but not until a half hour ahead of time. The wedding gown hung on the back of the door. The florist would deliver the flowers to the church. The cake was waiting at the restaurant.

Cherity would wear an ivory christening gown, bonnet and slippers, a gift from Daddy and Mom, given with a wonderfully understanding note to Valeta and a welcome note to Cherity.

Date with Responsibility

Four hours to wait.

Four hours instead of the four years she had expected. She closed her eyes, and behind the still weary lids a slim, happy-go-lucky cheerleader tossed her long blond curls as she was introduced to a tall, dark-haired Marine. The same carefree girl shopped for the latest borderline-immodest styles, flirting innocently with the boys at high school. The blithe spirit partied, surfed, ate pizza, rode horseback in Oahu's back country, sun bathed on Oahu's white beaches, and snorkeled wave-washed reefs, equally at home in every element – untroubled – lighthearted and breezy.

She opened her eyes, and let them critique the turret suite. Baby clothing and toys filled the oak chest, inside and out. A diaper pail and a clean litter box shared the corner near the bathroom with a box of plastic gloves and bags. A divided hamper sorted baby's clothing from mother's clothing, and a changing table – height of relaxed living – exhibited diaper rash creams, extra diapers, plastic pants, lotions, and wipes. The closet in the larger room held brand new baby clothing on small hangers, but on larger hangers, used mother clothing selected at a local thrift shop.

Still nearly four hours to wait. Valeta placed the baby on the big bed, and picked up a book – a book on how to be a good mother. She read to the end of one chapter.

Then she got up, wondering as she fingered the heavy white wedding gown, if every bride felt this way on her wedding day – or if it was only because she was a teen bride and an unwed mother. She opened the luggage again, certain that she would forget something vital and Edwin would think she had been careless.

Closing the bags and turning back to the big bed, she stopped, her hand flying to her mouth to stifle an exclamation. There on the bed, one eye tenderly watching the baby girl and the other scanning for danger, Leo lay in royal pride – his first opportunity to be near the infant.

Valeta hurried to the bed, whispering, "Leo, you and Cherity belong to one another now, to have and to hold until death do you part. I want you to be gentle with her, though she may not be very gentle with you while she's little."

A nervous giggle escaped her lips, and she petted the big cat, listening to the grandfather clock downstairs as it chimed eleven times.

Three hours to wait.

Outside, the bright sun called to her, and smiled on her wedding day as forecast. "That," she thought as she looked from the window, "is the omen of a happy marriage. I'm wearing something old – the gown; something new – my white shoes; something borrowed – the gown again; and something blue – the blue eyes of the tiny lamb, which I removed from the key chain and attached to a silver bracelet. Superstitious, maybe, but this must be my only wedding, and it must be perfect."

Valeta lay down on the bed with the cat and the baby, pulled a warm blanket over her, and closing her eyes, let excitement carry her where it would.

Sometime later, she awakened with a jerk and said aloud, "Oh! What time is it?" Then she heard what must have awakened her – someone knocking on her door. "Come in," she called softly.

The door burst open, and the room filled with chattering girls, ages ranging from teen to sixty something. Cherity awakened crying, for which they each and everyone apologized, and in a moment someone had taken her gently in their arms and hurried to the changing table, while Valeta still lay in a stupor.

"It's time to get ready," said Grandmother Davidson, "and to get the job done, we are maids and matrons of the bride."

Valeta sat up and rubbed her eyes. They all were dressed for the wedding, including Penny, whose light burgundy gown enhanced her long veil of coal black hair. She was beautiful.

"Here." Eager hands helped her from the bed, arranged cushions on the rocking chair so that she could feed Cherity, removed the plastic cover from the wedding gown, and began laying out the baby's christening outfit.

As she fed the baby, Valeta directed the packing of the diaper bag, which Alicia and Catherine handled with excitement, and Penny brushed Valeta's long hair, threatening to turn it into a halo of pure gold. Aunt Margaret and Mom spread the gown on the bed together, sharing a few memories of their mother who had first worn it. Grandmother Davidson bustled here and there in the crowded suite, trying to help in any small way she could.

The moment Cherity had been burped, Valeta was hustled into the bathroom, and the door closed. Baby Cherity was gently dressed in the ivory silk gown, ivory socks, and the tiny ivory slippers, and by the time Valeta returned to don the white wedding gown, Grandmother Davidson was rocking the baby, cooing softly.

It took them very little time to get the long wedding gown fastened up the back, despite the interminable row of pearly white buttons, and the many fingers that insisted on being involved. Catherine volunteered to slip Valeta's white shoes on her feet, and exclaimed at the lamb bracelet, which now adorned her ankle. It and the sparkling engagement ring were the only jewelry she would wear today – until she received her wedding band.

Date with Responsibility

She arrived at the church just one half hour before the ceremony was to begin, wishing she had waited to nurse the baby just before walking down the aisle, but then thinking that one did not nurse a baby while wearing a wedding gown.

By the time Edwin arrived with his parents, Valeta was in the church, secluded in a tiny back room that barely held her, the big gown, and Penny. It certainly did not admit anyone else.

"Are you excited?" asked Penny.

"Excited doesn't begin to express it," said Valeta. "I don't know if I'm going to get through it, Penny. Did you know I fainted yesterday? I'm just hoping I don't faint halfway through the ceremony."

"I'm sure Edwin will catch you in his strong arms if you do," Penny comforted her, "and tell the preacher to go on with the vows. I warn you, though, if you don't come to in time to say your vows, I might say them myself. Your Marine is nearly as handsome as Andrew."

Caleb's prelude suddenly became the bridal march and Penny gave Valeta a quick squeeze. "See you at the front," she said, and stepped out into the aisle. A moment later, Valeta followed, and in a few steps, was standing at Edwin's side.

The short ceremony passed as a dream, in the twinkling of an eye, and Valeta found herself being kissed by Edwin. Then – the words she had so often imagined hearing – "I now present to you Mr. and Mrs. Edwin Laroque."

Caleb's nimble fingers began playing Beethoven's *Ode to Joy*, and the newlyweds swept back the aisle of the tiny church, their eyes fixed on one another, their faces wreathed in smiles. Edwin hugged her and kissed her again, and in a moment, they were receiving their guests' best wishes – Mom, Mother Laroque and Grandmother wiping away tears – Daddy and Father Laroque letting their tears sit in their eyes – Aunt Margaret and Uncle William glowing as though it was their daughter who had married.

The last well-wisher had just stepped into the chilly November afternoon, the photographer announced that he was ready for outdoor photos, when Cherity began to cry.

"The baby's hungry," Valeta told Edwin.

"It won't take long to get the photos," he said, "and then you can feed her. Come on." He let her precede him through the small doorway, and helped her down the steps.

The photographer took several photos of them together and with their parents, and then said that he would like to try a few shots of Valeta alone, with leaves in place of her bouquet.

Valeta stared at him. "A wedding photo with dusty, dry, dead brown leaves?" But the sooner he had his photos, the sooner they could leave. Valeta hurried into the leaves, turning to left and right, stooping, picking up leaves, and throwing handfuls of leaves into the air at the photographer's request. Her ears rang with the rising cries of her baby girl, and the light in her eyes faded even as the smile left her lips. As the cries became screams, a tear trickled down the bride's cheek, and turning suddenly, she dashed into the church, Edwin close behind her.

She took the infant into her arms, sank onto a narrow pew, and fumbled with the bows on the front of her gown. Edwin gestured Alicia from the church and closed the door. Then he sat beside his little bride, and once the baby began to feed, supported her back with his firm shoulder as he told her, "Mrs. Valeta Laroque, my beautiful bride, and mother of the little girl who will soon be my daughter, I love you both very much." He kissed Cherity on her tiny head, but he kissed Valeta on the lips.

Later, the door of the church opened again, and the knot of well-wishers turned to see a tall, happy young man usher forth a radiant, petite bride who held a sleeping baby girl. "Ladies and gentlemen – my family," he said with bursting pride, and led them to his car.

Have you read...

Passport to Courage
Character-in-Action Series #1

What readers are saying about <u>Passport to Courage</u>

M. Everett:

"I read the whole thing last night — just couldn't put it down until I had finished it and found out what Andrew decided to do! I think it's a fantastic read ... I loved the book!"

K. Pitts:

"I thought this book was great... heart-pounding at times... a wide range of vocabulary, so it's good for older people as well as teens. I would rate it 5 stars for suspense, vocabulary, and pure feeling!"

G. Borlase:

"David just could not put it down and finished it very quickly, and then it was my turn and the same could be said."

E. Coppin:

"I read the book in two days! ... plenty of action and suspense."

A. Marshall:

"Just received your book a couple of days ago ... already finished it ... really enjoyed it!"

Be sure to visit us on the web at

www.character-in-action.com

...and look for

other books about

The Four McKeans
and their friends

in the

Character-in-Action™ Series

by Elizabeth L. Hamilton